ERE THE COCK CROWS

ERE THE COCK CROWS

Originally published as Før Hanen Galer

Jens Bjørneboe

Translated from the Norwegian by Esther Greenleaf Mürer

With a Recreation of the Original Play by the Translator

Frayed Edge Press
Philadelphia, PA

Original title: *Før Hanen Galer*
First published in 1952 by Aschehoug Oslo

English translation ©Esther Greenleaf Mürer
1st English Language Edition
Published by Frayed Edge Press, 2021
With the kind permission of Therese Bjørneboe

Cover illustration by Bruce Orr
Cover design by A.R. Melnik

This book is printed on acid-free paper

Publisher's Cataloging-in-Publication Data

Names: Bjørneboe, Jens, 1920-1976. Før hanen galer. | Mürer, Esther Greenleaf, translator.
Title: Ere the cock crows / Jens Bjørneboe ; translated from the Norwegian by Esther Greenleaf Mürer.
Description: Philadelphia, PA : Frayed Edge Press, 2021. | Includes a re-creation of the original play. | Summary: Presents the moral dilemmas, or lack thereof, of scientists performing human medical experimentation on prisoners of war in WWII Nazi Germany.
Identifiers: LCCN 2021930265 | ISBN 9781642510294 (pbk.) | ISBN 9781642510300 (ebook)
Subjects: LCSH: Human experimentation in medicine -- Fiction. | Medical scientists -- Fiction. | National socialism -- Fiction. | World War, 1939-1945 -- Prisoners and prisons -- Fiction. | Germany--Fiction. | BISAC: FICTION / Literary. | FICTION / Historical / World War II. | FICTION / Medical.
Classification: LCC PT8950.B528 F67 2021| DDC 839.823 B557E--dc23
LC record available at https://lccn.loc.gov/2021930265

Contents

FOREWORD

Joe Martin

I have always been fascinated by the manner in which the controversial and socially engaged author Jens Bjørneboe (1920-1976) imbued his many works with elements of his personal journey in life and the events that contributed to the evolution of his world-view. It is of particular interest that in his peculiar literary "method" he is often a profound presence in his fiction, unlike other authors whose personal biographies and even their personal "voice" vanish from their art. The fact is that his character-narrators in his most important works, often stand-ins for himself, may have been born of necessity—in order to get around the limits set by the marketplace in art and literature early in his career.

To better explain the paradox being discussed here, let me turn to some other great modern European writers. Bertolt Brecht was an important influence on Bjørneboe, but his personal life was almost entirely absent from his works—in which he (and his collaborators) strove to take an allegedly "scientific" approach to story-telling and the nexus of personal and economic relations. In Norway, Ibsen's earlier realism also made every attempt to remove the author's life from his portrayal of individuals in the matrix of social realities. This was also the case with Balzac in his vast cycle of fiction, *La Comédie humaine.* On the other end of the spectrum, as a novelist and sometimes in his more famous work as a playwright, the prolific Swedish author August Strindberg wrote his own life story into many works he presented as fictional such as *Inferno* and *A Madman's Defense*. These novels contained thinly disguised events emerging from his own life (including distorted perspectives due to his protagonists' overheated mental states or unsettling spiritual quests). In *Inferno* Strindberg's main character embarks on journeys through various landscapes in Europe which resemble awakened dreams, and the narrator Strindberg often describes real events, but colored through various altered states. He refers to his family members and his own literary works. His *Road to Damascus* trilogy of early expressionist plays made use of some of the same events. There the protagonist was called "The Stranger."

In *Keeper of the Protocols* (*Protokollføreren* in Norwegian), my earlier exploration of Bjørneboe's works, I drew from a scene in Strindberg's *A Dream Play* in which the Advocate defending the oppressed says that he keeps recorded accounts of injustice. At one point he asks Indra's Daughter, an avatar who bears witness to humankind's suffering, to "look at these papers where I write histories of injustice" (". . . se på dessa papper där jag forfatter historier om orät"). The Advocate is one of several stand-ins for the author-playwright, this time a socially engaged figure, as Strindberg also devoted a lot of his works to such concerns as a young radical and again later in life when he launched a great political debate on behalf of democratic socialism now called "the Strindberg feud."

Jens Bjørneboe's Servant of Justice—the narrator of his master-work, the trilogy known as "The History of Bestiality"—keeps the written "records" of some sort of real court of justice as well as a sort of court of history, investigating the sins of cruelty, oppression, and tyranny arising from all corners of Western civilization, never giving the writer's last name. He does, however, bring in various doubles with international first names (Iwan, Giovanni, Johannes, etc.) that can be rendered in Norwegian as "Jens." The internal narrator of the trilogy relates some episodes that appear to be from Bjørneboe's own life, but also from the annals of history. These are works on not only barbarous totalitarian movements like those of Fascism, Nazism, and Stalinism, but also witch burnings, the cult around execution as punishment, and the depredations of colonialism in the developing world.

Esther Greenleaf Mürer—the creator of loyal and dynamic translations of Bjørneboe's major works *Moment of Freedom*, *Powderhouse*, *The Silence*, and *The Sharks*, as well as some of his important essays and works for theatre—has turned here to the author's early novel *Ere the Cock Crows* (*Før hann galer*). The book is not ranked in Norway or Europe in general with those other novels as one of his masterpieces, but as the first published novel from the pen of a rising figure in Norwegian literature. Mürer has also reconstituted his earlier work with the material in which he attempted to put it into dramatic form.

In the early 1950s, during a period when Bjørneboe published his first breakthrough poetry collections, he also published *Ere the Cock Crows*, which represents his first published confrontation with systematic human cruelty. His earliest understanding of Nazi inhumanity came about as an adolescent when he read Wolfgang Langhoff's book *Die Moorsoldaten* that described the earliest concentration camps, specifically the camp at Oranienberg from which Langhoff had escaped. According to his own report, Bjørneboe was shaken to his core. This was especially so because in his youth he was profoundly influenced by German culture. Thus began his devastating insights into what a culturally developed nation is capable of when they are overcome by a cult of ignorance and glorified ruthlessness towards enemies, be they real or imagined. Insights into the broader trajectory of the history of the Western world were to follow.

Before the seeds of this insight took form artistically, he fled the Nazi occupation in Norway to Sweden where he studied painting and was mentored by the painter and Matisse disciple Isaac Grünewald. He has also described this period with a somewhat self-accusatory irony—noting his own obsession with Byzantine painting in the year Auschwitz was liberated and publicized—even as nuclear bombs were dropped on two Japanese cities. However, soon after the war ended he launched upon a journey, traveling as a journalist to the ruins of the German cities where—as Esther Mürer outlines in the essay also included in this volume—he received from a medical official the court records of the trials of physicians who had engaged in medical experiments on living human beings both outside and inside the concentration camps.

Mürer has taken a very particular angle on the project. She knew that Bjørneboe's first attempt at a full-length play was submitted and rejected for production due to its subject matter: the Nazi medical experiments on captive human subjects. As she describes it, she discovered through the commentary of a Norwegian critic that the central chapters of the novel were built on that lost play, involving the Nazi doctors, their circle of collaborators, and family members. The central physician involved is portrayed as a respected and well-liked member of the community and as a warm and engaged family man. As she explains in her rich and detailed essay "Jens Bjørneboe's *Ere the Cock Crows*: The Novel and the Play," the records of the medical trials in Germany focused on a Dr. Rascher (who becomes Dr. Reynhardt in the novel and play), the man who led such "experiments," and these provided the source material for the original play. Not content to simply undertake the first English translation the novel, she has proceeded to work down to the earliest layers of Bjørneboe's project, as I see it, uncovering the roots of his later literary method. This is a truly unusual project of literary excavation.

I am suggesting that there are some other facts here that will interest readers of Bjørneboe in terms of his better-known works, mentioned previously. Mürer makes us aware that this is the first attempt to consciously weave his own life and explorations into fiction—including his own willingness, like so many others, to look away from the darkest events of the time: a profound abandonment of conscience that swept so many people in Europe. Later his "journey in the land of Chaos" as he referred to it, will give his fiction the qualities sometimes associated with Franz Kafka's "Josef K" in *The Trial* and "Surveyor K" in *The Castle*, who had suffered from the delusion that they were free. Kafka's narratives are wanderings in a landscape of the absurd, resembling that of Kafka's own Prague.

The opening chapters of novel *Ere the Cock Crows* begin with a journalist-narrator, Bjørneboe's thinly disguised stand-in, arriving in an unnamed German city where he is given material from the court cases of Nazi medical experiments, with a focus on one particularly heinous case involving a Dr. Reynhardt. The frame device of the novel allows him to show how an investigative writer—a journalist or novelist depending on how one looks at it—might undertake a personal journey to investigate such evil. What we find here, again, is an early example of the author Bjørneboe inserting himself into a literary presentation about the origins of evil—originally done in order to make a novel out of a rejected play. The dramatic work it seems originally took an objective point of view, without an internal narrator, on "professional" and personal relations within the world of these Nazis and the compromised people around them—including those who try to resist compromising themselves. Mürer's project of literary excavation has culminated in this volume that contains both works: a loyal translation of the novel as published, and an attempt at reconstruction of the play in English. And here we see how a misadventure in an author's choice of genre may have given rise to similar and more sophisticated devices in his later works. One can imagine that the dialogue of the original play might even provide English-speaking theatre artists (with the aid of elements included in the novel) the opportunity to make use of the English-language reconstruction of a play that is no longer available to us, but based on historical fact. From this material a production or performance-piece speaking to our times might be constructed.

I suggest this possibility as the material is relevant for an America that has recently passed through a traumatizing period—one that has provided a warning of how the strategies of fascist and racist regimes of the past can be introduced like a contagion into a democratic culture. Ere the Cock Crows is an artistic rendering of a worst-case scenario, of the institutionalization of cruelty under the auspices of the state. It's a danger alive in the present.

After the creation of American detention facilities for migrant and refugee families led to forced separations of many hundreds of children from their parents who were sent thousands of miles away from each other, removing all data or information that might allow them to find each other, we find ourselves subject to a playbook that has been used before. Where migrant women are subjected to sterilization and hysterectomies for reasons never made clear—and where the women who suffered these medical violations of their lives and bodies are deported before they can tell the tale, we must not ignore that this playbook has been documented and exposed before. Who could not have known Americans were on a precipice similar to that over which an entire European culture fell headlong into barbarism? That we have not yet fallen over the precipice and into barbarism and universal violence, that we have seemingly preserved a society of law, does not negate the fact that we have come close. And the phenomenon has not just appeared recently in America. There is a similar dynamic abroad that also should have been purged by the warnings of history.

In Bjørneboe's first script for theatre, and later in the novel, he bears witness to just how such social and humanitarian catastrophes happen—and continue to happen—in authoritarian systems and even in modern and mature democracies.

After *Ere the Cock Crows*, Jens Bjørneboe would raise his literary warning to a pitch of even greater clarity, in an increasingly masterful manner until his death in 1976. The centenary celebration of his life in 2020, in publications, in forums, and in theatres in Norway, revealed that his voice remains a provocative one and his message prescient. A great part of that message is that we must bear witness to history, even if we weren't alive during those past events or part of them. Because nevertheless, we are part of the processes of history. We can shape our destiny and claim our true freedom only if we realize that.

Joe Martin is Senior Lecturer in Theatre Arts and Studies at Johns Hopkins University and a Fulbright Specialist in Theatre. He is the author of *Keeper of the Protocols: The Works of Jens Bjørneboe in the Crosscurrents of Western Literature* (Peter Lang, 1996) and has translated Bjørneboe's play *Semmelweis* (Sun and Moon Press, 1999).

Ere the Cock Crows

Part One

1. THE COMPATRIOT

I WAS THINKING of the incident with the rat the whole time. Even as I followed her through the bombed parts of the city, I couldn't get the animal out of my mind. I just saw Frau Müller's back ahead of me, moving up and down, up and down, right and left—however she had to bend to avoid railings and studs, beams and doorposts, or once in a while clamber over heaps of stone and plaster. And I followed half mechanically after her.

I had wakened unusually early that morning. It was still dark, but I felt that there was something alive in my room. When I turned on the light, I saw that the clock showed just after five. The lamp on the nightstand cast a faint yellowish light out into the attic room, a little of it across the worn floorboards, but mostly up toward the sloped ceiling. What was moving in the room I couldn't see. It was just as invisible as in the dark, but it continued its business undisturbed, with a strange squeaking and snarling sound. Presently I understood that the sound was coming from the rat trap which I'd set up over by the door, outside the gleam of the lamp. And when I stood barefoot on the floor, I saw a strange sight: in the trap lay a rather large rat, its head swaying. It was the source of the cries. Beside it stood another rat. At first it looked as if it were sniffing at its imprisoned comrade. Then it turned its head, and stood calmly looking at me. With tiny, glittering eyes. I'd never before seen a rat which didn't flee at the sight of people, and of late I'd certainly met a lot of them. Only when I got almost all the way over to them did it turn and scurry away with the usual rustling sound. The rat in the trap went on squeaking. The steel spring had caught it across the back, but too far down. Its spine was snapped and its hind legs paralyzed, so that its hindquarters just lay like a bloated, dead sack out over the rim of the trap. It was full of small, shiny flecks of blood. But its head and forelegs were alive enough, and it was trying with all its might to get free. I looked around for something to kill it with, and on the top board of my improvised bookshelf I found my hammer. I aimed carefully and struck, but the blow glanced off, so that I only crushed its snout. I swallowed my nausea and struck again, quickly and instinctively, without aiming—I felt a boundless relief that the rat was dead, and I decided to leave it there until I had gotten up for real. Besides I could only get rid of it by carrying it down five flights to the trash cans in the yard. A while later I went back to sleep.

When I next awoke, it was seven-thirty. I turned on the electric hot plate and started dressing. But when I glanced toward the door, I saw to my astonishment that the dead rat was not alone. Its comrade from last night was beside it. I couldn't understand what it was doing. And it was most unwilling to flee. I was no more than two feet away when it snarled at me for the last time and vanished into the hole by the door. Only when I bent down to take away the dead rat did I understand why the live one was so loath to leave it. The head of the dead one was transformed into one big bloody lump, no, to a bloody shred of skin. And over the floor were strewn tiny pink bits of flesh.

Frau Müller led the way through the ruins. She walked quickly and purposefully, but always in her quiet, listening way. Had we been strolling through the half-cleared streets, we would have walked side by side. But as it was, she kept taking shortcuts straight through the leveled blocks. So I walked behind her on the path, which was already well-trodden. You can't converse when you're walking single file like that, and without exchanging a word we went across foundation walls and courtyards, around collapsed buildings and between piles of wrecked furniture and crushed bricks. I thought that there must be thousands of rats under the foundation walls.

Does it rain more on ruins than on other landscapes? I don't know, but I think so. Or perhaps it's just because *this* image sticks in the soul better than other images do: Wet, sticky wet, glistening blocks of ruins, full of viscous ash. The saddest thing on earth is a wet wasteland. And the remains of the bombed city are our wasteland. They are Frau Müller's wasteland. They are my wasteland.

Flat, flat may the wasteland be, but there grow trees in it, trees which need no sun or nourishment. The wild growths are the remains of twisted water pipes and steel skeletons bristling toward the sky. Here and there a tottering chimney points upward—to show where the great change came from. Here and there one wall of a house is left standing, with the wind blowing through dead windows and with the scars left by the floors. From the wall you can see how the rooms were laid out: *here* was a kitchen, *there* was a bathroom. The tiles hang in pale squares, and gas and water pipes draw strange ornaments against them. To the left stands a huge, old-rose rectangle. That was a parlor. Farther left, a blue rectangle. That was a bedroom. There were people living everywhere, folk who mostly slept and worked. Where are they now?

Some are still lying under the rubble, but the others? The miles of dust-gray cemeteries, where cornices are tombstones, and rusty bathtubs are cisterns half full of yellow rainwater—the fields of ruins haven't swallowed them all. Where are the grandmothers who lived here? Where are the women who were always fetching bread and milk? And the fathers with their evening papers in their hands? Where are all the little girls with thin German braids hanging down over their shoulders? And the schoolboys with short pants and scars on their knees?

I walk behind Frau Müller, and our path winds through the remains of a courtyard. Across the path lies a mutilated doll with a faded celluloid head and wood shavings oozing out of its belly. Further along I find a doll buggy without wheels or hood. A roofing tile has laid itself protectively over a charred volume of Jules Verne's *Twenty Thousand Leagues Under the Sea*. Once you've become aware of it, you don't see anything else—marbles, a magnifying glass, something which was once a pocket knife—intimate, earthly remains of many childhoods. I even saw the wreck of a mechanical building set during this first trip with Frau Müller. It was lying at the bottom of a perforated leather chair.

But it's odd and absurd how much I see which has to do with bathrooms, again and again; gas heaters, showers and bathtubs. Bathtubs. You wouldn't think people had done anything but bathe. Against what was once a foundation wall, I find seven whole bathtubs inside each other, all nicely stacked. They had never been installed. And one and the same bomb fragment has gone through them, has cut seven triangular holes in seven bathtub bottoms of cast iron. Further off lay a rusty water pistol.

The trip with Frau Müller had a definite goal. We were on the way to Max.

I knew that he shared an attic room with three other living corpses from the war. They lay there year after year, but wouldn't die. Max was an SS man, a ruin of a human being, worse than any of the ruins we had to clamber through to get to him.

Frau Müller still keeps in touch with them; visits them regularly, puts up with their insults and curses, and sees that they don't starve to death. She probably knows more than a hundred of them in all, and spends whatever time is left over from the visits begging food and money for them.

The worst case of them all is probably Max; a very young cripple. He is paralyzed in both legs from being shot in the back. But despite the dead lower body his head and arms are living enough, and had he been in better shape he would have murdered his three roommates to get more space—a plan he has mentioned often. But it is postponed for the nonce. Max was trained and educated at a concentration camp, and was only sent to serve at the front toward the end of the war. It was to him, then, that Frau Müller was leading me that summer day we went together through the ruined city. From now on we shall call her Eva.

However, Eva has one weakness. Even if she is penniless today, she comes from rather high middle-class circles. And she can't stand obscenities. Max and his peers didn't take long to discover that, and every time she appeared in the doorway, she was deluged with foul language. The complaints about the food packages and the cigarettes she brought with her were liberally mixed with everything of that sort which the paralyzed spiritual ruin could produce. It was no different the first time I went along.

I stood in the half-darkness by the door while Eva went from bed to bed and dispensing what she had brought. Her round, friendly face was immobile under the flood of words.

When she came to the SS man she stopped:

"That's enough now, Max! I've brought you a visitor."

Max stopped talking and turned his head. When he caught sight of me standing under the pitched ceiling, he stuck out his lower lip and smiled. His head was tilted, and in the sharp, focused rays from the skylight the smile became a strange, friendly grimace. He had grown fat from lying there, but would still have been a handsome man had the folds in his face not been so unnaturally deep. He wasn't more than twenty-four.

"Hello!" he said. "Yankee?"

"Sorry, no," I replied, and explained that I was Norwegian.

The smile changed to a fleer, at once scornful and inviting.

"Oh," he said. "From an occupied country."

All Balts resemble each other as if they could be from the same family. Max too had the family looks: ash blond, Finnish hair and a square, light face. He was very broad across the shoulders. His hands had short, broad nails with blackened quicks.

"But we make very good Virginia cigarettes," I added, and threw a pack of Cravens onto the blanket.

"Sit down!" he replied, and pointing to the foot of the bed. "Don't worry if there's a foot under your behind. I won't feel it."

I sat down on the bed, while Eva went out to empty the urine bottle. He nodded after her.

"She's nuts!" he said calmly.

The room was filled with a compact, intense stink. And when Eva came in again, she opened the hatch in the roof. Amid protests from the sick people. Even the dusty, exhaust-filled summer air

which streamed into the room felt like manna from another world.
It was six o'clock in the evening. Then Eva introduced me to the
other three inhabitants, with commentary from Max.

"This is Willi," said Eva, "Twenty-one years old."

"Leaky roof," said Max.

"Fractured skull," continued Eva.

"Idiot," added Max.

"He's done for, poor thing," said Eva.

The boy in the bed was yellow-faced and seemed dull-witted. He
would never get up again.

"It's him that pisses himself," continued Max. "We'll never get rid
of 'im unless we kill 'im."

The man in the third bed was blind, and his features had the strangely
loose, soft quality which the blind often have. His skin was moist and
pale as flour. He spoke a broad farm dialect, and kept thanking Eva for
the food. He had to keep it by him in the bed so the others wouldn't
steal it from him, he explained. Then he thanked her again.

"Jus' listen to 'im!" said Max. "Yecch!"

And he rained obscenities over the blind man like hail, while we
greeted the next one. The fourth man in the room was of Max's type,
but of smaller build. The crutches by his bed showed that could walk.
Max used him to run errands.

Eva asked Max not to plague the blind man any more.

"Go to hell, old woman!" he replied calmly. "And don't you plague
us! Yeah, go away, so that for once we don't have to look at that ugly,
pockmarked mug of yours!"

It hit home. For Eva actually had a number of small scars on her face,
something she had never entirely got rid of. She looked away.

"You prolly got scars all over the resta you, too," he went on. And
suddenly he raised his head, gripped by a strange excitement:

"Damn it to hell—it's a pity they stopped the euthanasia! You should
damn well be gassed, the whole lot of you! Yecch! You should be done
away with! Hypocritical old bats and Jew devils. What the hell do you
think you're doing here, you Jewish shit?"

The last was to me, and it was hard to find an answer. In a way he was of course right to ask what I was doing there. Eva laid a finger across her lips. Max lit a Craven and lay back in the bed. Then he laughed, a bit embarrassed and clearly out of control.

"You use such fine foreign words," I said; "*Euthanasia*—where did you learn that?"

"Worked in a place like that meself," he replied. "We burnt up hundreds in a coupla days."

His face was utterly distorted as he looked at me. It was meant as a kind of smile. And slowly it dawned on me how sick he was. I found it difficult to breathe.

"Too bad it's over! Too bad it's over!" he repeated. "We had booze and a whorehouse every blasted day—and all fulla Jews. That was a fine time, when we worked for Dr. Reynhardt. Hard, but fine."

Eva suddenly sat down on the bed, her face as white as cotton. I thought she was going to faint.

"Did you know Dr. Reynhardt?" she whispered to Max.

"Hell, yes! *That* was his name."

Max looked at her with curled upper lip and a fixed stare. The memories lived so strongly in him that his youthful face was almost lifeless. He was far, far away in a world which no one could share with him.

The effect on Eva was so uncanny that I no longer noticed what was being said. That must have been why the name didn't strike me as familiar. It went by me like an empty sound, like a ball thrown into the room. Only later did I realize that I knew the name Dr. Reynhardt from before, and that all of us had something to do with that name.

It was getting darker in the room.

And in the twilight Eva gradually came to herself again. She turned on the lights and went on putting the room in order. But before we left I was already clear that I must come back and speak with Max—alone. And what Eva later told about him confirmed me in this.

When we were back on the street, I asked how she could stand to work under such conditions. A little nervously she answered that the reward was meeting such people as Lüngbü.

"As who?" I didn't get the name.

"As your compatriot," she answered; "Lüngbü. I've told you about him."

Then I remembered that she had mentioned him before. Lyngby was his name.

And suddenly she looked at me with all that blue in those irises:

"He's a saint!"

Now I *knew* Eva; she thought that most people were wonderful. And I must not have looked especially convinced, for she repeated what she had said:

"Yes, he's a saint. I've never met such a person before. And what he's done for our relief work, nobody can imagine."

The German passion for Northmen at times becomes intense, and Eva was a passionate soul. As we walked through the streets in the dusk she told about Lyngby. And gradually he began to interest me. If only the half of what she said were true, my countryman must be an very remarkable person. And if he was a saint, then he was a saint of a new and exceptional sort. At least there's something peculiar about a man who doesn't bother to come home after several years' stay in a German concentration camp, but who instead puts all his energy into relief work among the German populace. Still, at the moment I was more interested in Max, and presently led the conversation around to him.

It was a long walk, and the warm July evening was now totally dark. Eva walked small and shadowlike beside me, a strange peace around her. She seemed tired and rather old, but her step was light.

"Max is twenty-three years old," she began; "and an Estonian. At the age of seventeen he had joined the SS, and had had two years of special training in a concentration camp. During this time and later he had taken part in special pogrom raids in Poland and Eastern Europe. He was first sent to the front in '45."

"What does 'pogrom raids in Poland and the East' mean?" I asked.

"It means massacres in the ghettoes," replied Eva. "There were specially educated SS divisions which were assigned to extermination campaigns against the Jews. They were first trained in German camps, then driven to the ghettoes in the East in sealed railroad cars. There they were filled with booze and let loose on the population without ammunition, but with bayonets on their rifles. It was both a kind of mass liquidation and a form of mental training to which the SS's elite troops were subjected."

I fought down the nausea which rose up in me, and took some rapid deep breaths. For a moment the houses, the streets and the lights around me were so unreal that I could stick my hand through them.

"Isn't it hard to have to deal with Max?"

"Ever since they killed Edward, I've tried to work at something," she replied. "And Max has never had the chance to become a human being."

Eva walked beside me and went on talking quietly, and her voice detached itself from her so completely that it permeated the air around me.

"And Max took part in the pogroms?" I asked.

The heels of our shoes clattered against the pavement while I waited for an answer. For a long time she walked on as if she were thinking about something else.

"Max can tell you about that himself," she replied.

"What would the police do if they got hold of him?"

"Death penalty."

"How did he get sent to the front?"

"It was the front that saved him. He was standing and smoking in an ammunition depot, and a watchman came in and said that that was forbidden. Max just laughed. But when the other went to report it, Max shot him from behind. They never got any real proof, but he'd become suspect, and so they put him in a different uniform. At the front he wore the common Wehrmacht uniform until he was shot in the back, and was put into an ordinary field hospital. As he was lying wounded out in the field, he regained consciousness and found two Russians bending over him—a young one and an old one. The younger wanted to kill him with his rifle butt, but the elder held him back. After talking for awhile they brought water in a helmet and let him drink. Max thinks they were nuts."

When we had come back to the populated streets it dawned on me that I'd meant to ask her about something. But it was only after we had reached the corner where we parted that I remembered what it was. And I would have run across the street after her, but just then a car drove between us, the traffic light turned red, and the car stopped. So instead I called after her, for we weren't more than five or six meters apart:

"What name was it he mentioned?"

She heard my voice through the street noise, but didn't understand right away.

"Who?"

"Max! He mentioned someone he'd worked for! Who was that!?"

I shouted at the top of my lungs, for more and more cars were collecting around us.

Eva looked around in the throng, as if she didn't want to say the name out loud. She was standing in the middle of a river of black car bodies. For the moment it was dammed up by the two red lights, and stood rising and rising as if it would overflow. She shouted something or other which drowned in the cascade of noise. And I shook my head to show that I hadn't heard.

"You don't know him!" she yelled so loudly that her voice pressed forward: "It was a friend of mine—a long time ago—many years ago!"

My heart began to pound wildly, and I raised my head so that she should hear me better.

"Max's employer?" I yelled.

"Yes!" she yelled back. "He's dead. He was killed. He was accused of every possible crime....But there was nobody who...."

Then the lights turned green again, and the cars started moving. There must have been over thirty of them waiting to go, and now they all began gliding forward at once. The noise of the motors strangled all sound from Eva, but I could see her lips moving as in a silent film. I shook my head and waved goodbye, and a moment later she was gone. As I jumped back onto the sidewalk a fender bumped me, but I didn't fall. I just made good speed over to the wall of a building, where I stood watching the procession of cars and headlights glide past me. The warm, hazy, dark summer evening was full of gasoline and exhaust, the big city's own exotic bouquet. For a moment I felt faint as I stood on the sidewalk. I would have liked to know more about Dr...., Dr..... I had no inkling of the name. Then I walked down, following the stream, around the corner and up into the dark streets. I lived not far away.

ⅎ⅓

IT WAS UNBEARABLY HOT in the stairwell, and as usual the lights weren't working. The loose, old-fashioned wiring had to be repaired almost daily if they were to work. And who has time for such things? The switches weren't good either. Either they wouldn't turn on, or they wouldn't turn off. And even when they were functioning, the system itself was still old-fashioned and clumsy. At every landing there was a double set of switches, so that you could turn off the lights on the floor you had just passed, and turn on the lights for the next one. When you got up to the next landing you had to repeat the process. This is common in Germany, and people have got used to saving. Thrift has become second nature.

Today nothing was working. On the third landing I stumbled in the dark over a pile of brick, and on the fourth there was a loose floorboard. Only up in the attic was there light.

I let myself in through the two flimsy doors which led to the attic room. The used rat trap was still standing on the floor. The warmth in the room was indescribable, and I hurriedly opened the window so that the room slowly filled with relatively cool gasoline fumes from outside. Then I discovered that the hot plate was on, which explained the incredible temperature. I had forgotten it after my morning coffee. At least the tea water was soon hot. After my tea I dozed off in the wicker chair.

But first I sat for a little and listened to the sounds in the house. It was built after the last war—an inflation project using cheap materials. At the beginning, say thirty years ago, the house may have been good enough, but today it's run-down. The plaster is falling off, often in strange big flakes which reveal the netting underneath, the floor sags mightily under your footsteps, and the doors and windows no longer shut properly. In winter the damp, short-lived snow comes in through the cracks around the skylight. And the house carries sound. The whole attic is inhabited. We live side by side and can keep up with each other's lives. From the other floors too sounds penetrate up to us. The hall and the attic are full of things, suitcases and books and bad furniture. Even the stairwell is utilized, and that's why it's so difficult to navigate in the dark. But there are altogether too many of us in the house, and we have no extra space in our rooms. In any other country it would doubtless be an evil that the house is so far from soundproof, but here it's different. Evening after evening I can hear Bauer's violin.

The evening after my first visit to Max, Bauer was playing something by Mozart two floors below me. It was the rondo from a concerto in A minor, and the music sounded wonderfully delicate and joyous—like a joy from a different star. I'd already heard it while I was still out in the dark hall.

I felt surprisingly weak as I drank my tea and ate a couple of pieces of *knekkebrød* with it. And I had a vague notion that it wasn't just Eva who needed a vacation. The first two summer months had been uncommonly exhausting, and August would be even warmer and dustier.

Then the violin rose into my thoughts. It stayed there and grew like a vine, a sort of musical creeper.

When I woke up, I was drenched with sweat and had been dreaming. It wasn't a pleasant dream.

I'd been sleeping in the wicker chair, leaning on my right arm, which was wedged between my body and the armrest. It felt numb from my shoulder to my wrist, and was wet on the inside. As I tried to rub life into it again, I went over the dream in my thoughts. I moved my feet down off the old piano stool which I used as a desk chair. The position had made my knees stiff, and all in all I felt pretty miserable. In the dream I was back out in the ruins. I was amid the remains of a courtyard and was clambering over a big pile of old bricks. On the way down I saw a dog's snout sticking out between the stones. It was the broad, dark snout of a bulldog. I thought it was a shame for the dead dog to be lying like that, and began pulling the bricks away. They were dark red with remains of mortar on them, and there were rags and scrap iron between them. Above us the sky had a strange windswept, hard blue color, broken only by small, chalk-white clouds. When I had dug the dog out, I saw that it was yellow and wet, its joints utterly slack. It was blinking its eyes a little. "So here's where the dog was buried,"[1] I said aloud. And though I was annoyed at the stupid pun, I couldn't stop laughing. I laughed and laughed, and my voice echoed from the wall still standing on the other side of the yard. I laughed until I cried. Only when the dog got to its feet was I able to stop. It looked at me for a long time, then went to the attack. I defended myself, but couldn't prevent its getting hold of my right hand, and the warmth and the slime in its mouth felt far stronger than the teeth which pressed in between the bones of my hand, then moved further up and bit through my forearm. Finally I felt the animal's warm, stinking breath as it bit me in the shoulder. Its face was now on a level with my own, and I fell back toward the sharp edges in the pile of bricks. That put the dog's head further away. Strangely enough the bite of the huge jaws didn't hurt. And high up I saw the sky above me. The bold blueness was gone now. Only through the holes in the cloud cover could you still see it. Otherwise the sky was a luminous white, with some of the bricks in the pile silhouetted dark and heavy against the air. I bent my head backward trying to catch sight of the sun. It had to be somewhere behind the clouds. I craned my neck with all my might to find it. Around me it was getting brighter and brighter. The sun was very near, and suddenly I was looking straight into it. With a fierce effort I opened my eyes and woke up. On the table before me the lamp was burning.

There was a knock on the door. It was Heini, the youngest of the Bauer boys. He shouted that I had a phone call. And I followed him down the stairs, fumbling in the dark, but relieved at being drawn out of the oppressive feeling the dream had left behind. It was Eva wanting to speak to me, and Heini's round, close-cropped head stayed in the

---

1. Norwegian proverbial expression equivalent to "there's the rub" or "that's the real trouble/hidden agenda."

doorway for a while before he returned to the parlor. The family quartet took a break while I talked on the phone.

"He's here!" shouted Eva.

Her voice sang more than usual. Through the glass in the door I could see that the light in the parlor was dimmed. They were saving electricity during the break, while they didn't need it for reading music. In the telephone alcove lay a well-sharpened pencil and a little trimmed toilet paper instead of a notepad.

"Who?" I asked.

"Lüngbü!" replied Eva, somewhat miffed because I hadn't immediately understood who she meant.

"Oh," I said, "Lyngby."

"He's in town now. You can meet him this evening, if you wish."

I looked at the clock. It was three minutes past nine. And I thought about the dream and about my room. The water in X-burg is chlorinated, so that the tea secretes a kind of oil-like skin on the surface, and gradually leaves a coating in the cup.

"Where in town is he?" I asked.

I had little desire to sit up in my room the rest of the evening, but the prospect of an hour's trolley ride didn't appeal to me either.

"We're at Dunkers' now," she replied.

That decided the matter. I would be spared the trolley. To Dunkers' house was barely a fifteen-minute walk. And the thought of meeting Dunkers cheered me up. He was an Englishman, a major in the same international relief organization Eva worked for—and clearly the same with which Lyngby too was involved....

ဆာ ငာ

WHEN I RANG Dunkers' bell, it was Eva who opened the door. She seemed elated and happy, the way she could be sometimes.

"I'm so glad you're finally going to meet!" she said.

I understood that she meant Lyngby and me, which underscored a certain uneasiness I'd felt on the way over—the unwelcome thought of

Eva's having already talked about me in such terms that Lyngby must perforce be disappointed at meeting me as I really was. Nobody can live up to Eva's description. And I felt as if I was on the way to an absurd and unnecessary exam, which I was certain to fail. I was so irritated that I would have turned tail in the corridor had I not suddenly heard Dunkers' laughter inside, soft and irresistibly friendly. So when Eva opened the door, I pulled myself together and went in. From Dunkers I had nothing to fear—he knew me from before, and wouldn't meet me with particular expectations.

In the dim German lamplight I first saw Dunkers' back, and next I caught sight of Lyngby.

Even before the men had stood up, I understood that even if I had come to see the Englishman, the evening was going to be totally dominated by the meeting with the other. Lyngby saw me the moment I appeared in the doorway, but instead of standing up he finished what he was saying:

"…and still I'm sure that no matter what sin a person commits— anything, anything!—he can be cleansed of it again!"

It wasn't the words which made an impression on me. It was the way they were spoken. It was the calm and the certainty, the gestures and the look. He spoke like an old sailor does about the weather. His gaze was absent and at the same time eerily present. It was as if he were recounting a memory—he could just as well have said:

"…in such and such a place the northeast trade wind blows."

It is very difficult to explain how Lyngby affected me, but I had the feeling that he was uncommonly big, that he filled the whole room. Later I saw that he was only an inch or so taller than me, in other words slightly over medium height. And around the same time I noticed the scar below his cheekbone. Well, it was more a deep hole than a scar— like a gouge in his face.

The whole evening we didn't speak one word of Norwegian. The conversation took place in German, only occasionally broken by scraps of English. Lyngby spoke excellent German. He spoke slowly and very distinctly, as if savoring the perfect sentences before releasing them into the room—something which many people do with a language they've mastered, but which is still not their own. His English wasn't as good. And the velar *r*, which sounded fine in German, was distracting when it came through in English. It surprised me a bit, but I assumed that he was born in Western or Southern Norway.

What did we talk about, that first evening?

The three of them kept coming back to things which they were interested in; always something to do with their relief work—especially the refugee problem. Lyngby seemed to know all about this, and I had a feeling that the others were using him like a reference book. But when I think about it, nothing happened that evening. Nothing except that I met Lyngby and that he made an inordinately strong impression on me. Eva made tea. Dunkers offered us cigarettes. That was all.

And it must have been the aftermath of my meeting with Lyngby which have since made me think of these hours as having special significance. It was a wholly ordinary evening.—If I were to characterize Lyngby with one word, it would have to be: vitality. But it wasn't ordinary vitality or power—it was an overwhelming spiritual vitality. When I try to say how Lyngby affected me, I must recall some words by a forgotten writer named Nietzsche: "I'm not a human being, I'm dynamite." But the strangest thing about Lyngby's greater intensity was that it didn't embarrass or oppress anyone. I've experienced "strong personalities" before, and for the most part they are annoying. The substance in them isn't clear. Lyngby was transparent.—But I'm forgetting the most important thing, some words which were uttered, and which perhaps give the key to Lyngby's whole character. In the middle of the conversation he went off on a tangent. He referred to a couple of unfamiliar names, and concluded with: "Once I was with a man day and night for two years. We had eight square meters to move around in, and got very little to eat. But he knew the Gospel of John by heart—word for word. And after a few months that took the place of both the motion and the food."

Of course similar things have been told of Catherine of Siena, but Catherine was a saint, and Lyngby—well....

And twice more it came up again, the same theme which he and Dunkers had been discussing when I came in: the question of guilt. And it must have been Lyngby who led the discussion around to it without the rest of us noticing. Later I realized that he had a definite reason for wanting to talk about it, but it's easy to have hindsight. In any case that's the only sign of weakness I've seen in him. That first evening I didn't attach any special weight to it.

After the visit to Dunkers several days passed before I had any more to do with Lyngby. And I hardly thought of him. I was much too preoccupied with Max. I thought about him by day, and dreamed about him at night. And it was one single word he had said, and which bound me to him: euthanasia—"death assistance." Max had worked at a station for euthanasia and experimental medicine. He had got his training there, the last fine honing which had made him what he was today—a man who would murder his mother for a cigarette.

Max had helped write one of the darkest chapters in world history. He was alive. He was free. And he had no regrets.

At this time I was probably the only person in Norway who had made a thorough study of the material behind the so-called "Doctors' Trials". When I was in Germany the year before, a German scientist had passed on to me documents concerning the medical experiments conducted in some of the camps during the Third Reich. I wrote a little about it in newspapers and magazines. But the material was of such a character that I couldn't get rid of it again. It sat fast in my body like a strange corrosive heaviness. One who has been inside the mountain will never more be glad. And that's how I felt back then. I had got a glimpse into human nature in a way that I wasn't prepared for; and I saw that neither will he who has met the Evil One be happy again right away. I felt instinctively that if I stopped halfway I would become, as it were, an invalid for life.

At that time I was still overwhelmed, dumbfounded; in my mind the crimes seemed fantastic and incredible—superhuman in a way. And the need to understand how they had been possible felt overpowering.

Max's role in the tragic drama wasn't large. He was an extra. But he had stood on the stage, and he had seen the stars close up. And he was still alive.

Two days after that first meeting I was again in the attic room. This time without Eva. Everything was the same, except that the stink was if possible even worse than before. Max smirked triumphantly when he saw me.

He had expected the visit. Somewhat taken by surprise I sat on the edge of the bed and unpacked the goods I had brought with me. Aside from Max there were only two in the room, the feebleminded one and the blind one. The one with the crutches was out shopping, probably for his boss, Max. The SS-man had been sure that I would come back, but he didn't know what I wanted. And I for my part had expected to have difficulty getting anything out of him, but I was wrong. Well supplied with Virginia cigarettes and strangely flattered by my interest, he was willing to talk far more openly than I had dared to hope.

Like so many cynics of the primitive type, he considered himself someone who had once and for all seen through life and human nature, and a strongly developed conceit was the inevitable result. Vanity was his weak point, and this vanity was *spiritual.* In fact we simply made a deal: He satisfied my desire to know, answered all my questions and placed his very good memory at my disposal—in return for my listening silently and accepting his commentaries. These commentaries were of a psychological sort and at times extremely penetrating and sharp, primitive and vile. Their weakness lay in a one-sidedness bordering on insanity. This one-sidedness consisted an ability to sketch with a few words an ice-cold and crystal-clear portrait of the basest qualities of human nature. These qualities were for Max the true and eternal ones. And from comments on his narrative he often wandered off into what was clearly his philosophy of life. The digressions were persistent, and since the philosophy was as boring as it was unoriginal, they often became an annoyance which I had to take with the rest. They grew irksome especially because this first solo visit of mine was followed by so many more, and because he understood so well how to get his generous share of our bargain. Over the summer I often sat for hours listening to him hold forth, unable to break off the stream of words. His need for an audience was just as strong as his vanity. And contradiction excited him so much that after trying it a few times I had to give it up for good. But if I kept my mouth shut and nodded acquiescence, he paid me by telling about his experiences. And then he was no longer boring.

As a narrator he distinguished himself by his great intelligence. By nature he was unquestionably endowed with far above average talents. Only his professed view of life and his perfect freedom from morality gave expression to his real spiritual sickness, his true mental illness. And as he told about his experiences it gradually dawned on me that this sickness had been consciously produced by the people to whom he himself had been subordinate. The name he had mentioned during Eva's and my short visit came to play an increasingly great role. Bit by bit Dr. Reynhardt became the main person in the narrative, until—along with a certain SS *Standartenführer* Paul Heidebrand—he finally dominated Max's horizon and his story. Of this Heidebrand he spoke amazingly little ill. And even back then I got the impression that the SS officer had been an unusual man with an equally unusual fate.

By this time I knew the name of Dr. Reynhardt very well. I had first stumbled on it while reading the documents which formed the basis for the "Doctors' Trials." Every one of the co-defendants had singled out Reynhardt as the chief culprit, but he was precluded from defending himself by the fact that just before the Allies arrived he had been killed by prisoners whose friends and fellow victims he had used for his experiments. According to the other implicated doctors, Dr. Reynhardt had been the prime instigator of the research.

That Eva could have been a friend of the same Dr. Reynhardt seemed to me impossible. But if she had nonetheless known him, no one would be better able than she to round out my picture of him.

So when, shortly afterward, I met her on the street, I had a hard time curbing my curiosity. Strangely enough she was with Lyngby, so I couldn't just start pelting her with questions. And besides she looked so poorly that one could hardly burden her with such things. She was pale as a corpse and seemed so weak that I felt as if Lyngby's vitality was the only thing holding her strange, melancholy warmth and vigor. And he seemed different out in the daylight than in the faint lamplight at Dunkers'. The scar under his left cheekbone was no longer so predominant, and despite his gray hair he seemed younger. Perhaps he looked more ordinary too, less fantastic.

Eva was overstrained. The last, baking months in the city had been utterly devoid of any respite other than a few hours' sleep towards morning, and now a breakdown was clearly on the way. They were en route to a travel bureau. Eva was finally going to the country, and Lyngby was going with her to buy tickets. It was obviously the last minute for her to get out of the city, though she herself would surely have preferred to stay. Lyngby was treating her like a sick child, and in fact she was already further away than any train could take her. Eva's vacation had begun long since.

It was impossible to ask about Dr. Reynhardt, but today it's grotesque to think that I was on the verge of asking Lyngby about him instead. But Lyngby was standing beside Eva the whole time, bent over the counter; and so I couldn't. I consoled myself with the thought that I'd find an opportunity for that later.

Once they had bought the tickets I said goodbye to them both at the nearest trolley stop. She would be gone for a long time, and I felt rather lost to be staying in X-burg without being able to see her now and then. Afterwards it struck me that I had now met Lyngby for the second time without one word of Norwegian passing between us. But of course it was natural for us to speak German out of courtesy to Eva.

The same afternoon I was again with Max. And for the next three weeks I visited him almost daily. It was a great strain to talk with him, but he went on giving me material which took me hours to write down afterward. It was only now and then that he fooled me and spoke instead about his "philosophy." Then he would go on for hours, getting more and more excited. After such evenings I felt spiritually dead. Yes, deader than after the most horrible details he sometimes told of his former work.

And this was one of the reasons that I dropped in on Dunkers again. I felt a need for the Englishman's neutral and friendly company.

The primitive sharp-wittedness behind Max's view of life was distinguished only by the great emotional charge which filled it. The views themselves I had met innumerable times before and in all kinds of people, among laborers and shopkeepers, and not least among that large group of human beings known as "intellectuals." The basic assumption is that people are impelled to act solely by egotism, or more precisely: a variety of more or less refined and camouflaged forms of egotism. Some enjoy killing, others enjoy tending the sick. An irresistible force drives you to do what you most deeply *want* to do. And since life is amoral—a jungle—it makes no difference what you do, for you always do the right thing, namely what you get the most enjoyment from doing, what you *must* do. All this is nothing but the doctrine of "unfree will", translated to the needs of practical life. There are people who enjoy things which are beneficial to society, and people who get more enjoyment out of things which are harmful to society—but the real difference between people lies in the fact that the gifted desire things which are advantageous *in the long run*—and the "dumb" want things which bring brief pleasure, or possibly no pleasure at all.

Max loved to talk about "the dummies." They included Eva and the Russians who had given him water instead of killing him with their rifle butts. He could talk about "the idiots" for hours, at first with relatively controlled irony, then with mounting scorn, and finally with senseless rage. I've never heard the same banal thoughts set forth with more energy than they were expressed by Max. Not even a Swedish millionaire at whose home I once had the honor to sup during the war managed to work himself into such a state when he talked about "the dumb vuns." This hate for "the dummies" is bound up with a peculiar, untiring obsession with oneself. And Max seriously believed that he was a Columbus among thinkers, a man who had seen through life to its very marrow. To say a word against his "philosophy" was to spoil any chance of getting facts out of him. In such cases he utterly refused to talk about anything else, and nothing was allowed to serve any purpose but to prove his view of psychology. And the intensity with which he presented it gradually transformed it from a bore into a monster, an ogre who plagued me by day and tortured me in my sleep. Whether the psychology was the cause of his sickness, or if it was the other way around, I never figured out. Slowly it turned into a nightmare, for in one sense his way of thinking had reality enough. His experiences as an assistant at the crematoria meant that for all his madness he knew what he was talking about. And the spasms in his face showed it outwardly.

This and much else I told Dunkers while he was making tea. He listened with a very faint smile. Of course I didn't say who Max was, or where he could be found. As an officer Dunkers would have been duty bound to do something about the case of such a well-qualified war criminal, whatever he his private opinion. But I threw myself all the more fiercely into telling about the SS man's experiences and fixations. And beneath his smile Dunkers' narrow face became deadly serious. Therefore my surprise was all the greater when he interrupted me.

"The tiresome thing, of course, is that your friend is right," he said suddenly, in a dry and earnest tone.

The room around me slowly began to turn, on some invisible axis.

"We are incapable of doing anything but what we most deeply desire," continued Dunkers quietly and with dignity.

"But then why in the world do you act differently from Max?"

"Because I want something different from what he does."

"And why do you want something different?"

"Because I'm not mentally ill."

For awhile he looked serious, almost perturbed. But the lamplight cast a soft and golden, rather romantic gleam on his face and his thinning yellow hair.

"Do you think it's normal to spend your life the way you're doing now?" I asked. "After all your wartime contributions you could now be leading a very pleasant life back home in England, respected and comfortable—in some nice job, and with plum pudding at least once a week. But you don't seem to want that.

"Instead you want to work your heart out helping German refugees. Instead you want as fast as possible to get just as worn out as Eva is. Do you think that's so normal?"

"No," he said, "it isn't normal. But it's healthy. I have a healthy soul."

"And the rest of the people, the normal ones, they're sick?"

He grew very serious.

"Yes," he said. "The rest of the people, the normal ones, they're sick."

It was a while before he went on. Now he no longer looked romantic.

"A man like Max is merely even more normal than most. You ask if I don't like plum pudding, but I tell you that eating plum pudding isn't healthy no matter how you eat it, it isn't healthy so long as you can in fact be doing something useful. Right this minute I think that working with refugees is one of the *least* crazy things one can do. Therefore I'm doing it.

"It *is* the others who are sick! It's pathological to be able to sit still today. If you don't take your stick and cape and go out to *change* the world—and if this isn't the only thing you want, then you're crazy, which means that you're sick in your mind. You have a tumor in your soul, a paralysis or whatever.

"Our friend Eva, she broke down as soon as she got out to the country. Her heart almost stopped, and the rest of her organs went on strike, each in its own way. Still she—and your countryman Lyngby—are almost the only people I know who can rejoice in true spiritual health. Lyngby is perhaps the healthiest person I know."

I looked at Dunkers; he was a person who had taken sides. And with painful clarity I felt myself in a highly ambiguous position, at some point midway between him and Max.

"And the rest of us," I said, "can we be cured?"

"No one ever gets completely well," he replied, "without a doctor. Nature doesn't heal, for nature herself is sick. Nature is fallen, and the fallen nature herself is waiting for the great doctor."

It grew wonderfully still in the room. And with uncommon clarity I saw the rats before me, one in the trap and the other eating it. I didn't contradict him, and felt no need to do so. It was quiet for a long time.

"I didn't know you were interested in theology," I said to break the silence.

He laughed.

"Theology is the queen of sciences," he replied.

"Believe me," he added suddenly. "I have a sister back home in England. She leads the best, most pleasant life you could wish; with a wonderful husband and healthy children, sweet children. And she prides herself on being happy. In fact her self-esteem depends on the idea that she is happy. In the old days she would have kept going by believing that she was respectable. Today she manages by believing that she's happy. She literally clings to happiness like an old maid to virtue. What's more, you can call everything else about her into question—virtue, honesty, abilities, yes, even financial circumstances and ancestry—so long as you agree that she's happy. If you ask her how she is, she *shouts* that she's happy. And yet she'll be going to a nerve clinic before the year is up, and at the clinic she'll keep churning on about her happiness.

"But that she's *going* to the nerve clinic in the first place is due to the little seed of health which she still has left. That health is staging a revolt.

"It rebels against her mental illness.

"For in the long run it doesn't do to force yourself to be someone other than who you are. You can *become* someone else, but to *be* him doesn't work. In the end you still do what you desire.

"And Max? He's no more immoral than most people—he's merely sicker. He is just crazier, and more normal."

Dunkers rose and poured more tea. Then he put two lumps of sugar in each cup. Just then the doorbell rang, and with a faint uneasiness I sensed that it was Lyngby at the door. The thought of my country-man, this personification of virtue and health, got on my nerves for a moment. But that wasn't what bothered me. The image of the pale, almost brutal Caesar face—as Lyngby's might look if he was standing out in the hall now under the dim yellow lightbulb—the semidarkness of the warm stairwell, the deep scar under the cheekbone, the faint smile, the hand gestures—it all gave me a vague, oppressive feeling of dread, a jittery sense of having *forgotten* something which there was a penalty for forgetting. For a while my heart was beating so hard that I could feel it all the way out into my fingertips. My mouth was dry and I took a sip of tea.

Then the doorbell rang again—a clear anapest: short, short, long. And now I knew for sure that it was him. I drank up my tea. Dunkers left the door to the dark, narrow corridor ajar behind him. It was a white-lacquered, high, old-fashioned double door, and the opening out to the hall was a narrow black stripe between the illuminated surfaces. Then I heard the steps of the two men approaching.

As I stood to greet Lyngby, I saw that he had changed. The shadows from the one lamp burning in the room etched themselves into his face. Never have I seen such a burnt-out face. It was as if made of ashes. And still it was round, thick and powerful. The blue eyes were wholly expressionless.

When we had sat down, Dunkers went out to the kitchen to put on more water for tea. He let the water run for a little while before filling the pot.

"Is Eva very poorly?" I asked Lyngby in Norwegian.

It was the first time a Norwegian word had passed between us. And he looked as if he'd been waiting for that. His figure sat heavy and dark in his chair, in front of the lamp so that I saw him against the light. Then he turned to face me, but I couldn't distinguish his features or see his expression.

"Yes," he replied, "she's very sick."

He spoke excellent Norwegian, a clear and forceful eastern dialect. But yet those few words were enough to give me a feeling that he might not be Norwegian. Lyngby looked at me. Then he suddenly laughed heartily—loudly and shamelessly. For some reason I laughed too. Then I heard the gas flame being lit out in the kitchen, and a moment later Dunkers was back in the room with us. It would have been most discourteous to continue in Norwegian which he didn't understand a word of, and the conversation proceeded in English. I felt rather dazed as Lyngby and Dunkers went on talking. In the hours which followed, the courtesy which Lyngby and I had shown the Englishman was not extended to me.

After a few introductory sentences about Eva they devoted themselves without further ado to their own eternal topic: the work, the work…. Perhaps they assumed that I was just as interested in it as they were. And of course it did interest me, but I was not initiated into the subject; they incessantly referred to words, towns and people I didn't know, and to my ear the conversation was full of details—and of half-alluded to, implicit details—which I couldn't connect with anything. In short, they were speaking a foreign language.

And still I was unable to tear myself away. I sat as if glued to this person, the compatriot who perhaps wasn't a compatriot. It was only when Lyngby emptied his briefcase onto the table and picked out six or eight pieces of paper covered with numbers and addresses that I found the situation so humiliating and painful that I wanted to get up and leave. The two of them bent over one of the papers, Lyngby pointed to the columns of figures, and for the first time I really noticed his hand.

It was big and powerful, with long fingers and brown, taut skin. It reminded me most of all of a seaman's hands, lean and plump at the same time, a fist to do a jolly and dangerous job with. It was a *joyful* hand— perhaps the loveliest I've ever seen. But it was the right hand, and I spontaneously compared it with the left. At first I thought I was seeing things in the poor light. The hand was in shadow, or half in the shadow— and it *could* be the lamp distorting it. But when he rested it on the paper for a moment, I saw that it *was* like that. The hand was broken in the middle, the whole metacarpal area was crushed, and the back of the hand was larded with white scars, small ones and bigger ones. The fingers were untouched and just as beautiful as on the right hand. It lay on the paper for only a second, then he hid it again. I looked up at his face; it was dark, strained and imposing. As I saw it—from below—it reminded me of Donatello's great statue of the horseman; with huge and emaciated, passionate eyes in the middle of a desert landscape of a face. Then I rose and took my leave.

The gentlemen seemed chagrined at my having been there so long without being spoken to, but Dunkers swiftly summoned up his usual friendliness and accompanied me out into the dark.

It had grown late, and I walked rapidly homeward through the empty streets. There weren't many ruins in this part of town.

But the next afternoon I again clambered through the wasteland, by the same route Eva had shown me the first time; between bathtubs, upholstered furniture, toys and all the other superannuated remains life had left behind when it withdrew. I was beginning to know the way very well now.

Even the eternal darkness behind the cardboard panes in the sewer-like stairway leading up to Max gave me no trouble. I had soon become just as familiar with it as with my own stairway. Not that it became a pleasure. And it was even less of a pleasure to walk into the attic room where the cripples lay.

You could certainly tell that Eva was away. The hot air was so foul that I didn't immediately notice that Max had a visitor. The atmosphere was yellowish and in an indescribable way seemed greasy. It was as if these dying human remains regarded their own emanations as part of their lives, something from their organs which could be kept in the room for yet awhile, held onto and lived with. For as long as I visited Max the skylight was never opened without protests from the inhabitants. The blind man and the feeble-minded one lay immobile and silent, each in his own bed. The boy with the brain damage looked yellower and closer to death than ever. Only Max smiled his customary derisive grin, but with an even more satanic expression than usual. And suddenly I saw *who* I had before me. All in a row they lay there, as in a symbolic medieval engraving, three allegorical figures: The blind—the man with the closed visor—in the middle, flanked by Death and the Devil. But Max's smile grew steadily more devilish. He was clearly laughing about something in particular. Only then did I discover that there was a guest in the room. And the guest was smiling.

The moment I saw the man, I knew where Max got his "philosophy" from. He was in his mid-forties, abnormally tall and rather plump. He was very pale and his face seemed strangely squashed. His features were so blurred that his face seemed almost malformed; if a toad could have turned into a person, it would look like that. His smile was fixed, glued fast to the lower part of his face, but his eyes were hard and cold. His hands were very small and white. And the teeth behind the smile were small, gray and bad.

He stood leaning against the wall, but was so tall that he had to bend his neck under the sloping ceiling.

"It's good to meet you," he smiled. "Our friend Max has told so much about you that I can truly say that I know you very well already—"

"And I gather that you're interested in psychology!"

He stuck his head forward with an obsequiousness so embarrassing and incredible that I had to force myself to take the hand he extended to me.

I answered somewhat stiffly that what *he* meant by psychology was not my chief interest.

Max looked at us from the bed and roared with laughter.

The guest went on smiling, the same smile as before.

"My name is Dr. Buntzel. Our friend Max may have already intimated that I exist."

"No," I replied, "he hasn't. My name is B...."

"Buntzel, he's been a race psychologist since '36," shouted Max, explaining with relish. "But in '45 he came to here, and now he's an ordinary shrink again. "Sides, he's helpin' me with some things for the time bein'."

And Dr. Buntzel looked as if he needed a little business; he was rather shabby. Smiling, he lit his cigarette from the match I held up for him. Then I threw the pack of cigarettes over onto Max's bed.

"I didn't know that there was a science called race psychology?" I asked.

"There isn't—not anymore," replied the doctor, and suddenly his smile broadened:

"Race psychology departed this life in the year 1945."

Then he went on:

"I thought that the work on other things was so important that I might as well play along and present a 'race-psychological result' once in a while!"

He said "race-psychological result" in such a tone and with such a grimace that I positively heard the quotation marks.

Max laughed. And there was open admiration in the laughter. I hadn't heard such a thing from him before. And to the admiration was now added pride:

"Buntzel comes and talks to me often, dontcha?"

They looked each other in the eye.

It was painful and grotesque to witness, and it irritated me beyond measure to think that Max and Dr. Buntzel had discussed me. It was all too easy to imagine how Max must have described me and my strange interest in his achievements and his past. And it was even easier to see how such a picture in its crazy onesidedness must have fit the psycho-analyst's stock-in-trade. In fact it was all too easy to reconstruct the discussions the two of them must have had about me.

To hide the annoyance I felt at being caught off guard, I sat down on Max's bed—and with all the graciousness I could muster I said everything I could readily think of about psychology; that one of the dangers of current trends was that people easily came to believe them-selves possessed of a knowledge of human nature which they didn't have at all—that the answer books sold so cheaply in all the kiosks and bookstores were after all much too cheap.

As soon as I had uttered the words I realized how revealing they were of the train of thought which had led up to them, and the awful clarity with which they showed my own feelings. Max didn't notice. But for a fraction of a second a gleam of humor lit up under Buntzel's eternal, dead smile. I almost liked him for it, and before I knew it I was laughing too.

Then he said:

"What you're saying is only true of textbook psychology. *Real* psy-chology is something wholly different. It's…It…depends on inspiration, on talent, on innate abilities…It's related to art—an inborn gift, just as literature is!" Max looked at him with half-open mouth and eyes big with admiration. It was obvious that he was reading something entirely different into the words than their actual content.

Buntzel sat down on the other side of the bed and continued:

"You need intuition. Intuition is what you need. Look at our friend Max! He's hardly ever read a book on psychology. And he doesn't need to, for he has a natural gift. Talent and experience! *That's* what it's all about!

"You can't learn much from books."

Max leaned back his head and closed his eyes, while smiling as if in a state of great ecstasy. Never was his primitive vanity so glaringly evident as when he was praised. Buntzel regarded the SS man with cold and scornful interest. Still smiling.

"So psychology is an art form?" I asked.

"No," replied Buntzel, "psy-cho-lo-gy is much more. It is the queen of sciences: psy-cho-lo-gy is *magic!*"

He spoke with a strange formal solemnity, and Max listened with an expression of wide-eyed, unnatural suspense. He had raised his torso as far up as the paralysis would allow, and now thrust his head forward.

"If you know the human soul," continued the psychologist, "if you know *that*, you can control it like a cash register. Yes, excuse the comparison! But every time you push a button, a drawer opens…."

We all turned our heads at once toward the next bed. The sound which had interrupted us came from the blind man. Shrieking loudly with rage, he had raised himself up and flopped over in the bed—so that his face was turned away from us. Through his thin hair I could see his scalp. The roar of laughter which followed from Max and Buntzel was unexpectedly violent and prolonged. And as they continued to laugh, the blind man raised the featherbed and pulled it over his head.

"Well, well," said Dr. Buntzel, out of breath from laughing, "Now he has the featherbed to fall back on!"

"What in the world is going on?" escaped from me.

"'S magic!" said Max and fleered again.

"Max has practiced quite a bit on him," the scientist explained.

For a moment I thought about the few words I had exchanged with the blind man, about his broad peasant dialect, and about his wife and children somewhere off in East Germany, whom he hadn't seen or heard from for a good six years; people with hollow cheeks and swollen bellies. Perhaps they were alive. Perhaps they weren't so far away. It wasn't impossible that they were among the emaciated refugees whom Eva and Dunkers and Lyngby were trying to help. But the blind, tortured being in the next bed would hardly meet them again. Germany is a big country.

Then Max turned to me again:

"We usually take away the blanket when we're gonna work on 'im. Then it ain't enough for 'im to do like this!"

He put illustrative fingers in his ears.

"He can hear anyways."

I didn't understand what Max meant, but Dr. Buntzel came to my aid:

"Our friend Max—with my help—is doing some small psychological experiments on him.

"Today, for example, Max told him what the Russians will have done to his wife and children, if they've happened on them while drunk. You know that Max himself took part in the pogroms in the Polish ghettoes, so he knows how such things go—in the most minute details he knows it. And you know how he can spin a tale!

"And him over there…" Buntzel pointed at the blind man, who was still holding the featherbed over his head; "…him over there, he was a front soldier himself long enough to know that it's true."

Buntzel would have said more, but Max could no longer control himself. Beside himself with excitement, he interrupted the other:

"'S magic, y'unnerstand! *Magic!*"

The words were directed at me, but without regarding the state Max was in, the psychologist corrected him:

"It is not magic. By no means—yet. We are merely creating an artificial conflict in him. He's a long way into a full-blown neurosis…."

Max wagged his head back and forth, unable to restrain himself. Then he seized the floor again:

"We done other things with 'im too! Last week, just after that there Frau Müller left, Buntzel came up and pretended he was from the police. Then he told 'im—no, first he asked 'im if him in the bed there wasn't the former farmworker Rinde from Oberschöneweide in East Prussia, and then after that he told 'im that a letter had come to 'im that his wife 'n' young'uns—four of 'em—was found in a refugee camp up in Holstein, and they was gonna come here in three days, and then he'd get to see 'em right away. Then he read the letter to 'im and gave it to 'im. And so the nut lies there with the letter in 'is hand for three days and talks about 'is young'uns. And the third day, when he'd been washin' 'imself all mornin', then Buntzel comes up with a revolver and says now they're comin'; they're right down on the stairs, so if he listens good, he can hear 'em! And just when he was lyin' still and listenin', a shot banged in his ear."

Max roared with laughter when he'd finished the story, and the other observed him smilingly and precisely. The blurred face showed an expression of great concentration and attentiveness. I got the impression that Max interested him far more than the blind man did, and that it was actually his pretended friend he was experimenting on.

I had already got up to go when I realized why I had come. The evening was turning out to be so detestable that I had forgotten it.

This Heidebrand whom Max had told about earlier had begun to interest me immensely. He was originally a high-ranking SS officer, but broke with the party in '43 or '44, left the country along with a Jewish friend, was caught during his flight and later ended his days in the same concentration camp where he had earlier been the commandant.

Max still had a few things to explain about Heidebrand, and as I stood by the bed looking at Dr. Buntzel and the invalid, I knew that it was my last visit to the Estonian. I decided to do everything I could to get the blind man out of the attic. But first I wanted to get the last word out of Max.

And it was amazingly easy, perhaps because now—having introduced me to Dr. Buntzel—he regarded me as one of the initiated, quite as one of their own.

When I had was partway down the stairs Buntzel came running after me. He caught up with me before I reached the door. He had to leave now too, he said; patients, and so forth. . .

"Max is in bad shape," I said.

"Yes," he answered smiling, "his whole sense of self is in rapid disintegration."

His voice was singularly dry and factual as he continued:

"He already suffers strongly from persecution mania. Can't stand being contradicted, for example."

 Dr. Buntzel laughed out loud:

"In a few weeks he'll have dissolved into wind and rain. Then he'll take the leap out into the cosmos!

"He's rapidly going into the great loss of identity, out into blessedness, but first the I-feeling in him will mount up to enormity, up into the Caesar stage. And then the leap can take place—from everything to nothing! During these years you can believe I've seen many examples of a similar development—between 1932 and 1945, I mean. Active politicians are especially susceptible, of course."

Oddly enough Dr. Buntzel was going the same way I was. We could walk together, he said. We were already standing on the steps and the blocks of ruins lay ahead of us.

"You would do me a great service by letting me go alone," I said.

And for the first time his smile disappeared. He hunched his back and opened his mouth.

"Don't you want…?" he said. "Don't you want…?"

All at once he looked like a man who has been kicked before, and who even has a certain practice in receiving kicks of that sort. It was as if he were submitting his back. And I felt rather unwell as I left him. But I had just gone a little way when he called after me.

"You mustn't misunderstand!" he shouted. "Listen! You mustn't get the wrong idea! What we told you…."

He suddenly came running after me. When he caught up with me again, he laid his hand on my shoulder and held me fast:

"I'm just doing it to help them—both the blind man and Max! It's a collective treatment—a collective shock therapy—which I'm giving them both at the same time! This is really the first time I've let any of my treatment go beyond the boundaries of the private. But Max told me you were so interested in…."

I interrupted him by saying that all the same I would prefer to go by myself. And when I had gone a ways, I turned and looked back. Dr. Buntzel was still standing where I'd left him.

But he wasn't looking at me.

It looked as if he had found something among the ruins, and was bending down to examine it.

As I walked on, I abandoned the idea of reporting the situation to the police. For a while I thought of going to see Dunkers to beg him to intervene on in the blind man's behalf, get him away and into proper care. But as an officer Dunkers would also be duty bound to do something about Max, to deal with him as a war criminal. And I didn't want that at all. It took me a long time to figure out what to do. Not until I was standing at the door to my own attic room did I think of Lyngby. And I realized at once that he was the right person to do something, and that if anyone were in a position to find the wife and children of Max's blind roommate, it would have to be him. That same evening I wrote him a letter, and took it to Dunkers' mailbox before I went to bed.

I felt queasy, sick, and almost senseless with fatigue as I pulled the blanket over me. And of course I didn't go to sleep, but tossed around in the sweaty sheets like a fish in a net. Had Eva been in town, I would have got up and gone to her. And as the night wore on I grew more and more miserable. With an almost hallucinatory clarity I saw the mountain before me: The plateau, the mountain lakes, the brooks, the pure air and the turf in the bogs, where your feet sank in deep. For a long time I was gazing at the bottom of an ice-cold brook, clear as air, which I had once waded through alone on the Finnmark plateau. But it was more of a river than a brook; a yard deep, as it was—and twelve, fifteen yards wide. The stones cut into my feet as if from far away, giving no sense of temperature. The pain of the cold inside my bones was the only thing I felt. But the evening air was mild for such an altitude. On the other side of the river grew cloudberries in a kind of bog. And as I lay there in the garret in boiling X-burg, the images from the mountain slid little by little into a half-conscious dream. The dark, ramshackle, oppressively hot room slowly disappeared, until I no longer noticed it.

But I'd gone to bed early, and far, far below me, somewhere under the cracked floorboards, one of the Bauer boys was playing the viola. The deep, vibrant tones pressed faintly into my dream and gradually gave me a feeling of peace and repose. And the pictures changed, went back in time and arrived at my childhood, my boyhood room and my first books, a pocket mirror which broke—and a garden and an old, bearded uncle who had been a ship captain. I myself was very small, and his beard was big as a bush and glittered in the sunshine pressing in between the dark, curly strands. He had on white pants, and a white, old-fashioned cap with gold threads around it. He was sitting on a green-painted garden bench, and round us grew masses of laburnum and lilac. I had heard that laburnum was poisonous. But I sat on his right knee and used both feet to make black spots on his left pantleg. He took great pleasure in these spots, for he himself had neither wife or children, and inside on his wall hung only brown photographs of ships and of men posing amid masts and winches. Several of these men were wearing caps like Uncle's. And many had beards. It bound us very strongly together that we were both named Jens and had the same name. Time pulled itself together in my breast and became a point. But soon it became less than a point and almost the reverse—a kind of hole in something or other. It went backwards. But right after that it went forwards again, and then I myself was Uncle Jens. Despite the fact that it wasn't easy to understand how I could suddenly be him, an old gentleman with a cane and a beard and sometimes very strong pains in his heart, such pains in his heart that he had to cry out—and then he always shouted a woman's name, but whose it was I never found out. For it was a name which was never named either by him or by anyone else, except just when he had those pains. But then right afterward Uncle was dead, and the house was filled with flowers and with all the people who came to the party and ate, except for Uncle himself, of course, because he lived underneath. And it was him the flowers were for. So I gave them a krone so that he'd get a rose from me too, and the savings bank which was just like a little red mailbox, I locked it again and then I hid under the bed. But there I got dust in my mouth, until finally I had to cough. And this cough lodged high up in my throat and hurt, so I understood that it must be Uncle Jens's heart which had gone over into me, now that it didn't have any place to be. For he certainly couldn't have it with him any longer. And for the first time I understood what pain he had been in when he roared with his deep voice and called so loudly for the lady. And all the dust stuck fast to my face…. Right up until I had summer vacation and was sitting in my room over the vestibule and reading. On the wall above my desk hung a map of the Pacific Ocean and all the islands there. And outside the window a birch tree was shining. The sun ran through the foliage as through a strainer, and my room was all green. School was out. I was fifteen, and it wasn't yet time to go to the country. The sun stood almost still in the sky. But as I read, it turned gray. For it was a strange thing I was reading; it was called *The Concentration Camp Oranienburg*, and it was the first political book I had ever read. It was written by someone who had been a prisoner there, and who had managed to escape. So it was all about people who had had their eardrums punctured because they couldn't stand straight in line, and who were beaten to death with leather belts because they were sick. And as I read I already realized that the things written there I would never be able to forget. And what happened in me as I sat reading on that still, shining afternoon could never be undone. But the whole summer long the others went around believing that the sunshine and the sea and the wind—that all was the same as before. I was the only one who knew better…. Then right afterward I was standing up in the attic room with Max and Dr. Buntzel again. Both of them were dead and in a state of advanced putrefaction. The stink was worse than ever, but the skylight could no longer be opened. I hit it and pounded on it, but it wouldn't budge. It just couldn't be opened. Only the sky overhead was deeper, clearer and bluer than any sky I had seen before. I could see into it endlessly deep and far, through layer after layer upwards. And slowly, slowly the stars became visible. But the stink in the room under the skylight became unbearable, and I tried to knock out the pane. But it was as hard as bulletproof glass, and I understood that if I wanted out of the morgue I would have to go down the stairs. But out in the hall there were no stairs, only a queer long sewer. And I quickly slid down the floor's slimy slope until I was bathed in sewage. Over my head a low ceiling arched. I could see light above the sewer outlet far, far away. Otherwise it was very dark.

The voice came very suddenly: a resounding, distant, mighty roar:

"Can you swim?" it shouted.

"I used to be able to!" I replied.

"So swim!" it rang back.

After great exertions I noticed that the water was getting clearer. Slowly it turned blue and acquired a faint salty taste. I called up the last of my strength and swam on. And finally I noticed that there were waves in the water, waves which were lifting me up and down. And now it was no longer a strain to swim, I could float and drift comfortably around in the waves. For a long time I lay facing upward, and behind the stars I gradually saw outlined the enormous figure of a man. Then I realized that this was the earth's spirit, the great healing spirit which Dunkers had been thinking of that time he talked about fallen nature and about the doctor. The water was crystal clear, blue as the sky and bracing as the sea beyond the lighthouse of my childhood. It was very, very salty, and above me the stars grew bigger and bigger.

I woke up with a start. And I knew that I had to get out of the city. The work which continued day and night, the summer heat on the asphalt, the meetings with Max and now with Dr. Buntzel as well, the nocturnal hours spent writing down the conversations with Max—the totality was such that I couldn't stand it anymore. I felt sick to the bottom of my soul, queasy and afraid. I wanted to get out of the city, and I knew who would help me do it.

Eva was not one of those do-gooders who can only stand to see the humiliated and degraded around her. She thought that rich and happy people could well be worth just as much as the poor and sick. And her extensive circle of acquaintances was just as diverse as it was wide. It embraced among others the actress Leonora L., a gifted and beautiful person. Actually Fräulein L. is perhaps the most beautiful human being I've ever met.

Already half a year ago, when Eva brought us together for the first time, the actress had offered to let me use her house in the Tyrol. She herself almost never had time to leave the city, and the house up in the mountains for the most part stood empty. Unless it was loaned to friends or relatives. I was later to find that Fräulein L's indifference concerning her summer house went so far that for months at a time she had no idea whether it was inhabited or empty—let alone who might be staying in it.

When I sought her out that boiling August morning five years ago, she received me kindly, replied at once that the country place was free, and handed me the keys on the spot. Then she wrote down a dozen names on a page of her almanac; names of inhabitants of the village, people who had always lived in that valley, to whom she wanted me to convey her greetings. Afterwards we drank a pot of tea and talked for a while—mostly about Eva.

What I found out was that Eva was staying in another Alpine village, in the next valley—not more than three or four hours from the place where I myself was thinking of going. Fräulein L. would write and tell her that I was staying in the vicinity, and that I would be ready to visit as soon as Eva's strength would allow.

When it was time to leave, Fräulein L. went with me. And we walked down to the main street, where the traffic was heavy. At the corner of Kaiserstrasse we stopped and said goodbye. I was standing with my back toward the street when she gave me her hand, and she herself was standing so that she could see right over the swarm of cars at the intersection to the opposite sidewalk. She wished me a good vacation, and started to repeat that she would let Eva know where I was staying, but the sentence was never finished. Suddenly she froze, and stood there open-mouthed and wide-eyed.

"My God!" she said loudly, aghast. She took a step backward and looked as if she were about to fall. As I gripped her under the arm, I looked over to the other side of the street. A well-built, uncommonly powerful man was walking rapidly down the sidewalk. He had gray hair and a strikingly straight back. And the melancholy, fairy-tale face looked strangely extinguished and burnt-out. This was underscored by the scar under his left cheekbone, a scar which was more of a hole than a scar. A huge moving van drove up between us and braked, and when it pulled away, the man was gone.

"Ghosts?" I said to Fräulein L.

She had quickly come to her senses, even though she still seemed somewhat frozen.

"Yes," she replied with a kind of smile, "it really *was* a ghost! The man who was walking on the other side has been dead for seven years."

"You mean the pale man with the scar on his cheek?" I asked. "The one who was walking down the street a moment ago?"

"Yes," she replied rather absently.

"Sorry," I said, "but I must disappoint you. He isn't dead at all, but quite alive in the usual way. He's a compatriot of mine, whom I've met a few times here in town."

"Yes, yes!" she said, "that's always the way it goes!"

But her voice belied her words; she seemed far more relieved than disappointed. Then she gave me her hand again, and we said goodbye. But after she had turned way, she abruptly spun around again:

"Anyway, that countryman of yours reminded me of something! Actually I've invited some distant relatives to stay in the house in the Tyrol. A widow who wanted to stay there with her son. But I haven't heard anything from them, so I'm sure you'll have the house to yourself. Have a good time!"

She waved and walked quickly down the street.

When I got home, a small unstamped letter was lying in the mailbox. It contained a note with a couple of lines in German:

> "I shall see what I can do for your blind man. In any case I shall get
> him out of the attic room.
>
> > Yours,
> > P. Lyngby."

Obviously you could say what you would about Lyngby, but he didn't bother playing on national strings.

Instead of starting to pack at once, I sat down on the edge of the bed. It struck me that perhaps Lyngby ought not to meet Max.

For that reason my departure was three days delayed.

2. The Chapel

When I found a place to sit in the corridor of the overfilled, boiling hot train, it was after almost three days of conversation with Lyngby. I was at once dead tired and keyed-up. What he had told me was so harrowing that I don't know when I've ever have felt myself in such a state before or since. But as I sat on my suitcase with my back against the compartment wall, waiting for the last bell to sound from the platform, my disquiet slowly gave way to a dull and painful despair.

Conditions were bad in Germany that summer, and the visible railway equipment was as bleak as a poorhouse. The unpainted stations, the pale people, the empty window frames—all conjured up thoughts of something midway between poorhouse and morgue. It was cramped around me in the corridor, stinking, dirty and insufferably hot. The journey would take us through large parts of central Germany, and would last almost twenty-four hours.

When the train pulled out, it was beginning to get dark. I had the night before me. And the train went southward and eastward. Hour after hour, now infinitely slow with hard, painful jerks, now with long, pointless stops. At the station in an unknown, wholly bombed-out city I spoke with one of the railway officials. He was pale and sturdy, with deep wrinkles across his brow and around his mouth, wearing a shabby black uniform. They are remarkably alike, all these thousands of railway workers.

Does any other country in the world have so many railroad depots? And everywhere they're so alike that you'd think you were continually stopping at one and the same station. Eternally and always at that one same station. I suppose one day they'll all grow together, into a single black, endless mass of coal and iron and old rail cars with some people sitting in them—like big, sick birds. Everywhere there will be the same anemic workers—the same threadbare passengers. Women with crying, sickly children and exhausted, unshaven men. And everywhere, for all eternity, there will be the same seats with the sign: Reserved for War Invalids. But cripples don't travel much, and so the seats stand empty, and of course nobody else can sit in them. For the others are merely poor.

The corridor where I was camped in was no longer too warm. It was now night, and the passage had long since turned freezing cold, drafty with the cold night air.

Only when I started coughing did I try to get into the compartment. Right by the door I found a place for my suitcase, and sat down on it with my back against the end of one of the benches. People were lying on the floor and under the seats. And you couldn't go through the car without stepping on them. So only the conductor does that. The room was almost imperceptibly lit by a blue blackout bulb, left over from the war. Here and there it glimmered on a hand or a face, but otherwise all was a sea of darkness and shadows. Most people were sleeping, but now and then one of them turned, or someone raised a head, a movement which was transmitted at random to the others. Amid the thumping of the wheels the room was full of sounds, the sounds of sleeping, breathing people. Somebody coughed or scraped with a foot. A man and a woman whispered together in the dark. And with absolute regularity, at even, measured intervals, there was someone who sighed deeply.

In contrast to the corridor, the compartment was warm. The air was dense with breath and body warmth. But the car must be half-dark in the daytime too, for the broken window panes had been replaced with sheets of cardboard or plates of fiberboard. Once we sat for a long time at a station, and suddenly there was a rushing and rumbling out in the night. Through one of the intact panes I saw the lighted luxury train from Copenhagen to Rome go by. In three or four seconds the whole long line of cars was past. Several people in the compartment woke up, and the woman on my right crooned to her child. But soon we settled back into quiet. The passengers were as silent and tractable as livestock. And the train jerked a couple of times and started moving. But we were traveling through one of the most dismal areas in Germany. One of the most notorious death camps was here—placed with a sure sense for effect; hell must have its own landscape. And the camp is here still—a huge, empty, starving organism. After all, it was created, and it can't be uncreated again. It waits. But the night lay merciful and opaque between us and it.

The future will know only two ways of dying. One will be the anonymous, pain-free hospital death. The other will be to perish as an involuntary guinea pig for science, for holy medicine. We still have a period of grace, a few years perhaps, and then it will be past. Never again will anyone die the way my grandfather did. Never again will anyone die as nobody on earth has ever died before.

The captain, the old one, had been sick. And he still was. The pneumonia had gnawed and sucked at him, but there some vitality still remained in his chest. He was lying in bed now, supported by the pillows. And he saw how the winter sun burned and glowed in the small rectangular window panes. Just before sundown the housekeeper had gone out to do some shopping. Slowly the sun went down, but outside the panes something thin and black hung and beat against the sill. It took some time before he realized that it was the flag line…the rope from the flag which was still up long after the sun had plainly set. The seaman felt a wonderful fighting spirit, an almost merry wrath at such an unheard-of thing. And it was so long since he had been angry. So now the flag was up after sundown! And so he called to his sons, to all of them in turn. He roared. And the anger grew red and hard inside him. It was no longer a festive wrath, it was a wrath as he had felt it a thousand times before, a rage which hurt his bones and midriff and which must find an outlet.

"Adolf!" he shrieked. "Adolf!"

But Adolf didn't answer.

For while the old man shouted with all the strength which was left in his lungs despite the fever, while the father hawked and roared and coughed, Adolf was in Buenos Aires. He ran a sort of bar there—not, to be sure, one of the wholly pleasant sort where people came in white collars and such, but at any rate a thriving venture.

And therefore Adolf didn't answer.

Then the father called for Jens; he, after all, was the biggest of the boys, a rangy lout with pimples and a stiff collar. *He* must feel some responsibility for the flag hanging out there and twisting in the dusk! The captain shrieked for Jens until the sun had fully set, and until his voice was no longer what it had been when he began. But no! The lummox was gone. And in fact he was long gone. The lout was long since a gentleman in his late fifties, living in a huge bachelor apartment in Antwerp, and also skipper of one of the biggest passenger ships then plying between the continent and New York. For this reason, and because he had so much else to think about, Jens didn't answer either.

He let his father lie there and yell. Without batting an eye he let the old man lie there.

And gradually his anger utterly sapped the captain's strength. He turned reddish-blue above his beard, and his scalp shone lobster-colored through the wisps of hair. Now he shouted for the others. First for Søren, the one who went to mate's school for a shorter time than the other boys, because he had a giddy head and was musical. But just at the time when his father was calling for him, or at any rate in the same month, Søren was buried at the consulate's expense in Chicago, so he didn't answer either—legally exempt as he was.

And the two youngest boys, Ingvald and Karl, neither of them made a sound. The poor little things, close-cropped and in baggy, hand-me-down knee pants /knickers, they had taken off long since. Always out! But this evening they weren't haunting the ski slopes outside the town; one was a civil servant up in Finnmark, and the other ran an insurance company in Liverpool. The old man shrieked so that it echoed through the house, and after every yell came a silence which was sheer torture to listen to. You bring five sons and a lovely passel of daughters into the world, and not one of them has the sense to lower the flag before they go dashing off!

And with a jerk he kicked off the featherbed. Then he perched on the edge of the bed and drew his nightshirt down over his white knees. To be sure there was no one to see him, but it didn't hurt for a captain to observe the amenities a bit even if he was alone. Indeed he hadn't expected to feel so dizzy and miserable as he did now that he was sitting up. And there was a remarkably odd prickling in his feet when he put his weight on them. He couldn't find his slippers. And someone had taken away his shoes as well. But at least his hat with the gold braid on it was hanging over by the escritoire. Good thing the housekeeper had had the sense to light the lamps before she went out. And so he finally made it over to his cap. But strangely it felt a little too big now, so that it sank down and rested on his ears.

On the stairs he stopped and looked out over the fjord. There was driving snow and much ice on it, but a little blue-black seawater was visible. The sea air really cheered him up! But his body felt strangely hot and stiff, yes, so hot that it was good to feel the snow under his feet....

The flag line was frozen solid, and it wasn't easy to get up onto the washhouse roof, so that he could reach it with his hand. And as he stood on the roof and stretched, he felt the wind under his shirt; it crawled around his legs and up his shaggy body. And the captain marveled at how little cold there was in the fresh breeze this evening. It could pass as a veritable trade wind. And strangely enough it grew warmer and warmer—it was downright cozy. He finally got hold of the flag, and got one more glimpse of the fjord and the salt water before he fell.

The snowdrift was soft enough, but he couldn't find his uniform cap in the dark. And besides, it was snowing quite hard now. It was only when he came inside, to the warmth of the stove, that he began to freeze, and so he took the hot water from the range and made himself a strong toddy with it. But when he came to drink it, he had completely lost his appetite. It was never drunk up.

And when the housekeeper came home again, he was lying in bed and glowing like a stove. He called her Eva Christine—which had been his wife's name —and growled something about how the rascals would get a licking as sure as his own name was Ole Andreas. Later in the evening he talked a little French, and more he did not say.

Only after bosun Nielsen had filled in the grave was the hat with the gold braid found. It was lying in the snow, right by the washhouse wall. And the same day the neighbor's wife told the civil servant from Finnmark that she had heard the captain calling the boys that afternoon. But she couldn't leave what she was doing just then, she said tearfully. And at the very end the cap made the rounds of the guests, so that everybody got to see it and hold it solemnly for a little while. For its owner had sailed with it on all heaven's seven seas, before his own life's ship had capsized.

But afterwards, out in the hall, the bosun said that the old one had been a hard man, hard on himself and hard on others. And the son, the one who was a civil servant in Finnmark, nodded without saying anything. He just thought a bit about his own childhood and about how the bosun had been on board with the old man for over a generation. In a way they were colleagues. But the bosun spat into the snow, out through the door, and added that now the skipper had gone ashore on a coast where there was no great difference between the forecastle and amidships, and when they finally met him again there, he reckoned that quite a few things would have changed.

The corpse factories and the big mass crematoria from the camps are transitional forms—stages on the way from the captain's deathbed to the future's departments for death assistance. You'll be able to die rationally in the future; free of pain—with a film showing and to soothing, state-controlled music, designed for deathbeds. Anonymously, quietly, *without being aware of it.* And without being a burden to friends or relatives. It will be a hygienic, humane process, just as natural as television and cancer. All this will be ours if we're among the constructive, positive citizens of society. In the opposite case—if one belongs to the enemies of society—one will be placed at science's disposal as a research subject. These are thoughts which are older than national socialism.

The night on the train was one continuous nightmare. And it was the conversation with Lyngby which had rendered my condition so acute. Everything I myself had read about the medical research in Nazi Germany, everything Max had to tell as an eyewitness, everything Lyngby had described—inside me it all hardened into a kind of skeleton of dread. I could have crept in between the warm, sleeping and breathing human bodies just to get away from this mill of thoughts which had been set going in me, to prove to myself by sight, smell and sound that the *human being* still existed; irrational, sick and old, smelly, unwashed, poor, suffering, abased, useless—but holy and eternal, bigger and more beautiful than mountain, sea and sky.

The night was long, and I sucked the warmth from the sleepers into myself; of children, the old, the cripples, the sick, of all the great, disorderly, accidental, unhygienic and blessed life—which is to be lived right up until you die the great, the mighty, blessed death. The death which nobody before you and nobody after you has died the like of. Because the genuine, the healthy death, it is your own, like your look, your handshake and your laughter. Like your handwriting and your life. Because you create it in your own image.

Most of those around me in the compartment will die the good, the healthy death. Only the children will one day be surprised by the social paradise's death, served by white-clad social workers. For them the old lie about our equality in the presence of death will finally become truth. Until their days it was the case that if people weren't different before, they became so when the hour arrived. When the hour came when the gestation was accomplished, when they brought forth their firstborn, their only begotten, their own death into the world. And the death resembled them—the way the child resembles the mother.

For some of the night I slept, leaning against the farm woman with the child. And around six in the morning I changed trains. The local train went due south, toward the Alps, and it was quite a climb. The cars were almost empty. The air was cool, but the sky was clear and clean. And then came the morning.

Like a king's crown it climbed above the horizon, a golden crown bigger than a castle. And the flecks of sun dripped and splashed and trickled around me in the compartment. It was like sitting in a rushing cataract of golden water with long, shining eddies in it. The train had long since left the big traffic arteries now. The stations we stopped at were no longer bombarded scrap heaps, and we stopped at all of them. We had plenty of time. And now and then I saw animals on the platform, horses and chickens and dogs and pigs and cats. After three or four hours we were up in the Alps. And the climb continued. The mountain tops grew higher and more pointed. The turns became sharper. And the train went more slowly.

The farmers I saw from the compartment window were dressed in Bavarian costume, with short leather pants and colorful shirts. They were broad and hefty folk, dark and serious. The houses were built of wood, unpainted and with massive eaves. The area was Catholic, and at the crossroads stood crucifixes. In the early morning sunshine the high mountains became a strange, heroic and tragic landscape. It was studded with small white chapels. The people here must be herders who lived on milk, fruit and cheese. It was all the past, the past....The night on the long-distance train and my thoughts there appeared now as if seen though the wrong end of a telescope, real enough, but far, far away... the Middle Ages and Antiquity. This feeling remained with me as long as I was in the mountains.

Around noon I got off the train. To the village where Leonora L's house lay it was now still half an hour's journey by car. First I ate at the inn. After that I climbed into the village taxi, a worn-out two-cycle DKW which coughed us up the road.

The landscape around me had now became altogether unreal, no longer comprehensible. Two of Europe's highest mountain peaks were a few kilometers away, and at their feet lay the chapels, tiny ones, often no more than eight or ten meters long. The enormous mountain massifs spread around them a world where everything stood still. But despite the altitude the vegetation around us was lush and summery. The actress's house was outside the village, right by the narrow motor road, but hidden behind a huge wall of deciduous trees. When the taxi stopped, I crawled out, and the driver sent my suitcase after me. Then he turned the car around and with his motor off coasted back down the hill.

In the massive hedge was an opening with a little gate in it. I went in. And before me, at the top of a grassy hillside, stood a large Bavarian wooden house. On the veranda sat a very young man, almost a boy. He was holding a flute in his hand.

He had heard the car, and sat looking toward the gate in the hedge. When I started up the grassy slope, he rose to greet me. He was perhaps a little over twenty years old.

It's strange to think that this first time I met Claus Reynhardt, I almost thought him unsympathetic. As he said his name he seemed embarrassed, perhaps because I had been counting on having the house to myself and now couldn't manage to hide my disappointment, tired as I was after the journey.

I introduced myself and explained how I came to be there. At the same time I took a closer look at my fellow tenant. He was somewhat shorter than I, pale and rather skinny. He had short pants and thin legs. And there was about him an odd mixture of youth and old man. In his expression and movements there was something faded, a kind of not being present, which didn't seem prepossessing—at least not at first glance. Later, when I had gotten to know him, this first impression receded into the background, and I came to value him as the alien in the world he was. Claus Reynhardt was one of those whose lives get ground to bits earlier than other people's.

He looked at the typewriter I was carrying and asked if I were a journalist. When I had answered no, he showed me the house. On the second floor I found a big unoccupied room with a bed and a desk. And I settled in there.

An hour later I heard a woman's voice downstairs, and knew that it was Frau Reynhardt, Claus's mother, who had come back from the village. I straightaway went downstairs to greet her.

She was already standing in the kitchen, busy making coffee. She was completely gray-haired, but hardly past her late forties, wore a well-made street dress and thick, sturdy shoes. She seemed brisk, cheerful and energetic, and soon all three of us were drinking coffee on the veranda, which extended around two sides of the house. For me the enormous mountain peaks were still a sensation, and several times I tuned out of the conversation and sat gazing at them. The valley below us was easily surveyable, and resembled a colossal bathtub lined with soft green velvet.

"If you want to go up in the mountains," said Frau Reynhardt, "you can go with Claus one day. A week never passes without his hiking up there."

"I'm afraid I'm not very good at climbing," I replied.

"You don't have to climb," said Claus. "There are fine trails all over."

Still it was more than a week before anything came of the hike. I spent the time sleeping and reading. Or I strolled around the village and the immediate vicinity. A couple of times I bathed in a mountain stream, and occasionally wrote a little.

Relations with Frau Reynhardt and her son were comfortable and free. None of us tried to get past the conventional stage, despite our drinking coffee together daily on the veranda. But this distance between them and me came to an end which could hardly have been more abrupt. It began with Claus's inviting me to go with him to the mountains the next day. And we were gone for nearly six hours. Two of these hours we spent in one of the chapels up on the mountainside—during the most sinister thunderstorm I can remember experiencing. The cloudbursts poured down over the valley in such torrents that it wouldn't have amazed me to find that the whole village had been washed away when the clouds drifted off beneath us. But what happened with Claus inside the chapel nonetheless made a far greater impression on me.

We had hardly begun the trip down when the first thunderclap came—followed by the first, leaden drops. The air and the light changed, it became brownish gray around us, and a moment later the storm broke loose. For the first time since I was a child I was really *afraid* in a thunderstorm.

"Come on," said Claus, "there's a chapel nearby."

We ran along a path for a few minutes, and arrived sopping wet at the tiny little white building. We took off our shoes and jackets and began the wait.

Almost immediately Claus became fidgety. He couldn't sit still and paced back and forth on what little floor space there was to move in. Faster and faster. And meanwhile the thunderstorm rose to such a height that it felt as if the mountains themselves were beginning to crack under us. The bolts of lightning followed so thick and fast that the chapel was often lit up for several seconds running by continual flashes. Now and then several bolts jumped at the same time, and the thunderclaps couldn't be told apart. It went far beyond the bounds of common sense. A few times Claus tried to sit down, but almost at once he was on his feet again. He paced back and forth, back and forth, mouth open, and wide-eyed. His hands ran like animals, independent of his own will, up and down between his pockets and the lapels of his jacket. Up and down. Up and down. For a while he stood at the altar fingering the painted wooden figures. They were simple baroque sculptures of apostles and prophets. A rather large Mary hung above the altar, adorned with a couple of modest bracelets and a few gewgaws. Claus plucked at the jewelry, and in the glare from the lightning I saw that he was standing with his eyes closed. All at once I understood that he was came here often, and that he was used to being alone. Without opening his eyes he picked up a candle lying between the figure and the wall. He lit it hurriedly and set it up in front of Mary on the pedestal base. Then he turned to me and smiled.

His smile was much more unpleasant than his earlier restlessness. He seemed almost calm again.

"One thing I don't understand," he said. "Why you act as if nothing was wrong. Why do you do it?"

He walked quickly over to the door and set it ajar. A cold and rain-wet gust of wind poured in. The candle almost went out. Then he lit a cigarette, and tried to blow the smoke out the crack in the door. Piety decreed that it shouldn't stay inside the chapel.

"Why do you do it?" he repeated.

I didn't understand what he meant, and he must have seen that. He formulated his question more precisely:

"Why do you act as if you don't know the whole story?"

"What story?" I asked with a dry throat.

"The story about my dear father," he replied with a grimace which showed the teeth in his lower jaw.

"I know nothing about your father," I said.

"Well," replied Claus with obvious disdain. "Then I'll help you, since you're too tactful to remember it yourself. You know, perhaps, that people do vivisection with rats? Or don't you know that?

"They do research, they experiment on them. Inject bacteria and vitamins into them, transmit diseases to them, remove their organs and cut them up and sew them together again. They do lots of useful things with them, but they don't ask the rats first. And besides, it's us it's useful for, not for the rats—But I don't suppose you know anything about that either?"

Without waiting for a reply, he went on:

"So *that* you've heard nothing about. But my father, my greatly beloved father, he'd heard it, you understand—so he did research himself. But unfortunately not on rats. He was ahead of his time, so he did it with people of sorts—not human beings like you and me—but at any rate with some kind of human. But my father, you see, he was so used to rats that he didn't see any difference at all—And that of course is a question in itself, whether there really is any difference. But this you've heard nothing about? Not a word, eh? Well? Well?"

Suddenly he turned to the wall, pressed his face against the cold masonry and sobbed loudly. As he stood crying, his knees gave way and he sank slowly to the floor.

At first I was much too stunned to be able to say or do anything. And soon Claus got to his feet again. He sat down before the candle by the Mary statue and turned his back to me while he wiped his face. The chapel shook with the thunderclaps.

Without turning around, he went on speaking:

"At least you don't have to leave those damned documents of yours lying around, to show that you know about it!"

A warm wave of shame washed through me when I understood what he meant. Two days earlier I had been sitting on the veranda making a fair copy of some notes from the conversations with Max. They were in Norwegian. But to clarify one piece of information from the SS man I had brought out some of the documents from the Doctor's Trials. They were of course in German. Then I went to the post office and left the papers lying beside the typewriter. That was all. But the trip to the post office lasted rather a long time; on the way back I took a detour, walked all the way to the neighboring village half an hour away, bathed in a brook and lay for a long time in the grass afterwards. The catalog of Dr. Reynhardt's crimes, among others, must have lain for several hours on the veranda.

There are moments when you could die of shame. But you don't die. The rest of the stay in the chapel is best forgotten. As soon as Claus was convinced that I hadn't left the papers lying around on purpose, I could think only of explaining myself to his mother. And we began the trip down as soon as the weather would allow. It was quite heavy going after the violent rain, and we didn't exchange many words on the way.

The same evening I talked at length with Frau Reynhardt, naturally about her husband. And she was greatly concerned to give an accurate picture of him; of this singularly complicated nature which had posthumously been the main figure in the great prosecution of the implicated doctors.

On top of the information from Max and Lyngby it was her narrative—and she continued it in the days that followed—which made it possible to reconstruct the events as they actually happened in a city in Germany at the beginning of the 1940s.

Ere the Cock Crows

Part Two

3. PROJECT CATALYST

And in that day—declares the Lord--the mind of the king and the mind of the nobles shall fail, the priests shall be appalled, and the prophets stand aghast.
—Jeremiah 4:9 (JPS)

THE MAN AT THE TABLE sat in his black uniform. He slowly set his glass down without looking up. Then he straightened his back and drew in his arms, so that his fingertips rested against the edge of the table. For a while he sat studying his hands. They were brown and very powerful, but strongly chiseled. He leaned his big head forward and screwed up his eyes, and his chin, which was round and plump, came far down over his collar. Finally it hid half of the two S's, the two sharp zigzags which were the order's sign and emblem.

In spite of its roundness the face was strongly delineated. The eyes were set deep in the head, and the folds around the mouth bit deeply into the plump cheeks. The dark blond, short-cropped hair showed an almost bullet-shaped head. The half-open mouth was large and very expressive.

Before him on the table stood three large glasses and a bottle of French cognac. Beside them lay a pile of papers covered with writing. The big room was lit by three naked electric bulbs, and the glare fell on an almost empty interior. The whitewashed windows were curtainless and were covered from outside. Under one window stood a large radio set, and further along the same wall was a small black coke oven. The long stovepipe twisted in stiff waves up the lemon-colored wall, passed over the door and debouched in the corner. The long wall opposite was covered with racks of files from floor to ceiling.

The worst, thought the man at the desk; the worst is that damned color on the walls.

He had raised his head and was peering out into the room. His glance stopped at the meticulous order on the shelves.

"Do you know if any of the vaccination records were *not* brought up to date?"

The question was directed to a man in his forties, attired in the same uniform as himself.

The forty-year-old, who was tall and thin, stood stiffly at attention in the middle of the floor. Aside from the obligatory emblem of the order he had no decorations on his uniform. He was a subordinate.

"Jawohl, Standartenführer! The transients are not included in the statistics. But all the fever experiments are registered and entered in the records."

The answer came as if read from a book.

The man behind the desk drew himself up. The squinting and slightly sleepy expression had disappeared.

"What does 'transient' mean?"

"That is the designation for those who are inoculated with the disease just so they will have it. They aren't vaccinated first. Dr. Eger says that he keeps the bacteria cultures alive in them, so that one can just help oneself when infectious matter is needed."

The man at the desk bowed his head so far toward the papers that his features disappeared in the sharp shadow from the light bulb above him. For a while he sat as if sunk in thought.

The third person in the room stood beside the subordinate on the floor. He was wearing the same uniform. This was a boy of eighteen, with a square, pale face and ash blond, Baltic hair. He was of medium height, but with uncommonly broad shoulders. Despite the much too deep furrows in his face he did not look older than he was. He too stood at attention, but swayed unsteadily, with a watery gaze.

The officer at the desk looked up at the boy. With his thumb he pointed toward the window.

"Have *the ones out there* learned the song?" he asked.

"It took a couple hours, but now them's singin' just fine," replied the ash-blond. He leaned forward quickly to keep his balance.

With his fingertips the officer meticulously drew a single paper out of the pile in front of him. He studied it for a moment before laying it carefully to one side.

"Were there more doctors involved in the experiments besides those listed here?"

The words were again directed at the forty-year-old.

"Jawohl, Standartenführer! A Danish doctor took part in the experiments, but he hasn't been here for a long time now."

The man behind the desk looked at his wristwatch. Then he turned again to the Balt:

"Obergruppenführer Dr. Scholz should arrive from Berlin before two o'clock. When he gets here we must have a little night-time roll call and welcome him with the song. We can let them sing it a couple of times first. He'll appreciate it."

The boy clicked his heels, the order was received. He fought to keep himself upright. And the officer's gaze did not leave him.

"Were you present at all the experiments for the Air Force?"

"No."

The attempt to seem sober made him speak much too tersely, and the forty-year-old came to his rescue:

"Not all of them, Standartenführer!"

"I don't mean every single experiment, but at all the different *types*."

"I was only at the frost and pressure experiments. But not the others."

The older subordinate looked at him, but without changing his position. His body remained at the same rigid attention.

"You can be glad of that," he said quickly.

The man at the desk let his glance glide over the one who had spoken. He thrust out his lower lip as he looked at him. It was a while before he said anything.

"Did *you* attend all of them?"

The forty-year-old knitted his brows as he thought about it. He bared his teeth with the exertion. First he looked up at the ceiling. Then he looked down at the floor. Finally he relaxed and slowly began counting on his fingers:

"Let's see: Air—one! The dry frost experiments—two! The wet frost experiments—three! Then we have the shipwreck experiments with salt water—four! Then there were the ones with distilled salt water! That's five. Chemical salt water—six! The others—the ones with mustard gas and the surgical experiments, they were for the Army.

"But I've been at all the types of experiments for the Air Force, yes."

During the tally the man at the desk had been listening intently. Now he slowly and carefully laid out a row of papers, so that they finally covered most of the desk. With his eyes on the documents he pointed with one finger at the glasses which still stood along the table's edge.

"Drink!" he said. "Help yourselves!"

It looked as if he were playing solitaire. But it was clear that it wasn't coming out right.

The two subordinates marched forward to the table, raised the big, half-filled glasses and drank simultaneously from them. But the elder man finished first, and when he set down his glass some of its contents remained. The younger drank it all up. He had a hard time standing straight when the glass was tilted toward the ceiling, and when he put it down it landed on one of the papers. The officer pushed it aside with annoyance.

"But then we have a clear overview. That leaves just a few little things!"

His tone belied the words. It was obvious that the game still wasn't coming out.

"To begin with, the wagon. It was hermetically sealed, so that the air pressure could be varied. And a window was built into it, so that one could see how the prisoner acted when the air pressure sank. How low could the pressure go inside the wagon?"

The subordinate thought about it. Then he turned to the younger man beside him:

"Do you remember how low it could go? Dr. Eger explained it once."

The boy woke up from his intoxicated state and answered with almost metallic precision:

"The air pressure corresponded to twenty-one kilometers above sea level."

Without looking up from the papers, the officer continued his questions:

"Could the temperature be varied at the same time?"

"No," replied the elder subordinate.

"So one couldn't do frost and pressure experiments simultaneously. That's too bad, because in fact you usually have to protect yourself against both at the same time."

"Dr. Eger thought that it was easiest to work with them separately."

"It's certainly *easiest*, yes. But for us here the point isn't whether it's easy or not."

It sounded as if the game was beginning to come out. He went on:

"Then there were the frost experiments. They were intended to establish exactly how much cold a human being can stand, and then to arrive at the best methods of treatment after the frostbite? Is that right?"

"Yes," replied the tall, thin one.

The man at the desk went on. He was calm, but now and ten his face twitched.

"The experiments in ice water I'm familiar with."

It was clear that the game was nearing a resolution, and he picked up a few of the papers, put them together and stuck them back in the pile.

"But how did the 'dry' experiments go? Only the results are written up here. Drink now, boys!"

He pointed nervously at the bottle and the glasses. The younger of the subordinates, the one with the Baltic face, filled the glass all the way up and drank again. When he had set the glass down, he pointed over his shoulder with his thumb:

"Them was just put on a stretcher and set outside."

"And there they lay?" said the officer.

"No," said the boy, "them hadda be tied to the stretchers, 'cause them din't have no clothes on—'sides it was kinda cold."

"How long did they lie like that?"

The officer swallowed a couple of times. He completely forgot to look down at the papers.

It was the older man who replied:

"They lay there from a few hours to all day and all night. And then their temperature was taken—Well, the ones who got chloroform had their temperature monitored the whole time, 'cause of course we couldn't tell when they fainted."

"They got chloroform?"

The man behind the desk sounded surprised.

"Yeah, Dr. Eger him coun't get to sleep! Hah!" The answer came from the Balt. There seemed to be new problems with the solitaire game.

"*They* got chloroform so that Dr. Eger could get some sleep?"

The underlings grinned nastily.

"And daytimes them coun't get no peace to work," cried the boy, "not him or Dr. Fritze!"

"Did it disturb them so much to think of the prisoners lying out there?"

The officer looked up with big eyes. They were blue and very clear.

"Imagine the doctors being so sensitive!" he said.

The two subordinates roared with laughter.

"Well, the subjects screamed so horribly," said the elder, when he had calmed down again.

And the other added, with a thick and indistinct voice:

"Yeah, them screamed so loud it was hell to listen to for everybody round. Ten, twelve of 'em at once. Wasn't easy to sleep when us was doing the dry 'sperments!"

The Balt was very drunk, and sank completely into the memory of the sleepless nights he had undergone.

"Yes, I see," said the officer. "But the chloroform helped?"

He had again bowed his head, so that his face was hidden in shadow.

"Yes, there was just a little gurgling still."

"The death rate?"

"A darn sight more'n half of 'em went up. Through the chimley…."

The boy had wakened out of his memories again, and threw himself into the discussion. His elder colleague amplified:

"Nearly seventy percent."

The officer picked up the bottle and poured more brandy into the glasses. He opened the cupboard behind him and put the bottle in it.

"Please drink," he said kindly. It looked as if the game had moved forward again.

"Then there were the salt water experiments," he went on. "All that's recorded here are ages, daily rations, results and so on. I don't suppose that proceeded quietly either?"

"I should say not!" replied the elder of the two on the floor. "They squealed like stuck pigs! Some of 'em went crazy, too."

"Those who got salt water screamed the most, I assume?"

"Yes, so long as they could. They got even thirstier from the salt. Yecch! Makes me thirsty just to think of it!"

He suddenly raised his glass and took a long swig of the cognac.

At the same time the younger one abandoned his rigid and exhausting posture of attention. He wandered around the room for a while, knocked over a chair by the radio, and knelt in front of the apparatus. The marches disappeared, and after a while he got the radio tuned the way he wanted it; very loud and midway between two stations. It picked up a tango and a Schubert melody at the same time. Moved by the music he made prolonged attempts to get back on his feet.

The officer paid no attention to him. Wholly engrossed in his thoughts, he continued to study the papers. Finally he pulled out a single sheet and held it up above the rest.

"And here are some more who'll be screaming soon," he said to the thin one. The plump face, totally expressionless, leaned forward.

"Is that the list of research subjects?" responded the subordinate. He looked at the Balt, who was dragging the upturned chair straight across the floor. The boy set it up in front of the desk and sat down on it, so that he was sitting face to face with the officer.

"Are you comfortable?" asked the man behind the desk. He looked up without raising his head.

The Balt's square, pale face sank down to his chest with a jerk. He didn't reply.

"He gets drunk fast," said the thin one and looked down at him without abandoning his motionless position. "He ain't no mamma's boy. When we were doing the pressure experiments for the air force, two of the other orderlies fainted —though they'd been in the service for a long time. Those fellows were much older than him. But Max, he took it like a man! He just threw up. Hah!"

He suddenly bent down and patted the sleeping boy on the shoulder.

But Max wasn't sleeping too deeply to be aware that something was going on around him.

"Go 'way!" he mumbled. And the pale face with the sharp, youthful folds contracted into an expression of deep loathing. It was a general loathing, a reflex of aversion to the world at large, a grimace which for a moment gave the childish face an expression of indescribable desolation. For a little while the half-sleeping figure in the chair looked very young.

The officer raised his head and looked at him. He had forgotten the papers and was staring at the boy.

"Just listen!" said the thin one. "After all, he ain't but a lad!"

The man behind the desk let his glance glide up to the elder soldier. Then he bent over the papers, and the game of patience resumed. Now it was stuck again.

"Right," he said. "This is a list of the research subjects. But there's only one page, and it only goes up to 'G'. There must be at least two more pages."

"They're in 106," answered the thin one. "I'll get them out."

He was already crossing the room, but stopped when he heard the voice behind him.

Without getting up the officer had kicked the sleeper. The desk was open, and the kick hit the boy below the knee. He looked around in confusion, squinting against the sharp light.

"*He*'ll go!" cried the officer. "Up with you, Max!"

"He won't find 'em, though," said the forty-year-old, who had turned so that he was standing in the middle of the floor. Once again the black patent-leather boot traveled forward under the table. It hit in the same place.

"Anyway, he's rested enough. Up, I say!"

The Balt got up and stood at attention.

"Jawohl, Standartenführer," he said. The boy stood straight and sure on his feet, as if he had never done anything else.

The officer cleared his throat and looked at him with wide-open eyes.

"So," he said. "You took it like a man?"

"Max takes everything like a man."

"At any rate you can't work at night. You can't keep awake," continued the officer.

The thin man had reached the filing shelves long since. He was leafing in a binder with loose papers.

"106," he said aloud. "105!"

"And so you only threw up?" said the man at the desk. He looked at the underling with intense distaste.

"There was one of 'em wasn't dead," answered the one with the young face. "Woke up while Eger was cutting into 'im. But Eger just went on, he did, and so I had to hold 'im. So I threw up on the floor, but I di'n't let go of 'im."

The thin man leafed further, and at last he seemed to be finding something.

"G—G—G!" he cried. "Now we're getting there!"

But the officer was still occupied with the Balt. He cleared his throat and drew himself up straight. His hands disappeared under the table. For a minute he looked at a loss.

"Dr. Eger didn't say anything about your throwing up?"

"No," answered the boy. He smiled nastily as if about to proclaim an intimate, indecent secret: "Dr. Eger just said that it did me good to see what Jews looked like inside."

But at once he grew serious again, and seemed to be sobering up.

"But there wasn't no trick to holding 'im," he went on without pride, "'cause after all he hadn't no strength left."

His voice was matter-of-fact, and he looked down. The officer swallowed a couple of times.

The man at the files had found what he was looking for.

"Here it is!" he called. "It begins with 'Goldmann'!"

The word worked like a revolver shot on the one behind the desk. He rose halfway up and sat down again. Then he quieted down. It was clear that the game was very nearly over, and as solutions often do it had come a little too fast, a little too inexorably, when it was finally there. It is exactly as with a revolver shot; even if you've been expecting it for a long time, it still comes with surprising suddenness, in a way unexpected, and always more violent than what you were prepared for. A shot is always future or past—never present tense.

And before he had collected his wits, he shouted the question:

"Does it say *Samuel* Goldmann?"

The thin one glanced at the document and looked quickly up again, wide-eyed.

"Jawohl, Standartenführer! *Samuel.*"

He tried briefly to control himself, but the temptation was too great.

"Did you know him, Standartenführer?"

"Oh—yes," replied the officer with much too great a show of indifference. "Many years ago. We studied together."

The subordinate crossed the floor quickly and laid the list on the table.

"As a matter of fact, I'm familiar with this list from before." His voice was low and confidential. He bent halfway down toward the seated man. "They'll get theirs next, the ones on that list. They're for the fever experiments. For the moment they're getting extra provisions."

The officer opened his mouth and raised his head. It looked as if the game still had a surprise to offer.

"What?" he said with undisguised astonishment.

The subordinate grew in his uniform. He straightened all the way up again.

"They get full soldier's rations for three weeks first," he explained. "Otherwise they have no resistance. Hah!"

One of the two radio stations had gone off the air. The other was playing a lively polka.

The officer knitted his brows. They made a thick, soft line across the wide bridge of his nose.

"No, of course not," he said quietly and thoughtfully. "Otherwise the experiments would be worthless, wouldn't they?"

The thin man nodded.

For a moment the officer sat motionless. Then he burst into laughter, loud and shrill. His face darkened and he ran his hands several times over his hair, but the laughter continued—sometimes almost in falsetto, which was ill suited to his uncommonly powerful and heavy figure.

"Lord God!" he said, when he had caught his breath. "It's just like Hansel and Gretel! First, they're fattened up, afterwards they go into the oven. Yes, afterwards they literally go into the oven!" The laughter rose up in him again, and the embarrassed underling tried to laugh with him.

When he was done laughing, he rubbed his fingers together for a while, then felt to see if his collar was straight.

"How long has Goldmann been getting extra rations?" he went on.

"For about two weeks," replied the forty-year-old.

The officer looked at his watch and ran his right hand over his face. He rubbed his cheeks energetically.

"We must lodge an appeal at once, then," he said. "Now we're ready for Dr. Scholz—You're so musical, Max, see about putting a little life into them."

The boy walked unsteadily across the room and took a riding crop out of one of the pigeonholes. Then he turned.

"I'm not afraid of night work," he said. "But I had too much to drink. I've never been able to stand it."

He looked at the whip and straightened up.

"Hell, I'll make 'em dance!" His voice was loud and furious.

Just then the door opened, and a tall, thin man came into the room. Without looking around, he peeled off of his wet raincoat. The two subordinates clicked their heels and saluted with outstretched arms. He nodded back and raised his head, so that his face became visible in the lamplight. He had a narrow, long-skulled head with finely chiseled features, a handsome, nervous face. He was remarkably tanned. He nodded again when he caught sight of the officer, who had already risen. There was a moment's silence. Then the officer turned to the boy. The new arrival, who was wearing a gray suit, stopped in the middle of the floor. And with a wholly expressionless face he listened attentively as the conversation which continued.

"Have you ever been whipped yourself?" asked the officer in a friendly tone.

The two underlings exchanged glances before Max stretched to his full height.

"Jawohl, Standartenführer!"

The Balt cleared his throat slightly.

"As a boy," he went on.

"When Dr. Scholz gets here you can both go to bed," said the officer.

"Thank you, Standartenführer!"

"Here we're all comrades," he went on. The newcomer looked at him. The subordinates stood motionless.

"Take the glasses with you!"

"Jawohl, Standartenführer!"

Max took two measured steps forward and collected the three glasses on the desk with his left hand. He walked backwards to his place again.

"Can we sleep in tomorrow morning?" he asked.

"No," replied the officer.

When the door slammed shut after the underlings, the other two stood looking at each other for a moment. The civilian glanced at the door, then he turned on his heel and crossed the room with long strides.

He stopped with his back to the filing shelves.

"You've found your conversational tone," he said guardedly.

The other lit a cigarette, shading the match with both hands. He bent his head to the flame as if he were standing in a high wind.

"He's a child of the people, Heinrich. They don't appreciate the finer things the way you and I do."

Heinrich looked at the radio.

"May I find something else besides this commercial music?"

The SS man bowed.

"I was just going to do so myself," he said. Then he lifted his cigarette and carefully blew the ash from it.

The man in the grey suit bent down and looked for another station. After awhile he found a Mozart concerto, and as he adjusted the tuning and listened to the first measures, the officer walked back to the desk. Without sitting down he put the papers in order, gathered them into a pile and quickly crossed the room with them. He put them in one of the pigeonholes and looked with satisfaction at the order which had now been restored. Back on the table lay a single sheet.

The other had risen; for awhile he stood silently beside the radio. Then he cleared his throat and looked at the other's back. It was a waiting back, but not a rejecting one.

"We keep meeting, Paul." The words were quiet and challenging. And indeed he took his pince-nez out of his pocket. He put them on as if he had finally got up the courage to do something which had to be done.

Paul turned quickly.

"Yes," he said, "again and again."

He took a couple of steps across the floor, heavy and sure. Then he stopped and closed his eyes. The radio was playing a flute solo and the sound rose up in him like a grapevine. It climbed and branched, put forth new shoots, stretched out for a moment and stood quite still again. For awhile it waited, then slowly grew some more.

"But always in new circumstances," he said abruptly. "Have you noticed that, Heinrich?"

The grapevine stood still again; then it calmly put forth another shoot. Tender and green it stretched out, bifurcated and acquired dark, cool leaves. The tips of the soft tendrils curled in the air without finding any anchor.

"Providential meeting!" he added suddenly. Then he walked slowly over to the desk. The other had turned darker under his tan.

"How long is it since we've seen each other?" he went on.

"Over six years," replied the other without a pause. "And you've been three days in your new position?"

The officer looked at the clock.

"We are two hours into the fourth day," he replied. Suddenly he looked the other in the face. His voice dropped.

"How's Gerda? I said hello to her a few days ago—"

"Thanks, things are quite…."

He was interrupted by voices from outside. There were loud, strident commands, followed by a rhythmic tramping on the field. For awhile they both listened to the shouts and the boots. The voices went up and sometimes way down, they made leaps and large intervals, long pauses and sudden, lonely cries. The sound of the boots was always the same dull tone—the sound of one foot and yet of many.

"May I assume that you're thriving?" For the first time the civilian spoke with a tone of undisguised scorn.

The other went over to the desk. He reflected before he looked up.

"It's too early for me to say yet," he said calmly. "But there's much to learn, much to fill myself in on. I've been trying especially to acquaint myself with the records from this winter. The scientific work which has been done here, the experiments I mean, seem to have been very interesting."

Outside the voices of command rose into yells, and the man with the pince-nez grimaced nervously.

"The experiments are of very great significance."

The SS man cupped his hands around the burning match, and when he lit his cigarette the draft was stronger than before. When he looked up again, he said:

"And how are things with you? I assume *you're* thriving?"

"I'm not here all that often," replied the scientist. "Of course it's exclusively as a scientist that I'm associated with this camp. And just for the fever experiments. My laboratory is in town—It was a surprise to hear that you'd taken over the position."

"It's a long story," replied the officer. He closed his eyes and listened again to the music. But the grapevine inside him was gone.

"A story of connections," he went on, and tried again to see it. But there was nothing which wanted to grow and move.

"But it's exclusively as an official that I sit here," he finished loudly and mockingly.

The voices from the courtyard again took the upper hand. The boots tramped faster and faster. They followed the shouts lightning-fast now.

"That's nothing to joke about," said the scientist. He looked pained and annoyed. His left hand was digging around in his pocket.

"I am perfectly clear what responsibility my work entails. One day it will indeed save thousands of human lives, but for the research subjects—*now, today*—the tests are both prolonged and painful. And even if it were only for their sakes, it is my duty to ensure that the work is done in a responsible, scientific manner."

The other looked at him.

"The mortality rate lies around seventy percent?"

"It will decrease—provided that the research is carried through."

The SS man looked down for a moment. Then he raised his head and looked the other in the eyes. The doctor turned toward the radio. His fingers glided over the mahogany.

"Do you know anything about the surgical insertions of gangrene and tetanus bacilli?"

"It was Dr. Eger who started those," replied the doctor.

"Do you think they're valuable?"

"They can doubtless become so." His fingers rubbed the mahogany energetically. Then he suddenly switched off the radio. Outside it had been quiet for a while. Now they were singing. It was a large men's chorus.

"Why in the world do you have them sing such mournful songs?" The doctor turned to the other. "This one is almost unbearable."

"It must be a very bloody series of experiments?" The officer looked at the other searchingly. Suddenly he stepped forward and took him by the arm. He thrust his head forward.

"Lord, Heinrich," he said, "this is an unappetizing business."

"So?" rejoined the doctor. He took a step sideways and pulled his arm away.

"Well," replied the other, staring down at the illuminated box with the stations' names: "I was thinking that it might not be absolutely necessary. At least not so necessary as the fever experiments."

"Nothing can stop it now."

The officer looked up and smiled. His smile was open and shameless.

"With your scientific and my political influence...."

The scientist took a quick step forward. For a moment he lost his reserve. His voice was louder than before.

"I have a responsibility to my family," he said. "I can't get mixed up in adventures. I can't allow myself to be frivolous."

The other had become serious again.

"Do you think I'm trying to trap you?" he asked.

The doctor removed his pince-nez, and as he polished them with his handkerchief he replied coolly:

"How in the world should anyone trap me? I'm a wholly unpolitical person."

He held his pince-nez up to the light and discovered more spots to be wiped off. As he continued his task, he listened to the other nervously pacing the floor. Suddenly the officer stopped.

"You mean you *were*," he said gently.

"I am a doctor," replied the other.

There was a long silence. Outside the singing continued. And the SS man walked around restlessly. Finally, he sat down behind the desk and rested his chin in his hand.

"You're so right, Heinrich," he said thoughtfully. "It *is* remarkable that we should meet like this!"

The doctor looked searchingly at him. After a while he replied gravely:

"Yes, it's strange, Paul. After such a long time!" He looked down at the floor as if he were looking for footprints which could yield an explanation of the question which had arisen. But he found no solution.

"I didn't know anything about you…." he said and quickly looked up.

"The funny thing is," continued the officer, "that we seem to meet at decisive moments. Isn't there something in chemistry called a catalyst?"

"Yes," the other replied. "Catalyst is the name for a substance which has the property of being able to accelerate a chemical process which would have happened anyway—only more slowly."

For a while they looked at each other.

"Well, well," said the SS man. "In any case it's remarkable that it's precisely we three who should meet again."

"I don't understand? We *two*, you mean?"

"No, we *three*."

"Are you counting Gerda as the third?" The doctor looked irritated.

"No," the other replied. "I mean Samuel. I found him on the list of research subjects. He's one of the ones you're getting for the fever experiments."

The doctor took off his pince-nez. He bit his lower lip. And pallor from the bite spread all around his mouth. He put his pince-nez back on.

The other was already on his feet. The paper which had been on the table was now in his hand, and without haste he crossed the floor and held it out to the doctor.

"You can see his name here," he said. "At the beginning of the G's."

The doctor looked at the paper and breathed a few times very deeply. The pallor fought with a couple of reddish-brown spots on his cheeks.

"I had no idea that he was here!" he said. And a little bashfully he added:

"I never look at the lists. I have nothing to do with that part of the job."

"Well," replied the officer indifferently, "these things happen. Anyway, I have good news for you."

Heinrich looked up in amazement.

"For me?"

"Yes," replied the other. "Your membership is in order."

"What membership?" The doctor drew himself up.

"Yours."

The officer had seated himself behind the desk again. The doctor lowered his head and stared at him.

"In what?" he asked quietly.

The man behind the desk leaned back in his chair and ran his right hand down the black uniform. He patted it lovingly.

"In our legion," he answered. "You're accepted into the order."

The other took an involuntary step backward. Then he walked all the way up to the desk and bent forward.

"But I've never asked to be accepted!" he shouted.

The officer smiled faintly.

"Oddly enough you are accepted all the same." The reply came almost pityingly, and the doctor ran a hand over his eyes.

"But I've never applied," he stammered. "I have never…."

"So you'll have to get a uniform," continued the officer. "And you'll naturally want it tailor-made, won't you? You must pay for the sewing yourself at the outset. But later we can doubtless find some line on the books to charge it to."

"I haven't applied," repeated the other.

"Don't forget about the tailor," said the officer calmly. "You must see about getting your measurements taken as soon as possible."

The doctor drew himself all the way up. He was a tall man.

"Hell, no! I said I haven't applied!"

"Calm down, Heinrich!" The SS man was suddenly very grave. But then he smiled again.

"If you don't like our black uniform, you can always wear your white lab coat over it!"

Suddenly he pushed back his chair and jumped up. From outside came a couple of sharp cries, and at once the singing started up.

"There he is!" cried the SS man. "Now the doctor's coming!"

For a moment they waited in silence. The doctor stroked himself over his face. Then the door flew open. A subordinate in a black uniform appeared for a brief second in the doorway, saluted stiffly and disappeared again:

"Obergruppenführer Dr. Scholz!"

The words were left standing in the air behind him.

The men who now entered the room were all in uniform. First came a stout man in his sixties. He bore a high-ranking insignia and several decorations. Right behind him came a young, blond man, also with insignia. And finally came a man in his forties. This last wore a white lab coat over his uniform. He was very dark and his face was so swarthy that his skin seemed like leather. It was not suntan, but rather a natural excess of pigmentation. He could have been an auto mechanic.

The greetings proceeded formally and thoroughly. They all shook each other's hands and introduced themselves by name and title. All of them but the man who had just been sitting at the desk were doctors. The stout one was Dr. Scholz, the blond one was Dr. Fritze, and the auto mechanic was Dr. Eger.

When the ritual was over with, the gentlemen grouped themselves respectfully around Dr. Scholz. He looked around, listened for a moment to the continued singing, and sent the layman a friendly, informal smile.

"Wonderful song, Heidebrand!" he said heartily. "Is it new?"

Paul Heidebrand smiled back.

"It's new here," he replied. "But actually it's very old."

The words from the song rang clearly and distinctly in the room. They concerned a knight and death and the pact between them.

"They sing it just splendidly!" said Scholz.

"We have such musical prisoners," replied Heidebrand. "And then we have Max, too—to put some life into them!"

The last words were followed by laughter from the two younger doctors.

"Max?" said Dr. Scholz. He looked around the room.

Dr. Fritze stroked the blond hair back from his forehead.

"Yes," he laughed. "Max can make them sing, all right!"

"We also make them sing—in our way!" Dr. Eger laughed silently at his own words. He had small, very even teeth which shone strongly against his dark skin. They all laughed except Dr. Reynhardt, the slim man in mufti. He appeared to be feeling extremely uncomfortable with the company in which he found himself.

"I don't have the pleasure of knowing Max." said Dr. Scholz. "But I understand that his acquaintance must be worth having."

"He's one of our boys, Oberführer!" Heidebrand stated this drily and matter-of-factly. "He is a Balt, an Estonian—and Dr. Eger has him as a trainee at present."

"We'll make something of him yet," added Dr. Eger. "But first we have to work on him awhile. He's still a bit of a nature boy. But Lord, he's so young!"

Heidebrand went over to the filing shelves and rummaged there for a little. When he had found what he was looking for, he laid it on the desk. Then he went quietly up to the superior officer. He touched him lightly on the shoulder.

"If you could spare me a moment first, Herr Oberführer?"

He bowed slightly.

"Of course, of course," replied the other good-humoredly. And they went over to the desk together. They whispered for a while over the papers.

The rest of the company went on standing in the middle of the floor.

"How is your son, Herr Doktor?" The question was asked by Dr. Eger and was directed at the civilian. "I hope that he continues to get better?"

"Yes, thank you," replied the civilian with reserve. "He's making progress."

"After all, he must be getting the best possible treatment!" continued the dark man, friendly and ingratiating. The bland tone appeared to arouse an even stronger distaste in the other.

"I'm not a neurologist," he said curtly.

But Dr. Eger smiled broadly and inclined his head forward.

"I would be glad to turn over any kind of case to you, Dr. Reynhardt!" he continued, unruffled.

"I don't doubt it," replied the other. His voice was ice cold: "But I doubt if just any patient would have the same comfort from it."

During the conversation the young Dr. Fritze had kept quiet, but the whole time he was excitedly running his fingers through his hair, which kept falling down over his pale forehead. He was enjoying himself.

Now they were interrupted by Dr. Scholz, who came walking across the room with outstretched hand. In a loud voice he said:

"May I congratulate you, Herr Doktor!"

The words were directed at Dr. Reynhardt. Without enthusiasm he took the proffered hand.

"On what, Herr Oberführer?"

Paul Heidebrand, gathering up the papers, observed them, smiling.

Dr. Scholz shook the doctor's hand for a while. Then he said:

"On your membership, of course! Of course we too should be congratulated. It is an uncommonly great pleasure to acquire a colleague with your scientific standing."

While Dr. Eger and Dr. Fritze in turn congratulated the scientist, Dr. Scholz went over to the side with the windows. He placed himself between the radio and the oven with his back against the lemon-yellow wall. folded his arms and leaned his head back. For a while he stood thus with eyes closed. It was as if he needed the weight of his whole large and heavy body to collect himself inwardly. He stood as still as a stone Buddha.

The others gradually quieted down, and stared at him expectantly. Heidebrand looked long at the man standing there, and thought that he was not merely fat. His mouth was large, coarse, painful in a way. His lower lip had a tendency to sag, revealing the long, powerful teeth in his lower jaw. His eyes set deep amid large bags and wrinkles. For all his ugliness his superior had something beautiful about him. The loose skin and the big eyes, the enormous neck and the bald crown—it added up more to a landscape than to an ordinary human being. Had he been dressed in civilian clothes or just in some *other* uniform than the one he wore, he would have seemed like an officer of the old school, honest and genial—but with small weaknesses for good cigars and ladies' stockings.

As it was now, an almost disagreeable energy flowed from him.

The singing had long since died down when the old man began to speak. First he cleared his throat, opened his eyes and saw that all were completely absorbed in what he was going to say. Then he drew himself all the way up and said in a forceful voice:

"And *so* to business, gentlemen! This time there is in fact an order from the Führer which we are to receive. It is definitely the so-called euthanasia program which stands on our doorstep. This has long been a matter close to the Führer's heart. The code name for the project will be: 'Catalyst.' You know that the Greeks (I mean the ancient Greeks), like the early Germanic tribes, used to 'expose' their sickly and deformed children in the woods. They did it in those times which laid the foundation for the later, great ancient and Germanic cultures. It was done while the races were still young. It was done to prevent those of inferior stock from burdening the national body and genetic substance. In other words, it was done for reasons of racial hygiene.

"Today, gentlemen, we are once again facing the formation of a new culture. And we are aware of the task which confronts us. We know that our movement, whether it is victorious or not, is a harbinger of those cultures which belong to the future. Under *all circumstances*, gentlemen, it is that. We pioneers, we who are present at this beginning, we bear the responsibility for that which is to come. The future shall hibernate in us!

"This is not about *ourselves*, gentlemen! We are servants. Our task is to ensure the evolution of a race which shall give birth to the future. And this race must be tilled like a field. It must be weeded and tended. It must be cultivated in its purity. We are gardeners, and our first task is a negative one. We must get rid of the inferior genetic material. Already nature herself is working in this direction. We shall merely assist. What is destined for destruction must be destroyed. The Germanic national body must be cleansed and purified. But—we will no longer be exposing children.

"Today we have other means.

"In 1935 the Führer received a letter from a father in Berlin. The man begged leave to take the life of his deformed and imbecile child. The child was completely misshapen and would never have become a human being. Well, he got the permission.

"'Mercy killing' we called it back then. That was the first case. Next the euthanasia program was worked out theoretically. And then came a difficult time. Everything was kept secret, and the program had to work invisibly. In one of the homes, for example, we had twenty-five Jewish children. That was in '39, and we still had to consider the foreign press and—above all, certain gentlemen in one of our neutral neighboring countries. The children had to die quietly and naturally."

Dr. Scholz drew a blue silk handkerchief out of his pocket and wiped the sweat from his brow. The last part of the speech had been a strain on him. Carefully he wiped the sweat from the corners of his eyes. For a while he surveyed the listeners, smiling.

"How do you suppose we managed it?" he went on.

Dr. Eger put his hand halfway up. Scholz nodded at him.

"They starved them to death?" asked the mechanic.

"And if so—*how?*"

The silence sang in the room. Only Dr. Scholz was still smiling.

"Hm—by cutting off their food supply?" Eger clearly knew that he was on the wrong track. Scholz smiled again. The guessing was obviously affording him unusual intellectual enjoyment. He threw out his arms and waved for the others to come a little closer, as if to tell them a secret. They came closer. Only Dr. Reynhardt stayed where he was. He was looking down, unmoving.

"No," continued Dr. Scholz, "*not* by cutting off the food supply— We merely cut down the daily ration—a little each day, until it finally came below the subsistence level. And then we kept it there. In practice this meant that each child had to have a precisely measured, definite number of calories per day. Each case had to be treated separately. But the payoff—and *this* is the main point, gentlemen!"

The doctor raised his index finger and looked around the circle.

The payoff was that one could have opened every single child afterward, and one would have found the remains of food in their intestines!"

He bowed his head and took a few deep breaths. Again he mopped his brow with his handkerchief before going on:

"It takes imagination to picture what this meant in practice. Something which today we could have accomplished in half an hour, as late as '39 had to be dragged out over several weeks. Quite aside from the screaming! You can imagine what it cost in time and money. But we learned a lot from it. We gained real understanding from it.

"I've mentioned this, gentlemen, to show how we began. It is probably new to most of you. But today, of course, things are luckily quite different.

"We are armed with all of modern science's technology and objectivity. And on this objectivity everything depends. We have no time for sentimentality. The program which goes into effect as of this evening, and which in the future will be realized on a steadily greater scale—for this program *I* bear the responsibility."

He raised his head and looked at the doctors.

"I!" he repeated: "I bear the full, human, medical and political responsibility. *I!*"

He touched a thick, well-manicured thumb to his chest.

For a while it was silent in the room. Then Eger cleared his throat. The others looked expectantly at him. Only Dr. Reynhardt still looked unmoving at the floor.

"May I ask what main categories the project is going to cover?"

Eger looked at his superior in suspense.

"Yes, my friend—that you may!" Dr. Scholz waited a bit before going on. "It will be first and foremost: Imbeciles, schizophrenics, mentally ill in general and then the deformed and crippled and incurably ill who are unfit to work. In general we will be removing inferior and superfluous human material. A certain number of war casualties we will regretfully be treating in the same way, along with two large population groups: the Jews and the Gypsies. That is the list."

He looked around expectantly.

Dr. Fritze had been pushing the blond boy-scout forelock back from his forehead. And when he took the floor, his face shone with eagerness and anticipation. The expression made him even younger than he was:

"And the technical side of it?" He looked around, groping for words. "The means of death, I mean—the cremation of the bodies? I mean, the development of the system itself? Has any decision been made about that?"

The words had come by fits and starts and with nervous resoluteness. Now, having got through it, he looked around at his elder colleagues and wiped his palms on his jacket.

Dr. Scholz smiled at the young man's anxiety. It was an accepting and encouraging smile, an appreciative smile which understood that he had really risked something when he threw himself into the discussion.

"I'm glad," he said, tilting back his fat, close-cropped head, "I am really glad you asked about that, Dr. Fritze. It is in fact our main concern at the moment."

He looked around energetically. And his gaze came to rest on Dr. Reynhardt, who was still standing apart, motionless and detached. His eyes dwelt on him, attentive and displeased. Then Dr. Scholz continued addressing Dr. Fritze, but much more loudly than before.

"It is first and foremost the technical side we must agree on here. The thing is that the action must be kept secret."

Shooting another lightning glance at the scientist, sunken into himself in his light grey summer suit, he turned quickly to Heidebrand. And the expression in the officer's hollow yet vigorous face was so tense that the doctor directed his final words to him.

"I've been thinking along the lines of creating big collection points all over the country. They must be built with crematoria. But to prevent the accumulation of too many people at once—which could attract too much attention—both the laboratories and the crematoria must have a relatively large capacity. It would be best if people could be liquidated the same day they arrive. So these stations must be a kind of factory."

For a while Dr. Scholz looked down the broad breast of his uniform. He rocked his head a little as if he were thinking of something else entirely, then straightened up again and went on addressing the officer.

"The extermination method is a problem in itself," he said, pulling the cuff forward under his uniform jacket. He planted his feet yet a little further apart, so that nobody in the world could push him over. "We can't let them go straight into the oven. They must be killed or stunned first, and that will prolong the process. The obvious solutions are gas or some kind of injection—*but. . .*" he emphasized the word strongly and went on in a louder voice: "it's possible that someone may find better and cheaper solutions!"

He raised his finger and smiled at Dr. Fritze, who was now consciously playing the role of the youthful enthusiast. Then he continued, first to the doctors in turn, and finally again as if he were talking just to Heidebrand.

"This killing procedure must under no circumstances be wholly mechanized, for we must not forget the double role these stations will come to play: first and foremost as extermination facilities, and secondly—and this is no less important!—secondly as training grounds for people we will need in the future. . . .

"Very young people can do a kind of military service at these stations, and we will be able in a relatively short time to harden them to a degree of callousness which we cannot imagine today.

"The main thing, gentlemen, is to begin the experimental spadework as fast as possible."

He leaned back, supporting himself against the wall. He was resting.

Dr. Eger looked at him, and the healthy whites of his eyes shone against his taut brown skin. He blinked nervously a few times, then rubbed under his chin with the back of his hand.

"It's a far-reaching plan," he said, and looked around. His glance lit on Dr. Fritze, who was pushing the blond locks back off his smooth forehead. His eyes flickered with excitement.

"Impressive!" cried Fritze. "Now we have a real task ahead of us!"

Dr. Scholz hadn't been watching as they spoke. He had clsed his eyes and was looking in an entirely different direction. In reality he was thinking of his wife on her bed at the maternity hospital—once again the mother of a strapping youngster. She was rather worn now—what with the children and all she had to do for them--and she had never succeeded in adapting to the social circles they had been moving in these last few years. She still looked like a workingman's wife, or at any rate like a wife from the petit bourgeoisie. There was something around her mouth and something about the way she dressed which incorrigibly signaled that they had bought their first vacuum cleaner on the installment plan. And she never liked to go out on the evenings he had free. Now that their circle of acquaintances had changed she liked it less than ever; she felt unsure of herself, anxious among these people who had grown up with such different assumptions. But she was faithful, she had been faithful through all these years it had taken him to work his way up. She had gone through fire and water for him— and she would do it again should it become necessary.

Lord, he thought, he must find something to make her happy this time. Buy something or other! But no. She never wanted anything—he must think of something else to do....

With a jerk he pulled himself together and was back in the circle of doctors.

"Since Dr. Eger has taken over the direction of the surgical researches," he said, turning to the blond—to the youngster, "I'm entrusting the administration of this work to you, Dr. Fritze. You seem to have a particular interest in it, too. And Dr. Reynhardt will follow it with his interest and good advice."

He turned to the civilian, and the fat face took on a weary, almost annoyed expression. He thought again of his wife; the tall, suntanned man before him belonged to the sort she would never learn to associate with. Then he straightened up, and his voice became clearer as he went on.

"You will be so kind as to keep an eye on the methodology, will you not, Herr Doktor?"

Dr. Reynhardt looked up without replying. His handsome face had a tormented expression. His mouth was ever so slightly open and his eyebrows knit together over the blue eyes. He fumbled uncertainly for his pince-nez and put them on as clumsily as if he had never clamped them over his nose before. Dr. Scholz, observing him all the while, slowly lowered his head and stuck out his lower jaw. Thoughts of his wife were very far away now.

Very quietly he continued to speak. His voice was calm and exaggeratedly kind.

"Do you have concerns, Dr. Reynhardt?"

The others in the room followed the incident wide-eyed. And Dr. Reynhardt took off his pince-nez again and drew out his handkerchief. He rubbed the glasses carefully while he looked around. The silence in the room was very oppressive.

Then he cleared his throat and began to speak in an uncertain, indistinct voice. After just a few words he had to clear his throat again.

"If these things," he said slowly, "if these things are not handled with discretion, they will lead to the creation of rumors and an atmosphere of panic."

He looked around the circle again. Then he polished his glasses again and stuck them slowly back in his pocket.

"In the hands of inappropriate persons they can cause irreparable harm."

Dr. Scholz had sighed with relief as the other was speaking. Now he sent him a friendly look and smiled.

"Don't worry about it, Dr. Reynhardt," he said, and his relief became even more evident. "I shall take care of the discretion."

He seemed almost to be enjoying himself. Then he went on:

"Now let's think of other things! For example—*for example* of how our taking the first steps to actualize the euthanasia program means far more than mere material progress. The euthanasia project is the symbol of an intellectual victory."

He paused to look around at the calm faces. Then he went on, and his face acquired a faint and happy blush. It gave warmth to his voice, and he continued from a full heart, his head tilted back a little.

"Yes, I will go so far as to say that it is first and foremost a symbol. It confirms that we—humanity—have finally become masters in our own house. We have overcome the deep, subconscious inhibitions, the old taboos which have hitherto stood in the way of carrying out such a relatively natural thing. We have taken a step which no cultured people before us have dared to carry to its full conclusion. We are the first fully mature beings nature has produced. The day the euthanasia program becomes a reality is the new humanity's secret birthday!"

He was no longer looking at those he was addressing. He looked up at the ceiling and felt a warmth growing inside him. Somewhere in his chest he felt a hint of the enthusiasm which these long years of political dishonesty and compromise had threatened to stifle in him, something which had just barely survived the endless, trivial political dailiness. And it mounted to his head as a light, jubilant dizziness.

"A scientist," he almost shouted the word, "a *scientist* who is privileged to take part in this, he must feel proud! The meeting of science with the practical man has made it possible to consciously set the future to rights—to create the biological and psychological preconditions for a future the way *we* want it! Oh, he who takes part in this, he must feel proud!"

Flushed, he looked around. Then he raised his hand, as if waving a flag.

"Proud, gentlemen!" he cried. "Proud!"

Slowly, and strictly concerned with what he was doing, Heidebrand bent down to the cupboard behind the desk and brought out a bottle of cognac. Along with five small glasses he placed it on the desk and filled the glasses slowly and carefully.

Dr. Scholz looked straight ahead and asked in a dry voice if anyone had more questions. For a while only the sound of the brandy being poured broke the silence. Then Dr. Reynhardt cleared his throat. Slowly and hesitantly, but with determination, he began to speak. It was already clear before he opened his mouth that he did not share his superior's enthusiasm.

"I find a serious problem in the business itself," he said drily. "May I be permitted to mention it?"

He looked up, firm and unequivocal. The slim figure drew itself all the way up as he let his glance roam over those present.

For the first time Dr. Scholz showed signs of impatience. The demonstrable lack of enthusiasm in the other's manner irritated him after he, Scholz, had given himself away so unreservedly.

"Please!" he said coldly and gestured nervously at the scientist. "Please!"

"What about the euthanasia project's purely juridical basis?" Dr. Reynhardt seemed quite unmoved as he posed the question. But it affected the other like the sound of a gunshot. At once the impatience was gone. And the hostile look was transformed into a collegial smile of recognition. Then he raised a finger and looked around in a didactic manner.

"It's strange," he said, "that a scientist with no political training should be the one to raise such a question. But it's even stranger that none of the others present asked it first. For that is one of the most important points of all!"

He looked in turn at the faces around him. Only Heidebrand's was invisible, bent over the cognac glasses. Then he went on talking to Dr. Reynhardt, but as if he again felt more uncertain about the other.

"I can assure everyone here," he said, "that our lawyers at the Department of Justice have long since taken care of the juridical side of the matter."

For a moment all were silent. Then he continued, addressing the scientist:

"What is your attitude to the plan on a purely emotional level, Dr. Reynhardt?"

Everyone started at the question. Even Heidebrand looked up before filling the last glass. The only person unmoved was the man he had spoken to.

"I am of the opinion," he replied calmly, "that one should restrict one's emotional life to the sphere where it has validity." He considered for a moment. Then he continued slowly, emphasizing every word:

"I believe that it should be restricted to one's private life—yes, perhaps to one's family life.

"One must draw *very* clear lines here."

Dr. Scholz's answer came fast and unreservedly.

"Splendid!" he said. "That is a weighty point of view—both scientifically and politically."

Then he turned to Paul Heidebrand.

"You have not expressed yourself, Standartenführer?"

The officer bowed and smiled.

"I have my duties as host, Oberführer! And first among them is to keep a decent cognac. The only thing I could add to what Dr. Reynhardt has said would be a few little things I found while going through the books."

He broke off and made an inviting gesture toward the glasses.

"May I?" he said. "I can really recommend it! My predecessor sold some of the ashes from the crematorium as fertilizer to the farmers in the neighborhood. And he got a rather large sum for it, as a matter of fact."

The men in the room had started moving and ritually each in turn took a glass from the desk. With the glasses at chest height they awaited the officer's further words. He went on quickly:

"I should think that something similar could be done with the waste products from the euthanasia facilities."

Dr. Eger held his cognac glass up under his nose, inhaled deeply, and moaned.

"Mm—ahh!" he responded, "wonderful old cognac!"

They drank.

"Ahh!" continued the mechanic, "lovely!"

Heidebrand smiled down into his glass:

"I always do what I can to keep a good cognac. This one is older than you are, Dr. Eger."

He continued staring into his glass as he spoke.

"But the facilities will of course entail production on a much larger scale—so one may perhaps expect them to pay for themselves, once they get going?"

He could feel the bitter aroma from the cognac all the way inside his teeth. And he lifted the glass up to the lamp, so that the hard light glittered in the airy, oil-like liquid.

The drink unites with your blood and presses into your very bones, he thought, looking over at Dr. Scholz.

"Your suggestions are just as distinguished as the cognac you keep," said the doctor. "Do you have any more?"

"Only cognac for the moment," replied the officer, and reached backward toward the desk until he found the bottle. He had used only his arm; the massive shoulders and the heavy body under the uniform were wholly motionless. Then he walked quickly across to Dr. Scholz and poured out a new glass for him. And while he refilled the glasses for the other gentlemen, he continued speaking:

"I daresay more suggestions will come later!"

And as he went from man to man, he smiled quietly at what he was about to say:

"And besides—the idea of delivering the ashes to agriculture almost has something pious about it! The deceased will get a chance to rehabilitate themselves with regard to society. They will be of use! They will pay for their own burials, so to speak. Yes, one can say that their lives have borne—if not exactly fruit—then at any rate cabbage and potatoes!"

All laughed loudly, except for Dr. Reynhardt and Heidebrand himself. They drank. Upon lowered his glass the officer turned to the swarthy doctor, the one wearing a lab coat over his uniform.

"I would like to be present at one of the experimental operations," he said, raising his eyebrows. "When is the next one scheduled?"

Dr. Eger had been watching Dr. Scholz and Dr. Reynhardt, who were now deep in conversation; the faint ill will which had been between them for a moment seemed to be quite gone now. Then he turned to the layman—the officer.

For a moment he had the impression that the other's robust and passionate face looked scornfully at him, but the raised eyebrows and slightly parted lips showed only interest and curiosity.

"Well," he replied, "we have a transplant operation early tomorrow. It will be very interesting."

When he saw the other prick up his ears, he explained a little more fully:

"We're using one of these Polish girls."

The doctor creased the brown skin of his forehead into a fishnet of small, deep wrinkles. He thought for a while. Then the fishnet smoothed itself out again.

"They have great vitality, those Polacks," he added, shaking his head. "It wouldn't surprise me if they started growing new limbs."

Again the officer stared down into his glass with lips parted. as if he had not quite understood what the other was saying. When the doctor noticed his posture, he clarified:

"After we've taken something away, I mean. We begin tomorrow morning at nine o'clock."

"It will be interesting to see some of this for myself," said the officer. He seemed a bit shy of the other. But Dr. Eger merely laid his hand politely over his mouth and yawned. He was tired. And the dark, close-cropped hair suddenly looked wet.

But Dr. Scholz's voice, elated and cheerful, rang through the room as the others fell silent and only he was still talking.

He hunched his round shoulders and swung his head back and forth a few times, as if in utter helplessness.

"I can't say how happy I am about this collaboration, Dr. Reynhardt. Indeed I can't find words for it!"

Then he lowered his shoulders again and craned his neck. With his forefinger he touched the other very softly.

"But you know what?" The words came almost as a whisper. "I felt in my bones all along that you would really go for this thing!"

While Heidebrand had again bent over the radio, Dr. Eger turned to his older colleague.

"It's late," he said. "And if the conference is over—is it? Well, Dr. Fritze and I have had a long working day. And we have a day ahead of us tomorrow."

The other laid a sturdy, reddish hand on his shoulder.

"Oh, Lord!" he said with concern. "Go to bed at once! You need it, gentlemen! And sleep well.

"Good night, good night!"

The two young doctors marched out, Dr. Fritze with blond enthusiasm, and Eger with a mixed, unclear feeling of disquiet.

"I wonder what we can expect of the new commandant," he said, as they crossed the dark graveled yard. For a while there was only the sound of their boots against the ground.

"I think Heidebrand's all right," said his colleague absently. But it was only when he continued that his voice became loud and enthusiastic again.

"But I'm impressed with Dr. Scholz!"

Inside the archive room three silent men remained. Heidebrand's back was still bent under the taut cloth of his uniform jacket. He got a clear and singing flute tone out of the radio.

"Mozart again!" he said and straightened up, turning to the others.

It was awhile before the eldest of the doctors replied.

"But the three of us must go the town for the night! Lord, we really have to get going."

For a brief moment the old man looked tired.

"I'll get a car," said the officer. When the door had closed behind him, the other two stood and listened—first to a solo of heavy steps receding over the gravelled barracks yard. Then to a high, dancing flute solo. Scholz closed his eyes and tilted his head. Gradually he began to sway in time to the music.

When he spoke again, his voice was indistinct. And the words were uncertain, fumbling.

"Lord, how pure and clear it is!—These pure, utterly pure single notes…one and one…"

As he spoke the last words, he grabbed at the air as if wanting to catch the notes carefully between his fingertips. Then he went on talking, and his voice became authoritative and aroused:

"…this is heaven, Dr. Reynhardt, this is heaven! So endlessly pure… this is blessedness, blessedness and purity! Oh, such unending purity!"

For a while he was silent again, and Dr. Reynhardt regarded him gravely with big blue eyes. For the first time the thin, grey-clad form was wholly without reserve. Dr. Reynhardt was once again a child looking with amazement at another.

Then the old man opened his eyes again, unashamed of having revealed himself.

"How are things with your family, Dr. Reynhardt? Is your son better?"

Reynhardt smiled. It was a crooked and very youthful smile.

"He's making progress. But it takes time….You know what a shock it was, and at his tender age! Besides he has an unusually sensitive emotional makeup."

For a while the doctor merely looked into himself, then he raised his eyebrows and stuck out his lower lip slightly. It gave his narrow face an expression of faint and dreamy melancholy.

"Do you know," he said impulsively, "that when he was a child he could throw up if he saw any of the boys fighting in the schoolyard?! It really happened that he vomited if the others were fighting!"

The other smiled:

"He takes after you, then?" he said calmly.

"Yes," replied Reynhardt, running a hand quickly and casually through his hair, "he takes after me. And besides, you have to think what a miracle it was that it happened just as it did! It actually exploded only a few meters away from him! But now at least he's reached the point of beginning to play again."

Dr. Scholz quickly stepped forward and grasped his younger colleague under the arm.

"I sincerely wish him everything good in life! Including a complete recovery!"

"And how are things with your own family, Dr. Scholz?"

The old man let go of his arm. He looked down and smiled, a happy, embarrassed smile.

"It has gotten bigger."

Then he turned toward the other.

"My wife is much younger than I," he explained. "My second son was born four days ago."

"Well, congratulations!" Reynhardt lit up. His smile grew cheerful and boyish. "And mother and child are fine?"

"Yes," replied Scholz, "they're just fine! He's a big strapping fellow."

For a moment he looked straight ahead, then he suddenly laughed aloud.

"He has a voice like a brass trumpet!"

The old man lowered his voice again. He took the other by the shoulder and turned him carefully around. Then he pointed at the portrait on the wall over the desk.

"Can you believe," he said quietly, "that he—*he!*—has sent me a private telegram of good wishes!—And my wife a *marvelous*...." He stretched out his arms, "...a marvelous bouquet of roses."

His hands sketched the bouquet in the air.

"Can you imagine him finding the time and strength to think about something like that? About me and my small private affairs! When you just think of all a man like him has to do..."

He moved his head back and forth with a shrug of his shoulders. It was a gesture of extreme helplessness.

"Yes," he said, shaking his head, "I—I!" The sentence was never finished. He turned to the radio and fell silent.

And suddenly and rapturously he cried:

"Dr. Reynhardt! Oh—Dr. Reynhardt! *Listen* to this rondo!!"

Outside Paul Heidebrand drove the car up in front of the door. For a little while he saw Heinrich Reynhardt before him, the way he had looked as a middle-school boy. With the strange, round cap which his father had brought him from England. All the others would have been teased had they worn such a cap. But with Heinrich it was different. If anyone tried to tease him, he just looked uncomprehending and a little disoriented. So that you got the impression that it was yourself you were making a fool of.

When the officer opened the door to the archive room, the doctors were still standing in front of the radio. He stopped on the threshold.

"Excuse me," he said softly, "but the car is ready."

And for a moment the scientist in the grey summer suit was so like the schoolboy with the round cap that the officer gasped for breath. But a few minutes later the car glided out through the manned gate, a fortress in itself—of barbed wire, machine guns and searchlights.

And while the sentries saluted, Dr. Scholz lay heavily back in his seat. He thought about his garden, and hoped that someone had remembered to water the two new bushes in the rose hedge.

4. Claus

I

WITH THE LAST DAYLIGHT still glowing in the music room's big window, the boy played the piece again. He bent energetically over the keys and worked his way forward several measures at a time. Then he stopped and repeated certain notes again and again, quietly, concentratedly and gravely. He might have been around seventeen years old, but since he was sitting in front of the window, it was impossible to distinguish any of his features. Only the silhouette was visible, and it showed a thin, very delicate figure—a neck and shoulders contrasted strikingly with his firm and decisive manner of playing. It was a piece by Schubert.

Through the window one could see roofs and chimneys on the other side of the street. They stood sun-gold and ready to burst against the darkening blue evening sky.

"I think something completely new has come into your playing since you were sick. You play more clearly."

The woman who had spoken was standing in the doorway to the big living room. She had a dustcloth in her hand and was leaning lightly against the door frame.

The boy turned to face her and smiled. He stopped playing and let his thin, idle hands rest a moment on the keys. Then he carefully closed the lid over the gleaming expanse of ivory.

"They say that at the conservatory too," he said. "I've definitely made progress."

He looked back at the music, which was catching the last of the daylight. Then he placed all ten fingertips on the black-varnished lid, and for a moment it looked as if he were counting them.

"But, mother, a usable soldier is something I'll never be."

The woman had come into the room and was running a cloth over the mahogany back of a chair. She looked up.

"In this country we have enough soldiers," she said. "But supper is ready, my boy. You'd better come and eat."

Slowly he rose and gathered up the music with care. He stood bent over the piano bench for a bit, then straightened up.

"But they must need others too?" he said hesitantly. "Musicians and… well, scientists, for example. Like Father, I mean."

He had turned was now leaning against the grand piano.

"Yes, more than they need soldiers," answered his mother.

The boy stood still for a while, staring absently out the window. Then he suddenly turned to her and spoke loud and fast:

"But Mother! One *has* to admire him!—Has he always been like this? When he was very young, I mean?"

She turned, leaving the dustcloth on the tabletop.

"He wasn't so *very* young when I met him, but he's always been admirable. I've been proud of him forever."

She resumed her work as she went on:

"Since you were born I don't think he's thought about much of anything but us and his work."

The boy frowned, staring into space. His expression was pensive and very grave.

"I *thought* so! The way he is, you have to be born like that. You can't *become* that way!"

His mother answered him just as gravely.

"You know people can become however they want, Claus. If they just *will* it."

"Do you believe that?"

He still looked very thoughtful, but had brightened somewhat.

"Do you really think that for instance *I* could become like—well, now, like for instance Father?"

She bent her head to hide a smile:

"I'm quite sure of it, Claus."

For a while he stood still, chewing on her words. Then he suddenly opened his mouth, crossed the room and grabbed her by the arm.

"But look!" he cried, "there's something the matter with him!"

His voice was ernest and hard. His mother quickly looked him in the face.

"There's something the matter with Father?"

"Of course there is!" He was gloating because she hadn't seen it.

"He's not happy anymore. Anybody can see that! He was completely different just after he came home—much happier, like."

She looked away and went on polishing the table.

"Father has too much to do," she said calmly. "And then he brings problems from work home with him. For a doctor there's no time off, my boy."

Thoughtful again, he slowly crossed to the window and looked out. The twilight was deepening. And when he spoke, his voice was different. His father's state was no longer just an interesting discovery. Suddenly it worried him. And he felt that if his father wasn't happy, then he himself couldn't be happy either.

"I don't think it's that, Mother. It feels like there's something else— something *weighing* on him."

Neither of them spoke. He looked out the window for a long time. Then he cleared his throat and swallowed. He swallowed yet again.

"Mother," he said in a thick voice, "I think I could do *anything* for him, if it ever came down to that."

"If you'd do what you could to get well again, that would be the greatest happiness you could give him."

"Then I'll do it."

He looked out the window, and his voice became soft and slow.

"But now it's getting dark, Mother. Such a fine, fine veil settling over everything. First it almost shines—blue! Then it gets denser and denser, and finally the houses grow blurry. The trees get so thin against the street. Look, it's as melancholy as that waltz of Chopin's!"

His mother drew herself up.

"Go and eat, Little Claus—don't just stand there being sad."

"I have to laugh every time you say 'Little Claus'—it reminds me of that fairy tale!"

His voice was cheerful as he turned.

"What fairy tale?"

"The one about Great Claus and Little Claus, of course! The one who gets sewn up in the black sack and thrown into the water."

"Then I'll never call you 'Little Claus' again."

He laughed.

"You might as well," he said. "After all, there's no Great Claus here." He looked down into the street again, and the last words echoed for a long time in the silent room. The he bent toward the pane as if taking a good look down the street. Presently his face contracted into a grimace of curiosity and repugnance.

"Yecch!" he said quickly. "There comes one of those insects! One of those in the black uniform."

She quickly went over to him.

"Don't worry about them, my boy. After all, there aren't so many of them these days."

"Oh, there are lots."

She took him firmly by the arm and tried to pull him away from the window.

"The tea is getting cold, Claus."

But he stayed put. And a couple of times he stroked his forehead in excitement:

"You wouldn't believe the things I heard about them when I was outside!"

"People talk so much!"

He pointed out the window.

"There, down by the chestnut tree!"

She bent forward and looked down, her hand resting lightly on his shoulder.

"There comes one, sure enough!"

"He's completely black," said Claus.

"Yes—ah."

Her hand was still on his shoulder. Suddenly she let it fall and straightened up. It was a gesture of the greatest helplessness.

"But it's *him!*" he said loudly.

Claus had turned, and he looked at her searchingly.

"Does he drop in just like that?" he demanded.

She turned her back and withdrew further into the room.

"Oh—yes, he's been here a couple of times now."

"But it's only a few weeks since he came to town."

Again the boy stared down at the man on the sidewalk. It was a heavy, black-clad figure.

His mother had stopped at the piano. A couple of music books were still lying on it; she picked them up and put them in the piano bench.

"Can't you learn to put your music away, then! I always have to pick up after you've been practicing."

She had spoken wholly without annoyance, and he answered her distractedly, still peering down into the street.

"All right," he said distantly. "I'll do that."

For a while he was silent, then he said slowly and anxiously:

"Oh! I think it's creepy!"

She placed the dustcloth on the keys and ran it energetically all the way up, from bass to sopranino.

"What's creepy?" she asked calmly.

"The uniform."

She continued as if engrossed in her own thoughts.

"I wouldn't call it that. I just think it's unbecoming."

"No," he repeated decidedly. "It's spooky."

She turned to face him.

"Can't you go eat, my boy!"

"It's not *my* fault!" he said furiously. "And then that death's head on the hat, too! What do they mean by *that?*"

"They don't mean anything by it. It's just bad theater, Claus."

His anguish and his anger had passed when he turned to her. He was merely uncertain, questioning, and somewhat impatient.

"But what kind of *people* are they, then?"

She had crossed the room. Now she stood smoothing the cushions in the easy chairs.

"I'll tell you something, Claus," she said very quietly. "There are all different kinds of people in this world. There's no such thing as 'they,' there's only 'this one' and 'that one.' And *he* is a person one can very well be acquainted with—at least he used to be."

He slowly left the window and followed her deeper into the room.

"Has it been many years since you and Father knew him?"

"Oh—yes. Quite a few."

"He may have changed."

"Do you think so, Claus?"

Her words fell quietly and probingly.

"But you said yourself that people can change."

"Yes, I did. For the better, I meant."

"They can just as well go the other way too!"

"Yes, they can," she replied calmly.

Claus hesitated for a moment before going on.

"Maybe that's what's happened with Heidebrand?"

"What do you mean, Claus?"

"That he may have changed for the worse."

She studied her fingertips for a while. Then she replied:

"It's a serious thing to talk like that about a person." There was clear reproach in her tone. And the boy became eager and quick:

"But I only asked a question, Mother! Maybe he didn't have the uniform back then?"

His mother was friendly but firm as she answered:

"Perhaps you should get to know him first, Claus, and then judge him afterwards."

But the boy wouldn't be put off. He stared at her for a moment and persisted with an expression of quiet, unsurmountable obstinacy:

"But did he have the uniform then?"

"Back then there were no such uniforms," his mother replied patiently. "They're a more recent thing."

For a while he was silent, thinking. Then he put his finger to his chest.

"There, you see!" he said triumphantly. "Maybe you don't think that clothes can affect the wearer *inwardly*?"

For the first time she showed signs of irritation. She spoke quietly and with great decision as she replied.

"Tell me, Claus! Have Father and I conducted ourselves toward you in such a manner that you have reason to look upon our friends with suspicion?"

He continued for yet a moment in triumph, loud and sure of himself.

"But I didn't know that Heidebrand was a friend! If I'd known that, then..."

Suddenly he stopped and stared at her open-mouthed. Then he quickly sprang forward and grabbed her by the hand.

"But tell me you aren't mad at me, then!" he cried. "For what I said about Heidebrand, I mean!"

"Not at all," she said seriously. "But I don't like to hear people judged by the clothes they wear."

At the doorbell they both jumped. For a moment she looked uncertain. Then she smiled.

"Now you can meet him!"

The boy looked at her thoughtfully.

"He must have a high rank?"

"Standartenführer."

Claus suddenly forgot his misgivings. Again he grabbed his mother's hand and leaned his head against her shoulder.

"Hey! Tell me a little about him!" he said quickly.

She laughed aloud, rumpling his hair.

"But he's here! It's too late now, Claus. If you'd shown some interest a little sooner, you'd have known a great deal about him by now!"

Feelings of umbrage and curiosity fought an unequal battle in him, but he managed a somewhat steady tone as he persisted:

"You can tell me more later! But just give me a quick outline. Something that can be filled in later!"

"It's hard," she replied. "There's so much to tell about him. He was born in Berlin, but then….He was kind of a celebrity back then."

"He was *famous?*"

Claus was wholly swallowed up by the question, and his mother laughed out loud.

"Only among us young folks," she said. Then there was a knock on the door.

"Come in!" she called, still laughing.

II

THE MAN IN THE UNIFORM clicked his high black boots together. The gesture contrasted strangely with his smile and the way he moved. He hunched his big shoulders and plump face forward as if he were trying to make himself a little smaller than he was. He looked first at the woman and then at the boy. Then he directed his gaze at her again, and the smile suddenly changed into loud happy laughter.

"What a treat it is to be human!" he said, throwing back his head. His uniform stretched tight across his chest. Then he quickly advanced and took her by the hand.

"Is it still a treat?" she asked, as he greeted Claus.

"Yes," he replied, withdrawing his hand. "It is simply unbelievable." They laughed.

"There are lots of us who think the party's over," she said. After a slight pause she continued:

"What's your excuse for celebrating today, then?"

The officer waved a swarm of mosquitoes away with his glove. Then he looked at her with half-closed his eyes:

"A mere nothing," he said. And his voice was strangely dry and flat. "It's just that it's so lovely to be talked about. To know that old Paul

Heidebrand is still expected and that people *talk* about him while they wait."

She looked down during the uncertain atmosphere which followed his words. Then they laughed.

Claus had been silent for a while, wholly taken up with the guest. Now he opened his mouth but it took some time before the words came:

"But how could you know it was you we were talking about?"

His voice was fraught with wonder.

The SS man smiled lightly. Then he bent forward and whispered:

"Because I am an old fox," he said. "The kind of really old fox who has been in the fire before."

After a pause he added, even more softly than before:

"That's *my* secret."

She looked at her son.

"You have just as much time to spare as in the old days?" she said to the officer.

"That depends on what you mean by 'spare'."

The answer was dry and serious. But when the bell rang again he looked hurriedly at the door. The mother turned to Claus.

"Now you must go and eat supper, son! You can get the door while you're about it, and if it's Aunt Emmchen, poor thing, you can help her off with her coat, please."

"All right!" said Claus and nodded. He shook the officer's hand. "Auf Wiedersehn, Herr Heidebrand!"

"Goodbye for now, Herr Reynhardt! We would certainly enjoy having a little chat about music someday—if we could find the time."

The boy turned around in the doorway.

"We *must* find time for that!" he said. And suddenly he was embarrassed. Even in the dim light both of them noticed it.

When the door had banged after him, his mother walked slowly over to the window. The dusk had become so thick that she stood like a dark column of shadow before the vanishing daylight.

The officer remained inside the room. He looked at her, rubbing his chin.

"Uh—Gerda?" he said quietly and thoughtfully.

She stood as if she hadn't heard. Then he cleared his throat.

"Gerda!"

The word was almost whispered. She didn't move.

"Gerda?"

He had said the name aloud. And suddenly she wheeled around to face him. Her voice was furious, choked with tears.

"You could at least have spared me the uniform! You see, I know what it means."

"I could have," he replied weakly. He looked down until she went on:

"It's just uncalled for to make me see you in it!"

His face glistened faintly in the bluish light from the window. He was sweating.

"You must forgive me, Gerda. But I've gotten so used to it."

She was still indignant when she continued.

"Yes, I imagine you would—eventually," she said loudly. Then she grew calmer. "It doesn't bring back good memories."

The man looked up. He smiled, the way people smile when they have hurt themselves.

"But it makes a statement!" he said.

"There's no doubt but what it's expressive!"

The words were almost spit out.

"And yet it's missing something," he said, as he looked down at the jacket and the black riding britches. He bent forward to see better in the dim light.

"I think it looks complete," she said.

"It's missing one color," he replied hesitantly and looked up. "It's missing red! It should really be black and red."

She took a step backward before she replied.

"It certainly should."

He bit his lip and screwed up his eyes. And in the twilight his eyes became two black shadowy holes.

"But the strange thing is that the red is there just the same," he whispered. Then he stuck out his chin and stretched both arms out to her.

The jacket strained at the sleeves, so that the round, dark-haired forearms came into view. He clenched his left hand and clasped his right firmly around his left wrist. He massaged it as if rubbing away the pain after being handcuffed. Then he switched hands and rubbed himself his right wrist for a while, and the motion became one of washing, smearing.

"The red is there just the same," he repeated softly. "And strangely enough it's invisible."

He quickly glanced down at his hands, as if to make sure he was right, while continuing to whisper almost inaudibly:

"And do you know where it is? On my hands and wrists, all the way up to my elbows!"

Gerda quickly backed toward the window.

"Paul!" she cried loudly.

He let his hands fall and dangle motionless at his side.

They were interrupted by a loud, rather shrill voice from the next room. And they both looked toward the door.

"You don't say!" cried the woman's voice. "Is he really in there, Claus? Yes, that's a man who's done much for our country!"

It was Claus who opened the door.

"Yes, in here," he said. "But don't turn on the light, Aunt Emmchen, we haven't blacked out the windows yet!"

"It's Aunt Emmchen!" he said to his mother. Then he drew back his head and the lighted doorway was filled by the tall, rather plump figure of a woman. She was broad-shouldered and very straight-backed. Her thick blond hair was knotted over her nape. For a moment she stood like a Wagnerian soprano before the royal box. Then she walked quickly into the room and closed the door behind her. The transition from the light to the dark room made her stare half-blind at the window. Only after standing there for a while did she spring forward and hug her sister-in-law. Gerda looked small and frail in the mighty embrace.

"Oh, how nice to be in your home again!" cried the newcomer, staring over her sister-in-law's head at the officer. Then she abruptly let go of her and tittered shyly.

"It's so dark in here," she said. "I could hardly tell you apart! Oh, God! What if I'd hugged you instead by mistake, Standartenführer! Oh, how awful!"

Her voice rose to an ecstatic shriek on the last words.

The officer stood wholly silent with his back to the window. His face was buried in shadow. Gerda straightened her hair and her dress.

"But I haven't introduced you to Herr Heidebrand!" she said to her sister-in-law. Then she turned to the man:

"This is Fräulein Reynhardt, Heinrich's sister."

Paul took a step forward, held out his hand and bowed deeply.

"We've met before, Fräulein Reynhardt. But we haven't seen each other in a hundred years."

He straightened up and smiled at her:

"But tell us where you've been?"

She took a step back and lifted her head. Now she was Wagnerian again, and looked around importantly.

"I have been in Berlin," she said solemnly. "At the Chancery. We paid tribute to him with songs and flowers. Thousands of us, women from all over the country! Hailing him for the bombings of Lübeck."

Her sister-in-law looked at her:

"You were hailing *him* because Lübeck was bombed?"

Fräulein Reynhardt turned to her. It was a wholly involuntary movement. Patiently, as if speaking to a very small child, she explained what she was trying to say:

"We wanted to show him that we women too are loyal—that we won't desert him because of a little adversity."

"Were people there from Lübeck too?" asked Gerda.

And the tall blonde turned to the officer.

"No," she said. "The rail connections are broken. Imagine, they don't have a train station anymore!"

"Won't you have a cup of tea after all your exertions, my friend?"

As she asked Gerda looked down, and smiling faintly. The blonde smiled back.

"Oh God! How good that would taste!" she sighed. "But I don't have time. I'm on my way down to the newspaper to give them my impressions. You see, I just stopped in to tell you from mother that the party won't be on Friday, because it's Good Friday this week. So it'll probably be tomorrow instead."

She looked at her watch.

"Oh God!" she cried. "I should have been there by now. Goodbye then, Gerda!"

She dashed for the door, then stopped abruptly and turned to face them again. She fixed her gaze on Heidebrand. Then she raised her hand in the Germanic salute.

He cleared his throat.

"'itler!" he replied weakly.

Then she turned to Gerda again.

"It's so long since Mother has seen Heinrich," she said. "So you must definitely come! She's hoping so dreadfully that he'll be there."

"I think it will work out," Gerda replied. "Give her our love!"

The next moment the door slammed after her sister-in-law. It was utterly still in the room.

"Can I offer you something to drink, Paul?"

Her voice was friendly and calm.

"Yes," he replied. "We could drain a glass of cognac to Emmchen's continued health."

She looked at the window and saw that the daylight was gone.

"If we settle for candles, we won't have to black out the big window," she said. "It's a lot of work. So we often do it this way in the music room. If that's all right with you, then please light the candles on the table!"

He took matches out of his pocket and lit two of the candles. Then he sat down heavily and slowly on the sofa. He followed Gerda with his eyes as she closed the ordinary curtains and got glasses and bottles out of the corner cupboard. Slowly she set them down on the table in front of him, and eased into the chair so that they sat facing each other.

She's moving blindly, he thought and offered his cigarette case.

"An Allied cigarette?" he said. "Captured in open and honest battle!"

As he leaned forward, the shadows from the wax candles etched themselves deeply into his plump face. He was black around the eyes.

He's grown old, she thought taking a cigarette. His healthiness is a sham.

"I didn't think you took part in open and honest battles," she said bluntly. There was no ill will in her voice, but still he avoided meeting her gaze.

"Heavens, no!" he replied quickly. "I didn't capture them personally. It's our simple but loyal countrymen who captured them for us."

He looked up at her, meekly and in earnest. She bit her lower lip and took refuge in picking up the bottle.

"Please!" she said, filling his glass. "This is Heinrich's special cognac!"

"Thanks, Gerda!" He looked away again. And he ran his hand quickly through his hair as he went on:

"Now *that* will perk us up!"

For a while he stared at his glass. Then his eyes slid upward until they met hers.

"I'm sitting here thinking," he said slowly, "that this isn't the first glass you've poured for Paul Heidebrand."

"And it probably isn't the first cigarette his simple, loyal countrymen have captured for him either."

He pretended not to hear. His feelings were focused elsewhere.

He looks tired, she thought.

"It's almost like old times," he said, closing his eyes before going on: "Candles and glasses on the table! It's like twenty years ago. Do you sometimes think about those days? Do you still remember them?"

She held her fingers up in front of the candle, as if it were hurting her eyes.

"It would be more to the point to ask if *you* haven't forgotten them."

He leaned back and crossed his arms. The cigarette lit up faintly when he inhaled. For a while he sat looking down his broad, uniformed chest.

"I haven't forgotten them," he said softly. "I often think of those days."

He was silent for a while, looking into the candle flame. "Especially of late it's been like that….I think of those trips down the Rhine and all over the country, the mountains, the woods—all the campfires in the dark, and the nights, the nights…."

He paused again. Then he raised his head and looked fixedly at her.

"All that has jerked me back to life!" he said loudly.

"You know," he added, "just as old people begin to remember more and more of their childhood, their first years, the first people they met. . . in the same way I've begun to remember my youth! I remember a stretch of road, an old tree, some twigs against the sky—but I've forgotten where in Germany—or in the world—I saw it. I remember the faces, the friends, the conversations, the songs….I remember a hand! A knee! Somebody's close-cropped neck!"

Abruptly both of them looked down, and she found nothing to say. She felt him waiting for some kind of answer, but knew that she couldn't give him one.

Suddenly he looked up. The words came loud and fast:

"Do you know, Gerda, that now and then the whole past wells up in me! And there's one song which haunts me."

He looked at her; his wide-open eyes glinted in the faint light. Then he picked up his glass and drained it at one pull. He stood up abruptly and started across the room.

He stopped before he got over to the piano, turned to her and planted his feet a ways apart—as if rooting them fast in the carpet to keep himself upright.

He looks better standing, she thought, his clothes are too tight when he's sitting down.

"It's nothing!" he said, "nothing!—I just can't get it out of my head!"

"What kind of song is it?" she asked.

"It's strange!" He looked around uneasily. "I can't get it out of my head. There were so many of them, you see! But this particular one I can't get rid of. You see, it pops up at the most unbelievably inconvenient moments. One of the freelance soldier songs. You must know it."

"But which one?"

She could feel herself sweating. Plainly something was in the process of cracking inside him; she could have pushed the heavy figure over with one hand. Then he took a step backward toward the piano, still facing her.

"Do you want to hear it?" His voice was almost beseeching.

She nodded, but without curiosity. One song was like the others. They were all about freelance soldiers and death and the made between them. All had the same blend of sadness and brutality, of loneliness and death.

Paul sat down at the piano; his fingers fumbled uncertainly over the scarcely visible keys. After playing a few chords he began the song. He played a bit stiffly from lack of practice. Then he sang loudly and monotonously:

> "On a coal-black horse rides Brother Death,
> his cloak is full of the dark wind's breath!
> His cloak is full of the long long sleep,
> full of the blessed peace.
> Brother Death, he gallops forth—
> wherever soldiers of fortune march,
> there he rides along…
> In Flanders we dance the meadow red—
> Flanders in distress!
> There it blooms double, with crimson thread!
> There in Flanders rides brother Death—
> To Flanders he rides along!
> His horse is as white as the snow so cold,
> and he is angel-fair to behold…."

"Stop! Stop!" She interrupted him, almost rising out of her chair. Her voice was high and furious. The man at the piano hit a discord and stopped playing. He was breathing heavily as he stood up.

"You remember that, Gerda!"

She looked down for a moment. Then she replied slowly:

"Yes, I remember it—and it has its prehistory—How in the world can you be so unbelievably cruel as to remind me of Samuel in that way!? After all, it was his song."

She hesitated, then suddenly looked up as if she had hit on an explanation. "Does it really help?" she asked. "Does it really help to have sung it?"

She looked candidly at him. He paced the floor for a while, and as he paced he began to speak:

"Dear kind Gerda! You can well imagine that nothing helps. Nothing helps against ghosts. I can see them all here—very, very clearly! Now and then I talk with them a bit. Well, only with the dead ones, of course; I never speak with the living. But for the most part I merely hear their names—Little Jacob, Samuel Goldmann and, well…there were so many of them."

"First they got their hands on Little Jacob."

The officer came to a standstill. He was suddenly calm again. And his voice was cool and mocking as he answered her. He was smiling.

"You don't need to be tactful on my account, Gerda. You can just as well say 'you got your hands on'!—But you're wrong, my friend, you're wrong if you think it was us he died of."

Almost with relish she felt the anger growing within her, mounting into a rage which made her dizzy and pale. And faraway she could feel the skin on her face and shoulders puckering, turning to gooseflesh. She felt cold.

"When someone is 'shot while trying to escape,' what does that mean? What?! *What does that mean*?" she yelled. "Even if it were really true that he was shot while escaping…even if he *wasn't* beaten to death with rubber truncheons…who gave you permission to shoot someone because they tried to escape?!"

She could feel something warm and dark flowing down her freezing cheeks, and the image of the man in front of her grew blurred. He floated off in big flowing waves. She heard only his voice. It was calm and quiet.

"That's part of the game," it said. "Just rules in a game, rules which we all know. Little Jacob knew them too. We're just men playing."

She hid her face in her hands and felt the wrath shriveling up inside her. Only a sick dullness remained. He went on talking.

"What you're saying is right, Gerda. It all adds up. But just the same it's wrong. It wasn't us he died of."

His voice grew softer—but stronger, more penetrating.

"He died of a sickness, a delayed childhood disease—one of those which hits much too hard if you get it as an adult. If the word weren't so ambiguous and so compromised, you could call it 'morality.' If he'd gotten over it, he could have been at liberty in just a few weeks. And if Samuel had managed the same thing a couple years ago, he would have been out today. He wouldn't be sitting where he is now. But you understand…." His voice became higher and thinner. "You understand—they had their morbid little pleasure in their ideals right to the end."

She raised her head and looked up at him. He had come closer. And she saw the broad face from below, the big, expressive mouth, the deep eyes. He was sweating.

"What kind of a human being are you, Paul?"

He drew in his chin and gravely looked down at her.

"You put it precisely yourself," he said, "one of those who marches in step—who collects his pay and wears a black jacket."

She opened her mouth halfway. Then she stretched out her hand and touched the uniform very lightly with her fingertips. Like lightning she jerked her hand back again, as if she had burned herself. Her voice was thick and indistinct when she spoke.

"And what made it possible for you to end up where you are today?— In *that*?"

"I pulled up stakes," he said.

"That's no answer."

"And that's no question." He leaned toward her and whispered the rest of the sentence:

"Because you know the answer yourself. You know it yourself, if you just think of what I attained by 'getting there,'—as you call it."

For a moment she thought about it. And she felt herself getting gooseflesh again as she replied. She was cold.

"You've succeeded in dirtying yourself, you've succeeded in sullying the old Paul, in befouling the image of you as you never were, but was only how Heinrich and I saw you! You've succeeded in betraying the ideals you talked about so much and so loudly!"

He closed his eyes.

"You're wrong again, Gerda, if you think that I betrayed anything. I didn't even betray my friends, let alone my ideals. And I didn't *lose* them either.

"I threw them overboard and choked and drowned them in cold blood. You mustn't believe for a moment that it was easy. They didn't let me kill them just like that! They still haunt me! Pale, shining ghosts from my adolescence. They're real ghosts, you see! They appear at night and in the gloaming. They've never been able to stand the light of day. No, I haven't lost them! What I've achieved is something quite different."

"And what's that?" she asked.

She looked up at the pale, closed face above her. The mouth and eyes were closed as if immured in a fortress, a huge, armored layer of flesh and bones which he had to work his way through in order to answer. Slowly he opened his gaze again and looked her in the eyes.

"Money and power," he replied calmly.

"And that's what you preferred!"

"Yes," he said taking a few steps across the floor. "I found that it suits me better than virtue and poverty."

For a while he stood still, reflecting. Then he raised his head and looked at her again.

"But it's not *that* simple either," he added, slowly and thoughtfully. His eyebrows drew together in a thick dark line. And for a while he was completely alone with something inside himself, something forgotten and at the same time unforgettable. She looked down at the floor at the way he was standing. The black boots creaked slightly when he lifted his heels off the carpet. For a moment he rocked on tiptoe, then the heavy figure sank back into place.

"I went to school barefoot," he said, still slowly and thoughtfully. Then his voice rose. "Barefoot, Gerda! You can think about *that*, when you start seeing my black uniform all too starkly against Heinrich's white doctor's gown!"

Quickly he crossed the room with long strides. Then he came back, bent over the table and refilled his glass. He held it out to her like a salute before drinking it up.

"Aside from the past two years, which I spent in a province up by the North Pole, I've been *traveling* all this time. I know Italy. Rome! Naples! Pompeii! Venice! Florence! I've seen the Balkans. I know Paris, London, Budapest! I've slept in the best hotels, eaten in the fanciest restaurants. That's what money can buy! And *power*, Gerda—power is a strange thing."

"And this was while Little Jacob and Samuel were in your camps," she said without looking at him.

He sat down on the sofa. And again they were sitting face to face.

"Jacob was your brother," he said. "And he was six years younger than you. I know that."

Again she felt the pressure in her eyes, and the man in the uniform grew foggy. He floated off into big gray shadows. She closed her eyes, and the picture inside her grew clearer. It was long ago, endlessly long ago—a summer day under an avenue of chestnut trees. The boy with the tricycle had a toy saber in his hand. And it would have been a lovely toy saber if the hilt hadn't come off. But as it was, where the wooden hilt had been there was only a piece of sharp steel, a long, thin point— the only point on the saber. And all would have been well if he hadn't taken the saber outside with him that day. Their mother had forbidden it, but the saber was so wonderful; he had to have it with him constantly. But the front wheel of the tricycle had lost its rubber ring, and the rim made a strange double line in the wet sandy earth. He was holding the saber in his hand.

"Gerda!" shouted the boy. "Look at the lines! See how Macedonia can draw!"

"Macedonia" was the name of the tricycle, and it would never have tipped over if the boy hadn't been so taken up with the lines. The point of the saber went through his cheek as he fell. And again, almost thirty years later, she felt all her sisterly pain as she held him in her lap and tried to stop the bleeding. But she couldn't do it. The big girl of thirteen couldn't do it. All she could manage was to hold him in her lap and say: "Little Jacob! Little Jacob!" And she said it over and over again.

"But he was twenty-four years old. He knew the rules of the game." The voice from the man on the sofa came barging into the picture. And she felt something tickle her cheek, stop under her chin and hang there. It was only one drop. But she could only just force the words out.

"While Little Jacob and Samuel sat in your camps...."

The man on the sofa sighed heavily. Suddenly he leaned forward and buried his face in his hands.

"That's how they wanted it," he said. "They wanted to lie under the wheel. And I wanted to sit up in the carriage."

Again she tried to see him, and now he was clearer.

"You were right not to visit us for so long," she said, and noticed a rush of something liberated and warm running down her cheek. The pain in her eyes was gone. "We were so fond of you, Paul! We were all so fond of you! And you've changed so!"

"Who hasn't?" he replied.

The warmth in her face was gone, and she quickly wiped her eyes. In her mouth there was still a slight taste of salt.

"Heinrich hasn't changed," she said calmly. "He's the same."

The officer looked up. He let his hands fall.

"Oh?" he said gravely. "Is Heinrich the same?"

He frowned and studied the flame of the candle. His look was at the same time distant and very present.

"I met him yesterday. And *I* thought he'd changed. He looked anxious and depressed."

She straightened her back, so that she was sitting higher in the chair. The broad face in front of her was knotted with concern. His eyebrows came all the way together. She smiled faintly.

"Inwardly he's the same," she said. "He's unchanged. He has the same character as back then, the same backbone. He's stayed out of the pigsty. And he's kept his ideals in spite of everything—I admire him more than ever."

The officer looked down.

"If Heinrich has ideals," he said decidedly, "then he too has changed."

"Heinrich's ideals relate to his work, to science. And he's always had them—even if they weren't so noisy as yours."

Heidebrand stood up. After maneuvering himself out from between the sofa and the table he rubbed his scalp. A ways off, almost wholly in darkness, he stopped and turned to her again.

"It's strange to hear you say that. Because in the old days he laid great stress on how there was very little room for ideals inside the frame of a scientific worldview. To tell the truth, our friendship with him was one of the things which helped me most in getting rid of my dreams."

She stood up so suddenly that he involuntarily took a step backward, bumping against the grand piano.

"I will not stand here and listen to you try to blame Heinrich for what you have become!"

He arranged himself against the piano so that the small of his back rested against the edge. Then he pushed back his elbow onto the black surface. And for a while his heavy torso rested against the instrument. The black boots seemed almost sharp against the red carpet. Then he lifted his eyes to her.

"Don't worry, Gerda! Of course I won't set my black-and-red paw print on that white gown of his. Actually I owe him a debt of gratitude, and I hope one day I can repay it."

"I'm not sure that he'll accept the kind of help you can give him."

She bent over the table and took a cigarette from the pack which was still lying there. She lit it from the candle.

"No," said the voice behind her. "That's what I'm afraid of too."

She turned slowly.

"I don't think that this is a topic of conversation for us."

She sat down again. After pacing the room uneasily for a while, he crawled back into his place.

"You must forgive me," he said. "But I've been thinking about him so much lately. Ever since he came home, or rather: since I heard that he'd come home. How are things going with his research?"

She answered very quietly, a bit troubled.

"He works so hard that I can't believe he'll manage in the long run."

"May I ask what kind of thing he's working on at present?"

She thought for a little while. Then she went on slowly.

"You know that he took part in the African campaign because he was a specialist in tropical diseases. And that was also the reason he was called home. They were going to do research of military importance up here."

The man on the sofa had laid both palms on the table. And it struck her that he still had the most beautiful hands she had ever seen. It was suddenly a colossal strain for her to go on talking.

"And so first of all they wanted to find vaccines for some of the most widespread fever sicknesses. And also to find new ways of treating those who had already been infected. On the Eastern Front there were whole epidemics of such fevers—especially in the big swamp districts."

Heidebrand was looking at her with wide eyes and an almost expressionless face. It distracted her, but she managed to go on.

"And now Heinrich probably knows more about these diseases than anyone else in this country. Therefore he puts all his energy into the work. Every single hour in the laboratory benefits somebody. Every moment can mean a life lost or saved."

She felt herself growing warm inside.

"And after the war the results will belong to all humanity," she added. Her voice grew eager. And suddenly her voice was loud and firm:

"Isn't it strange to think that in the midst of a world of corruption and inhumanity there is one single person who is trying to do something worthwhile?!!"

The officer drew back his hands and let them fall into his lap. He lowered his head and nodded affirmatively.

"Absolutely," he said.

"I'll tell you, Paul, that it's Heinrich who sustains me through these times. I don't see much of him, but I know he's there. And I know what he's doing."

Heidebrand, still looking down, reached for his glass. But his fingertips met it too soon, and the glass overturned. The clear, oily drink flowed over the table.

"Oh!" he said. And, producing a big handkerchief from his uniform, he quickly mopped up the brandy.

"And Heinrich's special cognac, yet!" His voice was apologetic, but very calm as he continued: "It'll probably take the finish off the mahogany—Do you think it's because of the strain that he looks so bad?"

"He's wearing himself out."

There was silence for a while. Then the officer spoke.

"Didn't he once think of becoming a prison doctor?"

"Yes," she replied thoughtfully. "That was years ago—just after Claus was born. Do you really still remember that?"

Her voice grew warm, confiding.

"But actually it was my idea! I was so taken up with social work back then, while it was still possible. Now of course everything goes through Party channels. —Anyway, he considered it seriously for quite a long time. But of course he had the inheritance from his father, and so he chose to go on and specialize in febrile diseases. And of course he never needed to practice."

"Had he become a prison doctor, many things would have looked different today." The officer smiled.

"Yes," she replied, "utterly different. Then he wouldn't have been working at the laboratory again this evening."

"No," said the officer drily. "He would have been at the front."

He refilled his glass and lifted it carefully with both hands. For a while he held it in front of his mouth, inhaling deeply. Then he tasted the drink, and the muscles around his mouth tensed slightly.

"By the way, do you know that Heinrich *isn't* at the laboratory this evening? He has a conference with my superior—Oberführer Scholz, M.D." He spoke the words casually, but the look he sent her was very alert.

"Oh, well!" she said. "Then it's a scientific conference."

"Not necessarily."

"What else could it be?" Again she felt irritated. He took another sip from his glass before replying.

"It could be scientific *and* political."

"Heinrich has never been political—least of all now." She tried to make her voice sound calm and undisturbed as she went on:

"Just what do mean, anyway, using a word like 'political' in connection with him?"

Suddenly he looked very grave.

"I was just getting around to what I actually dropped in to tell you. I wanted to let you know that you shouldn't worry tonight."

"Worry?"

He smiled, as he set down the glass.

"Yes, you see; Heinrich may be called away a while after he gets home this evening. If anything comes of it, he'll probably get a call around midnight. But there's no reason for anxiety. We don't suspect him of anything. It's a purely routine matter. Purely routine.

"But you know, in such inhuman and undemocratic times as ours, it can happen that people disappear that way—so I just thought I could spare you some anxiety and agitation if I told you in advance that we don't wish him any ill. And then I was in this part of town anyway...."

"And what kind of routine question is it that has to be dealt with after midnight?"

"It would be another conference with the same doctor, Obergruppenführer Scholz."

"And I suppose *that* will be of a scientific and political nature?"

"It may be, yes." He looked at her. "Now perhaps you understand why I brought it up?"

She rose swiftly.

"Yes, now I understand! Now I begin to understand!"

He looked up, surprised at the harsh tone.

"What's the matter?" he said.

Her voice turned soprano when she answered him.

"You said you owed Heinrich a debt of gratitude?"

"Yes?"

"Because you've become who you are today?"

"For that too. He undoubtedly helped me on my way." The officer looked at her uncertainly.

"But I don't think I quite understand…." he continued hesitantly.

"No, but *I* understand! You're repaying your debt by trying to drag him into your swinish affairs! Now I really begin to understand who you are!"

He raised his glass.

"Nonsense!" he said and drank it down.

She laid her fists on the table and leaned forward toward him.

"Now I know what you meant by talking about 'the old days'! And why you wanted to spare me worry! Have you always, always put on a comedy act like that?"

He raised his head abruptly and looked at her. The strong, emaciated face turned black and red.

"I've never hidden who I am!" he said aloud. He let his index and middle fingers glide down the breast of his uniform. "And I go around dressed like this so that everybody can see it. It isn't everyone who does that. Is that a comedy act?"

His voice became calmer as he went on:

"I've admitted that I'm power-mad and greedy. That I've swung myself up using others' misfortune. That I wallow, gorge and enrich myself. Is that a comedy act?"

She had straightened up again. She looked at him in confusion.

"No, that's true," she said. "You've been very frank. Very frank. You always have been, Paul."

"But now when I tell you not to be afraid if they come to get Heinrich tonight—when I tell you not to be afraid that he'll be shot or put in a camp or God knows what—that's suddenly putting on a comedy act! Is it?

"But I'm telling you: Nothing bad will happen to him."

She let her arms fall to her sides in resignation.

"But what am I to believe, Paul? You've been away for so many years. And you've had such a strange career!"

"But now I've come back."

"What am I to believe?"

He raised his eyebrows.

"You should believe what I said a little while ago: That my underwear is stained red and that I kill Jews and socialists with gas."

"Paul." She almost whispered the word.

"And that I eat children at night."

She smiled.

"And that I kill Gypsies with chlorine."

She looked pleadingly at him.

"Please, Paul!"

He closed his eyes.

"And that just now I'm bored and have found my old friend Heinrich Reynhardt to experiment on."

"Shut up!" she cried.

"...to stain my old friend's lily-white soul and gown with blood."

"Now that's *enough!*" She was white with rage.

He pulled up his sleeve and looked at his watch.

"Yes," he said. "Now that's enough. It's late, and duty calls. Coal-black duty. Just as black as my uniform."

He looked at her, and his face changed. The jovial, mocking expression had disappeared. He looked tired and hard.

"We live during a perpetual solar eclipse, Gerda."

He closed his eyes again:

"If you just had an *inkling* of why I came?"

She bent forward.

"What is it, Paul?"

"I hardly know why anymore myself," he replied weakly. "But I think I came so that you should see me—and so that I should see you."

The words came more and more slowly. Then he opened his eyes again.

"You must forgive me, Gerda! But the day began so strangely. For example, I attended an operation this morning. It was nine o'clock, and I had just eaten breakfast."

"Haven't you ever seen an operation before?"

"Yes. But it was strange all the same. It was a Polish girl they were operating on. I threw up my breakfast afterwards."

"How was the patient?"

They both turned at the knock on the door. Fräulein Reynhardt entered the room, pushing ahead of her a heavy-set man in his forties. She was elated and lively.

"Good evening! We've just come from the newspaper. Editor Schneider has written such a lovely article about me—about *us*, I mean. About those of us who went and paid homage to the Führer. Imagine, it was already finished when I got down there. It must be mental telepathy, because he knew it all in advance! It'll be on the front page."

She looked around breathlessly.

"The editor has just now finished working. I hope we're not disturbing you?" She introduced the journalist.

"You press people must always be working at night?" Frau Reynhardt smiled at the newcomer.

"Journalists have many duties," he said, looking around. He went on apologetically: "It's so dark in here. It takes awhile for one's eyes to get used to it."

He stared half-blind at the man in uniform.

"But you're sure we're not disturbing you? It was Fräulein Reynhardt who invited me up."

Fräulein Reynhardt sighed.

"Standartenführer Heidebrand is a man who has made great sacrifices," she said to the journalist.

"Yes, he was just talking about his duties," replied her sister-in-law smiling, "right before you knocked."

Fräulein Reynhardt looked at the clock, then gave a deep sigh of admiration.

"Imagine, have you been talking about your duties the whole time!"

The journalist had his note pad in hand and was rolling the pencil between his right forefinger and thumb. He had placed himself next to the officer, who had risen. Then he bent toward him and said confidingly:

"I would very much like to hear a little about your appointment…."

The SS man cleared his throat. Then he said loudly:

"Well, I'll tell you! Just before you came, we were talking about duties. We agreed that there are different conceptions of what 'duty' is. As an example, it was mentioned that there are men right in their prime, who think that it is their duty not to be at the front. There are men like that who think that they should go around demonstrating their patriotic sentiments with their mouths. You know, there are men like that who think that they can serve their fatherland best by lying in their good warm beds and thinking up lead articles."

They both looked down at the journalist's lapel and at the enormous party insignia he was wearing.

He blushed slightly and grasped his necktie, while the note pad slid back down into his jacket pocket. He fingered the knot on his tie.

"The press fulfills a great task in such times," he replied. "It criticizes—where criticism is appropriate, especially of the enemy and of malcontents. It admonishes, it arouses. It keeps the people alert."

He looked nervously at the big man in front of him. What does he have against me? he thought. What can it be? Sometimes people were so insolent when they were being interviewed.

"The press's eyes are always watching," he said aloud, and felt that the pressure under his ribs was coming back. The pains always came when something like this happened. The distant, sharp pain grew rapidly stronger, and he involuntarily laid his palm against the right side of his diaphragm. He pushed, and it eased a little. At the same time he straightened his back, because it hurt less like that.

The officer looked at him, cool, but not unfriendly.

"There are men like that who think that there are no older colleagues, unfit for battle, who can keep watch instead of them."

The journalist looked down. He felt that his liver was getting worse; now it dissolved inside him and his whole belly became soft and helpless. At this stage it was better to bend forward a little. He bowed slightly.

"I'm a sick man," he said. "A sick man, Standartenführer."

Fräulein Reynhardt looked gravely and a little sternly at him.

"You mustn't take it personally," she said. "Herr Heidebrand always makes great demands on people."

"I'm a sick man," he repeated.

"Sometimes it's good to be sick," replied the officer kindly.

The journalist looked up at him. His eyes screwed up with pain.

"I have to eat white bread," he said.

"But it can happen that someone is sent to the front all the same—without white bread." The officer studied his fingernails. Then he polished them slowly against his palms.

Frau Reynhardt had fetched more glasses. She offered the tray with the filled glasses between them.

"Will your stomach stand a glass of cognac?" she asked quietly.

He looked gratefully at her.

"Lord!" he said. "That's medicine, Frau."

The officer had quickly caught up his own empty glass from the table. Now he held it out to the hostess.

"I'll gladly take twenty drops with him," he said. He blinked at the journalist. "Then the editor and I can empty a tablespoon for the soldiers."

He stood still and straight-backed while she filled the glass. Then he stretched out his left arm, so that the sleeve rode up and showed his watch.

"But we must be quick," he added; "our duties await us!"

III

IN THE MUSIC ROOM the only lights burning were the lamp over the pale rococo sofa and the small, unshaded bulb over the music stand on the grand piano. The spacious, well-furnished room lay in a pleasant half-light. Dr. Reynhardt had just come in. Throwing his light raincoat over the back of a chair, he turned his thin, handsome face toward his son. The boy had asked him about something, and now he was gathering his thoughts for a reply. Two narrow wrinkles formed between his blond eyebrows, and the yellow, slightly grizzled hair caught the light from the sofa lamp. He stretched out his left hand and stroked the boy's head. The right hand groped in his breast pocket for his pince-nez. When he had found it, he quickly clamped it onto the bridge of his nose and tilted his head slightly to one side. Then he answered the question:

"Well, son, he's certainly gifted in his way. He's a very gifted man."

The boy was not satisfied with the reply.

"But what's he like?"

The doctor took off his pince-nez. He squinted and peered into the darkness. He looked through the room and far back into the past.

"He's the kind who upset the chessboard when they lose at chess," he said.

His son was still not satisfied with the answer.

"But what kind of a *person* is he?"

The scientist looked at the boy. He'll soon be grown up now, he thought. Damnable that he's met Heidebrand!

"There are people," he said slowly and with emphasis, "there are people whose personal morals are not entirely on a level with their talents."

Now the boy was growing impatient.

"But is he evil or good, I mean! Is he a good person—like—well, for example, you, Father?"

For a moment the man stood and looked gravely at his son.

"No one is wholly good or wholly evil, you know—And it isn't for me to search people's hearts—but getting mixed up in politics has hardly improved him."

"But maybe he's an idealist?"

Dr. Reynhardt hesitated for a moment. I'm too late, he thought. The boy likes him already; he's looking for mitigating circumstances. There suddenly arose a faint memory that he himself had felt something similar the first time he met Heidebrand. How many years ago was that? How many? He himself must have been fourteen at that time, and Paul a little younger. Claus was seventeen. Paul had come climbing up over the edge of the balcony—that was the first time. Today my only son has met the only friend of my youth, it said inside him.

"Idealist, Claus? Idealist!" He heard his own voice the way it was when he began a sentence without knowing how he would end it. Then he went on, more attentively:

"All respect for ideals, Claus—all respect for them! But you understand that when ideals come together with politics—well, those two things don't mix very well. And the ideals usually get short shrift—Everything and everyone has two sides, Claus. And one of Heidebrand's sides is shown by the fact that he quite openly, you might say shamelessly, goes around in this uniform."

The boy looked at him, astonished.

"But surely it wouldn't have been better for him to wear civilian clothes?"

The doctor stood quite still for a moment. Then he took the boy by the lapel and shook him gently.

"I think you'd better go to bed now, son. We mustn't forget that you've been sick."

Then he turned his back.

"Besides, I didn't say that that must necessarily be a bad side!"

Claus grabbed his wrist with both hands.

"But you're in the lab all day, Father! I never get to see you. And we have so much to talk about!"

His father laid a hand on each of the boy's shoulders. He laughed.

"Listen!" he said. "Actually I'm *two* people: One doctor and one father. One and one are, as you know, *two*. And the father is glad that you sit up so late waiting for him—but the *doctor* would feel safer if you got more rest."

With his hands still on the boy's shoulders, he turned him firmly around toward the door. Claus resisted feebly. He looked around over his shoulder.

"Will you come up then and say good night?"

The father let go with his left hand and crossed his heart.

"Absolutely!" he said.

"Is that a promise?"

"Yes!"

He pushed him toward the door. And just before they reached it, it opened of itself. The mother stood there.

"Well?" she said smiling. "Have the turtle doves found each other?"

"We were just waiting for you," replied the doctor. "Claus is going to bed now."

Claus went over to his mother and kissed her on the cheek.

"Good night, mother!—See that Father comes up to my room in a while. He *did* promise!"

"Good night, Claus!"

When the door had slammed shut after Claus, she took her husband by the arm. She laid her head against his shoulder.

"Couldn't you spend a little more time at home, Heinz? He gets completely beside himself when you're away for so long at a time."

He blew something or other out of her hair. Then he arranged his face in exaggeratedly sorry folds.

"And his mother—how is it for her when I'm gone?"

She kissed him on the neck.

"She's also a little bit beside herself, Heinz."

He drew her to him and put both hands around her waist

"It will be better in a while," he said. "I'm working on a series of tests now, and I must do as many as possible every day—But, say! Do you know what I'm thinking?"

She shook her head.

"I'm thinking that you and I—our marriage, it's like an old, impregnable medieval fortress! The kind which rises up proudly on a cliff, with ruins all around."

She leaned her head back and looked up at him.

Many things around it have fallen into ruin," she said gravely.

He let go of her. And his right hand found his pince-nez again.

"And there will be more ruination, Gerda—in every sense of the word."

She stared ahead.

"Paul was here today."

He took out a cigarette and lit it. The cigarette case was old and heavy, and of late it had been reminding him very much of his father. It had originally belonged to old Dr. Reynhardt, and Gerda kept it so shiny that he could always see the gleam of his own face in it. And this face—especially the narrow nose—had become very like the old doctor's, his father's beard notwithstanding.

"Yes, Claus told me that Paul had been here. What did he want?"

"He seemed to have come mainly to talk about the old days. And he was in a dreadful state. Then he asked after you—he thought you were looking poorly."

Reynhardt had been pacing the floor. Now he stopped. He drew himself up in indignation.

"He thought I was looking poorly?"

He thought about it a little:

"Actually, he's the one who's looking poorly. He's pale—and even if he's stout and vigorous, he looks kind of emaciated just the same."

"Paul has always been like that," she said. "He can change his appearance completely in a few minutes. He can look glowing with health one moment, and wrinkled and ashen the next. He's always had that quality. Actually he's as strong as a blacksmith."

"I'm healthy too," muttered the doctor.

"But Paul isn't altogether wrong."

She went over to him and stroked his cheek.

"I've seen it for a long time, Heinz! I don't mean that you're *thin*, that doesn't matter. But I have the impression that there's something weighing on you."

"Well, you're wrong, my friend."

"But everybody can see it! Even Emmchen has noticed it!"

He patted her hair. Then he laughed.

"But little Gerda! Emmchen, poor thing, you don't take her seriously!"

But she stuck to her guns.

"Today Claus spoke of it too. He doesn't think you look happy any more, he said."

He took her hands and swung them back and forth.

"This sounds like a conspiracy!" he laughed.

Suddenly he opened his mouth and stared at her.

"Oh!" he cried. "I've forgotten something!"

And with one bound he was over by the chair, lifting up his raincoat. First he felt in one of the wide pockets. Then he drew a package out of the other. He quickly twisted off brown wrapping, which sank to the floor between his legs, and held up a tissue-paper package above his head.

In triumph he bore it over to her and offered it ceremoniously.

"Here!" he said. "This is from me, just from me."

She felt the package.

"Oh!" she said.

Out of the tissue paper came a purse the shape of a drawstring bag, in thick red leather.

"The strap is to go around your wrist," he explained, and bent over it.

She held the red Russian leather up to her nose and inhaled deeply.

"Oh!" she said again. "How in the world did you come by it?" She closed her hand around the soft leather.

"You are a prince!" she said, enchanted. "A prince above all the other princes on earth!"

"I came across it in the station this morning," he replied. "There was a man selling things from Russia. There were a few other things too, but most of them were ordinary tourist stuff. This purse was the only really pretty one he had."

"And the prince swooped down on it with his unerring falcon's eye!"

Again she held the purse up to her face and breathed in the smell of the leather.

"Hey," she said. "They must use red leather in their boots, too?"

"Yes," he said.

She looked up.

"Think how different everything would be in Germany if we used red boots here—instead of the black ones! Here they always wear black."

"Yes," he said. "Here they always wear black."

He looked gravely at her.

"Did Paul tell you that he'd taken over the position of commandant at the camp out there?"

She put the purse down on the sofa before she looked up. For a moment she was dumb. Then she spoke with mounting distaste.

"And where Samuel is, yet! But that's disgusting! That's disgusting! Paul and Samuel in the same camp! The one as commandant and the other as prisoner!"

He looked calmly at her. His handsome face was clear and solemn.

"He is said to have introduced a pace of work out there, a tempo in the camp administration which is scaring the subordinates out of their wits. He works day and night."

She had collected herself somewhat.

"So he stands in high favor with his superiors, then?"

"They're delighted. They believe they've come across an idealist." He paused for a moment, looking at her. "But you're not particularly surprised. I was afraid it would be a shock for you."

She looked straight ahead and shook her head slightly.

"Oh—no," she said.

He felt rather relieved.

"I'm glad that you look on Paul with a certain tolerance. Such a case absolutely does have *two* sides."

Her head jerked up with keen decisiveness.

"No," she said firmly. "It does not. Such a case has only one side. If it doesn't come as a shock to me, that's because this position of his is only a logical consequence. Everybody who works with them has sold out. So it's really nothing new."

He stopped in front of her and grasped her by the hands.

"So?" he said slowly. "*I* work with them too in a way. We must be objective, Gerda. A little bit fair! Do you think that I've sold out too?"

She answered quickly and with some irritation as she looked at him.

"You work to save the sick. There's nothing wrong with giving them medicines. Nobody can misuse that."

"You're right," he said thoughtfully. "Perhaps I have a bedrock in the work itself. One must have trust in science—that it will *bear fruit* in itself."

He was silent for a while, pacing back and forth. Then he stopped and raised his hand. She looked expectantly at him as he continued.

"But—one must have trust in *people* too! In a man like Paul there's so endlessly much that's complex, all mixed up together. After all, he has…."

"With Paul it's different," she interrupted him.

But he continued undisturbed.

"Paul may come to prevent many wrongs—perhaps set some things to rights. He's not a fiend, after all…. At least one wouldn't think so."

"He can make small reforms in hell? Is that what you mean?"

He frowned, and the two delicate wrinkles appeared again.

"I mean that with as the years go by you grow modest; a small, decent action counts for infinitely more than a big, beautiful dream."

He took her again by the hand.

"Let's not be too one-sided, Gerda! There's no patented way through life. The side roads are there, tiny narrow paths and long, crooked detours. And everyone has his own. Paul has his own. And he must walk it alone. What will come out of it, no one can say beforehand."

"There are roads which nobody needs to walk."

He sat down on the sofa before replying. He ran his hand over his forehead.

"Dear little Gerda!" he said. "It's easier to judge others than to live yourself."

She stood right in front of him.

"That sounds almost like a defense of Paul."

He sighed heavily.

"It is, too." he replied. "But it's just as much a defense of myself. Who can be human at all today without feeling like an accessory?"

She quickly bent down and ran a hand through his hair.

"Lord, Heinz! Is that what's bothering you?"

He looked up and laughed at her tone. She had spoken as if to a sick child. He pulled her down to him on the sofa.

"Is the conspiracy beginning again?"

She nestled her head against his shoulder as she looked up.

"Don't laugh, Heinz! A true marriage is always based on honesty. Tell me what's the matter!"

His tone was still jovial as he replied:

"Gerda—my friend! A man must have one secret from his wife!"

"But now if I *beg* you? You often look so downright desparing."

They both jumped when the telephone rang in the next room. He was already on his feet when he turned to her again.

"There, you see!" he laughed. "I don't *get* to answer!"

And as the telephone continued to ring, he ran out of the room. She sat and followed the conversation:

"Yes, hello! Yes, it's me. Please!—Now, this evening?—Yes, but it's very late!—All right! .Hmm?—All right!—Mm-hmm—And it's already left? Any minute?—Jawohl!—Fine!"

He looked older when he came in again.

"I would have enjoyed getting some sleep tonight," he said. "But *no!* Lord, Gerda! I have to leave at once. A car is coming for me right away; it's left already. Oh, for a chance to have a good rest!—These eternal conferences, now they're beginning at night as well!"

She listened to him in silence. He looked childish and old at the same time. And it was so seldom he complained about anything that he must be allowed a few words. But he was finished already. She rose and kissed him.

"You must eat first," she said.

"What vitality these people have!" he replied quietly.

"Poor Heinz! I'll make a couple of sandwiches."

"There won't be time," he replied absently. "They'll be here any minute."

He looked toward the window. Then he woke up again.

"But a cognac, now! That I think would help."

While he was getting into his light-colored raincoat, she got out the glass and the bottle. She poured a glass and held it out to him. He took it.

"Don't you want to join me?" he asked.

"I've already had a drink today," she replied. And abruptly, forcefully she went on: "It's terrible, Heinz, that you never get a good night's sleep! Tomorrow evening we'll leave the party early."

He put down the empty glass.

"Tomorrow evening I'm not going to any party at all!"

"What do you think it's about tonight?"

"It's a Dr. Scholz from Berlin. I'll be talking to him about the possibility of mass producing the fever preparations. He's leaving at six in the morning."

A car horn tooted energetically and pointedly from the street.

"See!" he said. "There they are. Goodbye for now!"

He kissed her.

"Try to think that all the drudgery will bring good to someone!" She almost shouted it after him. And he stopped for a moment in the doorway.

"Yes," he said thoughtfully. "Hopefully someone will reap benefits from it."

When he was gone, she went over to the window and pushed the curtains a little to the side. Then she opened a little crack between the window frame and the blackout paper and looked down to the street. Four stories below her stood a big, black Mercedes. The faint light from the shaded headlights drew a pale fan on the asphalt. From the doorway came a tall man in a light raincoat. He bent down and said a few words to the driver. Then he opened the door and crawled in. She heard nothing from the motor as the car began to move. The street was completely empty. And still she went on standing there. There was something about the situation which reminded her of an incident several years before, while Claus was still small. It was during an auto trip she and Heinrich had taken in Italy. While they were staying in Florence he had been called away in the middle of the night for a sick visit to a German diplomat. His wife had gotten sick, the diplomat had said on the telephone, and he was afraid she was about to die. She was completely unconscious, and Dr. Reynhardt was the only German doctor in the city. He had no confidence in the Italian doctors. Three days earlier they had been at a party at the diplomat's. Heinrich got up and left. And that time too she had stood like this at the window and looked after him—only the house farther down the street had been the Strozzi palace and not the secret EPA store. But she had not been able to sleep while he was away in the strange city. Only toward morning he got home again and told that when he arrived at the diplomat's, the official himself had disappeared, and the only person remaining with the unconscious woman was her Danish lover who didn't understand anything but Italian and Danish. The diplomat's wife had been unconscious for two reasons: In the first place she was dead drunk, and in the second place she had taken a triple dose of sleeping powder. With the aid of a Danish-German dictionary he had explained to the cavalier what he must watch out for the rest of the night. While Heinrich was telling her this, they drank chianti out of the common tooth glass and swallowed a big piece of *bel paese* without bread.

The memory of that night rose up overwhelmingly in her, the empty streets in the clear, foreign stone city, Heinrich sitting on the edge of the bed in his shirtsleeves and telling about it—it was all suddenly with her again. She remained standing at the window for a long time.

She started when the door behind her creaked. In the lamplight inside, between the door and the sofa, stood Claus, barefoot and in his pajamas. He was standing very still, with his eyebrows drawn together and his face down. The light hair fell down over his forehead.

"Where's Father?" he said. "He promised to come up and say goodnight."

She let the curtains fall into place again. She felt her own heart pounding so strongly that it almost took away her breath.

"Father had to leave," she said and cleared her throat. "He got a phone call. But I was supposed to say goodnight from him, Claus."

He stood without moving. Still by the door.

"They phoned, you see," she added by way of explanation. But she saw that he didn't see. Not completely. She looked away, and finally her gaze lighted on the red purse on the sofa.

5. Friends

I

It was on one of the last days of the summer vacation that he had been standing so long out on the balcony off the second floor. It was quite late in the evening, down in the garden it was pitch black, and his parents doubtless believed that he had gone to bed a good while ago. But the August night was so warm, it was so full of insects, and the warmth on the dry porch floor felt so wonderfully good against his naked feet. The old, dark suburban villa had high ceilings, and the fire rope which he had amused himself by sliding down was still hanging out over the railing. That summer he had been abroad for the first time, with his parents at an Italian beach resort—far—far away, by a dazzlingly blue, briny ocean which was called the Adriatic Sea. In four days school would start again. To be sure, Jan went to Holland every single summer to visit his grandparents, but no one else in the class had been to Italy. He thought awhile about how he would do it. For the first few days he wouldn't say anything, then he'd mention it to one of them, as if by accident—let it shine through that he'd been there. It would trickle out slowly, and finally when they asked him about it, he'd nod and say: Yes? And look questioningly at them as if wanting to know why they should ask about something so everyday as traveling to the Adriatic Sea. It was while he was engrossed in thinking about how impressed their faces would be that he noticed the vibration in the railing. The rope was pulled dangerously tight, and was quivering with a fine, irregular tempo. Icy cold ran down his back when he understood that someone was hanging onto it on the other side. For a moment he wanted to call for his parents. And the shriek was already in his throat when it came to him that if it was a burglar, that would be even better than a trip to Italy. But the vibration grew stronger, and now he heard a very faint sound. It was a kind of scratching at the wall, sole-protector against wood. And the next minute a head came into view. Quick as an ape the climber swung himself over the banister, and before he could say "Jack Robinson" they were standing face to face. He had again been on the point of shouting, it happened so fast.

The burglar was his own age, around fourteen. But he was dark-haired, a little shorter, and much heavier and broader. His hair was cut short and stood straight up. Beneath the short pantlegs were two (albeit somewhat bowed) calves, and the calves impressed him more than the climbing ability—for they had clear shadows of a dark, sprouting growth of hair. No one else in the class had that, least of all himself. The thin, blond doctor's son knew very well that he himself was no picture of robust masculine activity. The climbing ape laid a finger across his lips and said: "Hush!" Then he smiled, and the moment the smile spread over that broad, tanned face, the boy on the balcony knew that he had never liked any other boy so much before. And it was very important to become friends with him.

"I crawled in under the fence," said the dark-haired boy. And the blond one understood very well which hole he had got in through.

"I just wanted to say hello, since you were standing up here on the veranda. It was easy to see you from the street. I live here now, you understand. A little farther down the avenue."

The blond boy felt his heart pounding, exactly as if it were himself and not the other who had climbed up the rope.

"Will you be going to school here?" he asked eagerly. And the dark boy looked around and thrust out his lower lip—as if he were making the decision now, right this minute. Then he nodded.

"Yes," he said. "I think we can say that."

"Maybe we'll be in the same class!" said the doctor's son.

The other looked at him and drew his eyebrows together, so that they formed a thick, soft line which undulated below his forehead. He thought it over.

"I think we can say that," he said decidedly.

"I was at the Adriatic Sea this summer!" burst forth from the blond.

"My dad's a musician," replied the other. "He's lived in Italy for twenty years. He is a great artist, but devilishly poor."

And Heinrich Reynhardt felt that what he wanted more than anything in the world was to be friends with the son of the great, but devilishly poor artist. And so it turned out....

⁕⁖

He leaned back in the car and closed his eyes. He stayed like that until he felt the silver of the heavy cigarette case against his fingertips. Then he took it out and opened it. As he blew out the match, he noticed that the memory of the meeting with the friend of his youth had made his hand shake. He closed his eyes again. For a while he heard only the sound of the rubber tires against the asphalt. It was a tone which rose and fell. And slowly another face rose up within him. He knew that it was the cigarette case's fault. Of late he needed only to feel the case in his pocket, and the image of his father was there. And it always gave him the same corrosive feeling of schoolboy dread and helplessness. It was incomprehensible that the memory of his father should be so painful; the tall, well-dressed man with the blond beard had never been anything but kind and considerate toward him. He was no strict, stern paterfamilias. He was a well-to-do, nay rich doctor with rich and neurotic patients. But he didn't regard them as hypochondriacs. He didn't smile over them after they left. He was fond of them. Cared for them. And thanks to them he never took fees from poor patients. For strangely enough the poor also had nervous illnesses. And the nerve specialist himself had a heart condition. Despite the fact that spiritually he had an uncommonly good heart, his earthly heart was really bad. He had always been himself. It wasn't just people he was fond of. He had a lot of love left over for animals, too. Moreover, this weakness for animals had almost cost him his doctor's degree once, at the end of the previous century. He had refused to substantiate his dissertation with experiments on animals. Rats or guinea pigs, which they used back then. His subject had been something about neural paralysis, and with experiments it would have been easy to prove the point he was trying to make. But the doctor's spirit had stood firm; instead of behaving more or less scientifically, he had mumbled something philosophical about "Divinity", and that as long as human beings couldn't create a rat, they could just refrain from rooting around in God's creation. In reality he had merely felt sorry for the pretty white mice. The academic gentlemen had looked at each other and tempered justice with mercy for the young scientist. . . .

The car slowed down before the gate; slowly it glided in between the machine guns and the searchlights. The sentries saluted until the car was far into the barracks yard. . . .

II

THE OFFICER STOOD in the middle of the floor in the archive room and received him. Against the garish yellow walls and in the sharp light from the bulbs, the black uniform looked strongly violet. The doctor stopped just inside the door and took off his light raincoat.

The officer's wiry black hair was uncombed and stood straight up.

"Welcome!" he said.

The doctor looked up. And slowly he drew out his pince-nez and set them in place before his squinting eyes.

"May I ask what you're laughing about?" He tilted his head and placed his feet a ways apart.

"You're looking at me as if you already had me under the microscope," answered the other. The doctor came further into the room.

"Have the others arrived?"

"No one else is coming," replied the officer and sat down on the desk. "It'll be just us two."

For a moment Reynhardt stared at him open-mouthed. A faint blush spread over the narrow face.

"Does that mean it was *you* who called me here?"

The other looked at him, teasing and friendly.

"That means it was *I* who called you here. But first I was ordered to do it by Dr. Scholz. You know I'd never spoil a night's sleep for an old friend of my own free will!"

The doctor took a few more steps into the room. Then he stopped and looked crossly at the other.

"Well, honestly!" he said. "What's so funny?"

The officer gripped the table edge and pulled himself further in onto the desk. He let his feet dangle as he laughed loudly.

"You did have social impulses once, didn't you?" he said jovially. "You once wanted to be a prison doctor and sacrifice yourselves for the prisoners, isn't that right?"

That's the way he used to sit on the railing, thought the doctor. Aloud he said:

"I considered it once; but it was actually Gerda's idea. Do you really think it's comical?"

The other went on laughing.

"Well, after all, in a way you've become one! You *are* in fact a kind of prison doctor."

Reynhardt took out his cigarette case. He didn't reply, and the other went on.

"Did you get some sleep in the car?" he said casually.

The doctor raised his head. He threw the match on the floor without looking around for an ashtray.

"Oh, yes!" he said. "I slept a little! And what if I did? I'm tired, Paul! Tired! Tired! Tired!" Suddenly he was furious. "So what if I slept a little? Don't you need sleep yourself?"

Almost soundlessly the other had jumped down from the desk. With light, quick steps he crossed the room and went over to the filing shelves. He turned, and leaned against the unpainted wood of the boards.

He looked very interested when he replied.

"The last few nights I've needed very little sleep," he said. "To tell the truth I've been rather excited." He grasped his hair and thrust his face forward toward his friend. "The very thought of sleep is physically painful. To relax—to close my eyes—lose consciousness—get away from myself! I tell you, Heinrich, I begin to be afraid every time sleep gets near. Going to sleep has something about it which reminds me so horribly of being broken on the wheel. In a way it's as if my limbs are pulled apart!"

Heinrich had turned after him and was following him with his eyes.

"If you have something specific to tell me," he said drily, "then I must ask you to make it short. Tomorrow evening I'm going to a party, and what's left of tonight I must use to get a little sleep."

The other straightened up. He smiled:

"You're going to your mother's, to the widow?"

"Yes," replied the doctor. "If it's about your condition, you know that I'm not a neurologist."

Heidebrand was again at the desk. He took an empty glass which stood beside the ashtray, and lifted it up toward the lightbulb. There were a few drops left in the bottom.

"It's not about my condition," he said quietly and seriously. "That's as it should be. On the contrary it's about *your* condition—or if you will, your position."

"With regard to that, I think that I'm already quite well oriented."

The SS man was still examining the glass. He continued to hold it up to the light, and turned it now one way, now the other.

"Not well enough," he said absently. "Not well enough. There are certain scattered features of the camp's history which will make you see it in a somewhat broader context."

He put the glass down and turned to the other. He smiled.

"It's been decided that you are to play a significant role for our beloved fatherland."

The thin fingers removed the pince-nez. Reynhardt took out his handkerchief and polished his glasses before he answered.

"Are you sure it will interest me?"

The officer had sat down on the other side of the desk. Now he bent down and opened the cupboard by the wall. With his left hand he brought out the cognac bottle, while turning his head toward the other.

"It would be a great shame if it didn't interest a man with your high military and political rank."

His voice was joking and frivolous. Then he slid down off the table and squatted in front of the cupboard. He was searching thoroughly for something, and everything he took out to look properly, he left lying on the floor. There were books, papers, and a couple of pairs of handcuffs. The other had straightened his back as he looked down on him.

"I have neither military nor political rank," he said decidedly. "Even if you appointed me Kaiser, that wouldn't even make me a sergeant. I am a medical man!"

The broad nape of the man hunkering behind the desk slowly turned dark and red.

"Hell!" he said. "There should have been a couple of glasses here!"

Then he stood up and kicked the cupboard door shut.

"Fine!" he said. "But then as a *scientist* you're at least interested in *knowing!*"

He picked up the glass he had been playing with.

"It looks like we'll have to drink out of the same glass, Heinrich. There's only one here."

The doctor noticed that the stream inside him had begun anew: "He is a great artist," said the dark-haired boy on the veranda, "but he's devilishly poor. He's so poor that I only have one pair of shoes. Which I wear on Sundays." And the fair-haired boy understood that it was Sunday that day. For now, during the summer vacation, the days were so alike that there was hardly any difference between Sundays and other days. Then he thought that of course he had quite a lot of shoes in his room, but that it would hardly do to offer a pair just like that. Some people were insulted by such things. It would be best to wait until they were better acquainted. Then he heard the officer's voice.

"You don't mind?"

"It doesn't matter," replied the doctor. And the officer smiled as he poured. Then he held out the glass to him.

"We've done it before," said the voice, "years ago. Please!"

Dr. Reynhardt took the glass. He looked at the other before he drank.

Lord! thought the officer. How much he resembles himself! If he just put on the round cap again. Aloud he said:

"I have a strenuous morning ahead of me, and therefore I must ask something of you in connection with what I'm about to tell you. That's why I'm keeping you up tonight."

He took the empty glass and filled it. Then he drank it up. He went on:

"Last year there was a group of about 150 Jews among the prisoners here. They worked in a quarry not so very far away. Now it happened that they were driven very hard—unusually hard, in fact—in this quarry. And there occurred an average of four to five accidents a day. The accidents happened when they, with their own or others' help, fell down onto the gravel from the top. And it was rather high, you see, so it always led to fatal accidents.

"The finished gravel was delivered to an ordinary private firm. But after several weeks of deliveries—and by then, of course, the supply of Jews had markedly decreased—a strange thing happened! The firm began to complain that something was wrong with the stone they received. They asked the camp to wash it before it was sent."

The doctor looked at him attentively.

"So—was it done?"

"Oh, no. The deliveries continued as before. And according to Dr. Eger you could study anatomy in the gravel. But eventually there were no more Jews, and then the complaints stopped as well."

For a while neither of them said anything. The officer cleared his throat and continued.

"You may remember my mentioning the ash sold to the farmers as fertilizer?"

"I remember."

"Well, it too led to complaints. The farmers kept finding teeth and bones in their fertilizer, and they didn't like it. After all, they had bought it fair and square and had paid for the goods. So the cremation must have been highly incomplete, and first one farmer complained, then another, another—and so on...."

The doctor grew red in the face.

"Why are you telling me this?" he said indignantly. "It doesn't concern me what these idiots have been up to!" He collected himself then repeated calmly: "Yes, you must pardon my saying it: These *idiots*!"

The man in uniform was clearly unfazed, for he went on as if he were talking about the current price of wood or the lack of good writing paper. His tone was somewhat plaintive:

"And then one day a sewer main got clogged. Absolutely watertight. It was so stopped up that they had to get plumbers from the town to clear it....

"Well, now! The plumbers got quite a shock when they discovered what was stopping up the pipes. Really fresh stuff, yet! The poor fellows were practically comatose when they were driven home—even if plumbers are used to just about anything."

The doctor bent over the table, leaning on fists clenched so hard that the knuckles shone white through the skin.

"But this doesn't concern me!" he shouted. "It has nothing to do with me!"

The officer looked at him astonished.

Then he went on coolly:

"Can you think of any connection between these complaints from the firm and the farmers, and what the plumbers got a glimpse of?"

The doctor was still upset.

"Nothing," he sputtered, "nothing but negligence, incompetence, and unforgivable stupidity in the camp administration!"

The other leaned forward toward him:

"*Nothing* but that?"

The doctor turned away. He walked out onto the floor. His voice was high and went almost over into falsetto when he replied.

"No, I'm telling you! No! And it offends me to hear it! I've just come from my home!"

The officer was sitting alone again on the desk, was following the other with his eyes:

"But what effect do you think it might have had?"

The other stopped abruptly and turned toward him again. He opened his mouth. But a moment passed before he spoke.

"Of course it would be whispered and talked about!" he said irascibly. "Whispers and talk!"

The officer continued to stare at him.

"And how do you think they feel, the ones who talk about it?"

He put his pince-nez back on. He was calm now.

"Well, the rumors naturally create a certain—a certain anxiety," he said casually. He slowly crossed the room again, all the way to the table. As he filled the glass, drinking up half of it, he heard the other say:

"And you don't think that could be the whole point?"

Without answering he held out the half-full glass to the officer, who took a swig of it before saying more.

"The people get totally paralyzed," he went on. "They go numb with fear. You see, they get a small glimpse of what happens to those who are don't obey."

The doctor stood in thought for a while. He could still feel the warmth of the cognac, the faint, pleasant burning near his diaphragm. For a moment he merely savored it. Then he raised his head, calm and thoughtful.

"I repeat," he said with dignity, "I repeat: It's nothing to me how one uses the remains." Then he took a step forward, stuck his head out and looked the other in the eyes. Slowly and earnestly he said:

"I'll tell you quite frankly, Paul, how things are with me. I am a physician. Actually medicine has always been an exception among the natural sciences. The conditions of research have been especially bad. In all other branches of science one could solve problems by experiment. But not us. In medicine we were cut off from that. We had to proceed with infinite slowness. Now and then we could do research with animals. But that was a long way round. It didn't help us much. We could never experiment freely. We could never get past the scruples we had to observe. Imagine a chemist having to experiment with phosphorus when he wanted to know something about sulfur! That's how it was for us."

He looked down. Then he again directed his look at the other:

"I don't give a damn about politics! I don't give a damn about the war! I don't give a damn about corpses and sewers and uniforms! *This* is what interests me. And it interests me *truly*! It has opened up whole new avenues for medicine."

He screwed up his eyes and grabbed the other by the sleeve:

"*It's so interesting, Paul!* It's so interesting. And therefore it's completely immaterial to me what they use the remains for. Utterly immaterial! That's the way it is."

He looked away after the last words, and very softly he added;

"You have no right to keep me awake at night with this." He was tired. And as he looked away, he suddenly yawned, a loud, pulsating yawn.

The officer sat silent for a while. He stared ahead with half-open mouth. His right hand was clenched around the collar of his uniform. His lit cigarette lay unregarded on the table surface. Only after a while did he notice the smell of the burnt wood, and took the cigarette away. But a piece of charred paper clung to the black mark on the table.

"Right," he said quietly. "I understand. I understand. And as a private person you are probably justified in that." And his voice suddenly became hard and determined. "But not in the position you are in today. Not there!" He slid down off the table again, and walked across the room to the wall with the pigeonholes. There he turned and stood with his hands behind his back as he continued the monologue.

"As a scientist, as a representative for today's intellectual elite, you stand only and solely in the service of the *state*—and you ought to be interested in what political aspects your work has."

He squinted eyes and inspected the doctor even more thoroughly.

"You ought to be flattered," he said, "that we have a use for you. As a professional man you possess an enormous asset in your reputation."

Dr. Reynhardt looked at the officer unmoved. The thin, tanned face had an expression of invincibly tough obstinacy. He leaned against the table.

"And as a private man," he replied, "I have another asset. I have my morality, my emotional life. I quite simply have my decency to protect!"

He raised the glass, and had almost put it to his mouth before he discovered that it was empty. With a dismissive gesture he set it down again. He drew himself all the way up, and raised his head.

"I will under no circumstances get involved in politics," he said. "That you'll have to manage by yourselves. Without me. I'm not taking one step in that direction."

The other sauntered slowly toward him.

"You won't be involved in it," he said persuasively. "You'll just be giving us some purely technical help."

He had come back to the table again. Now he grabbed the bottle and poured another glass. He held out the filled glass to his friend. He himself lit a cigarette and stuck out his lower lip as he blew out the smoke in a think white stream. Without turning his head, he looked obliquely at the scientist.

"You know these surgical experiments Eger is working on?" The words fell quietly and probingly. "They would acquire an enormous psychological clout if they were to leak out as secrets. As secrets, mind! Dr. Eger can't do it himself. He's been so compromised for so long that no one will believe a word he says. But if secret, purely factual reports about the operations were to leak out, that would be more effective than anything else. And a man with your scientific prestige would be very well suited for just that sort of thing.

"You understand that there are certain officers' circles within the Wehrmacht who could doubtless use a little enlightenment on what happens to rebels. And of course you could make a show of indignation over these experiments."

Dr. Reynhardt looked at him with big round eyes. The pince-nez which he was trying to clamp in place absolutely refused to stay put.

What blue eyes he has, thought the officer. The round cap was also blue, but much darker.

The doctor was still having trouble breathing evenly. He stammered faintly when he began to speak.

"But th—th—that would be a misuse of science!"

"It's not a misuse at all," replied the officer. "It's in perfect accord with the scientific spirit. After all, it's just a matter of conveying the pure truth: This is what happens to rebels. And that can be a good thing to know—if one is a rebel. An excellent thing to have before one's eyes."

He poured a new glass for himself. He went on confidentially:

"How might these things get into their hands, Heinrich? How could we arrange it?"

The other turned his back to him.

"I'm not employed by the Ministry of Propaganda."

"But that's exactly what you are!" The voice sounded loud and surprised. "You're employed by the backside of the Ministry of Propaganda. One could say you're employed as a public bogeyman: Watch out! Or science will come and get you! We have negative propaganda, and it must be managed in tandem with the positive. For example, you could just inform one of the army doctors, show him a few documents and a couple of photographs. Everything is at your disposal. The rest will take care of itself. It will reach the appropriate people, and it will help them maintain the right attitude. You will help us, Heinrich?"

The last words were spoken with warmth and emphasis. The doctor paced the room restlessly. He made a big circle around the other.

"I can't," he replied decidedly. "I cannot drag my private person into this. If I do just one single thing which goes beyond the purely medical, then I've involved myself politically. I have my family, Paul. And as its head I have very definite obligations."

For a long time neither of them spoke.

"Has the husband and father told his family about his scientific work?"

The words fell so coldly, and came so surprisingly that the doctor involuntarily stopped pacing. He stood stock-still.

"Those things have nothing to do with each other!" he said dismissively. "Be so good as to keep them separate!"

"Why haven't you told Gerda about your experiments?" The SS man stood importunately before him, with feet placed wide apart on the floor. It was obvious that he was speaking to a subordinate.

The scientist thought it over.

"If I were experimenting with rats," he said calmly, "I wouldn't entertain my family with that either. There's no reason for her to know."

"Still she's bound to hear about it someday!"

The doctor curled his upper lip when he answered. He stuck out his head and went right up to the other.

"Did you mention anything today?" he said softly. He licked the foam from the corners of his mouth.

The other just stood there.

"Gerda has no feel for our disciplines. I'd never dream of talking shop with her," he replied smiling. For a moment he looked at the other. Then he raised his voice in triumph. "But this is interesting! The paterfamilias does not acknowledge the scientist! Not even the vivisection of rats does the paterfamilias find wholly fitting!"

The doctor frowned. He felt was astonished to feel irritation almost winning out over anxiety.

"Of course I acknowledge it!" he said. "My work has the very greatest significance for the future...in a purely human sense."

But suddenly he saw her face as she bent over the soft red purse of Russian leather. She was smelling it.

"What did you mean, she's bound to hear of it?" he went on. It hit him with certainty that never again could she take such pleasure in a purse were to find out about the experiments.

The officer didn't reply. He turned on his heel, sauntered slowly over to the desk. When he had seated himself there, he drew the cork out of the bottle and poured. He drained the glass, and filled it again. Then he held it out at arm's length. The doctor took it, and swallowed the warming contents.

"You're enchanting, Heinrich! I'll always keep a soft spot for you. You have a peculiar fossil charm."

The officer had spoken with a strange, alien clang in his voice. And suddenly he stood up, white with anger. He roared the words into the other's face:

"Why in hell should anyone have a decent private life? I thought your race was extinct!"

"Well, it isn't."

The SS man was already far out on the floor. He tramped around rapidly.

"No, that's clear enough," he said, continuing to pace. "It certainly makes itself noticed. It has its second youth now!"

He paced and paced. For a while he held his thumb against his chest.

"Thanks to us!" he said loudly. "We gave you another chance. But just wait!"

He suddenly stopped and stared wide-eyed at the other.

"Just wait!" he repeated absently. And quietly, hesitatingly he went on:

"Which actually came first, Heinrich? The white coat or the black uniform?"

For yet awhile he was lost in thought. And a couple of minutes passed before the doctor interrupted him, cool and collected:

"So you won't be so good as to tell me what you meant by saying that Gerda is bound to hear it? It's an extremely painful thought, for I don't believe she'd be able to understand it quite—quite objectively."

"I meant that you should have a chance to tell her about it yourself—before others do."

"What others?"

The officer was quite himself again.

"Sooner or later Dr. Scholz will make sure that Gerda is carefully informed. Carefully! And he will have his reasons for doing it.

"Therefore you should put her in the picture yourself."

The blond man looked at the other in consternation.

"But it's Dr. Scholz who bears responsibility for the work!"

"Well," replied the officer casually. "Then of course it's a question whether Gerda will understand *that*."

The doctor went up to him grabbed him by the arm.

"But this is inhuman!" he said. "Gerda won't understand anything at all. She'll judge it by a standard which is alien to our work —*She* can't understand that it involves another world with different values than hers! She won't understand that, Paul!" He raised his voice. "She *can't!* After all, she's a romantic! She's a child!"

The other looked gravely at him.

"It will be worst for her to hear it from outsiders. You must do it yourself."

The doctor looked at him in bewilderment. He opened his shirt collar, and the button fell to the floor with a sharp little sound. For a moment it rolled around on the wooden boards, the spirals growing smaller and smaller, and for a brief second the sound of ivory against wood reached a climax. Then it was still.

"You can't demand such a thing of me!" said the physician. "It would destroy my home."

"We aren't *demanding* it," replied the officer. His voice sounded tired. "No one is demanding anything of you. I just think it would be best if she heard it from you."

Dr. Reynhardt had turned around. He looked down.

"There must be a way to avoid it," he said uncertainly.

The other looked at him, still tired.

"Dr. Scholz will certainly understand your situation, but he meant what he said—he was completely frank about there being no room for sentimental considerations. There really isn't any place for them. Not in his book—He's a hard man, Heinrich—and just as hard on himself as on others."

"But what can I do?"

"Tell her yourself."

"I can't do that."

"It would be the wisest course."

The SS man suddenly found himself on the other side of the desk.

"I *can't,*" repeated the doctor. "It's wholly out of the question."

"And then there's one more thing," said the officer abruptly. "You have a grown son!"

For a second they looked each other in the eyes.

"*Grown* is putting it strongly."

The officer shrugged.

"He's at most a couple years younger than Max. You should tell him about your work."

The doctor stood for a moment as if thunderstruck.

"Are you crazy?" he said almost inaudibly. "Don't you know the boy's sick?"

The words were hoarse and spasmodic.

"You'd better tell him all the same," said the officer. "That would be best. If you do it yourself, if you steal a march on them, then you can tell him in a way that softens the shock."

Dr. Reynhardt bit his upper lip. A strong whiteness was spreading under the brown skin. It drew a kind of polar map over his face. The North Pole lay somewhere near the mouth, and the white boundaries spread outward, past his cheekbones.

When he spoke, his words echoed in the deserted room.

"Claus is much too nervous to tolerate anything so upsetting. You know that very well! And besides, he's nowhere near mature enough to understand it."

"He's old enough to begin to understand."

The doctor haltingly walked the few steps over to the desk. He laid his hands on the surface, and leaned forward. His hair suddenly fell down into his face.

"Lord God in heaven, Paul!" he said. "He's sick. And besides, he's hardly come up against reality yet!"

The officer held out the full glass to him.

"Sooner or later the boy must learn about the world."

The hands which lay on the table surface bore the whole weight of his body. He refused the glass, and the other drank it himself.

"It would destroy him!" he said.

When the officer had drunk up, he replied:

"You're the one who's destroying him—shutting him up in an ivory tower."

The father leaned even further forward.

"He'd kill himself!" he said. "He'll misunderstand everything—my position—the work—everything, everything!" He took a couple of deep breaths. Then he went on:

"Just think how he clings to me! Think what I *mean* to him!"

The other shrugged his broad shoulders again.

"As you will," he said indifferently. "But I have to tell you that none of this cuts any ice with Dr. Scholz."

The other straightened up. His face was rigid, as if he hadn't slept in a long time.

"But Dr. Scholz?" he said mechanically. "Why should he…. What pleasure would he get from informing Claus and Gerda?"

"Dr. Scholz isn't after pleasure," replied the officer drily. "Dr. Scholz is after *results*."

"But what benefit can anyone get from destroying and sullying my family life?"

The officer looked even more tired than before. He breathed deeply and groaned.

"To make a long story short, Heinrich! I'm speaking here on behalf of Dr. Scholz himself: He values your work, and can certainly appreciate your point of view. He is glad that you're helping us. He is grateful for your exertions.

"But he is your superior.

"And now he wants you to do him a service."

"And that is?"

"That you tactfully turn certain secrets over to your colleagues, the doctors inside the Wehrmacht."

Reynhardt looked calmer. He said definitely:

"But I've already said that I can't engage myself politically! That is out of the question."

"And therefore he is going to inform Gerda and Claus. That is: Provided that you don't change your mind."

The doctor took a step backward. He tore his hair.

"But that's blackmail!" he cried. "So he's trying to force me to do it!"

The officer bent forward and put his elbows on the table.

"You can't call it blackmail," he said. "You have a perfectly free choice."

The doctor threw out his arms:

"Yes, between two impossible things!"

"No," replied the officer. "Between two possible things."

The doctor squinted at him.

"And you go along with things like this!" he said.

A clear red spot under appeared under the officer's cheekbone.

"Now don't forget that I too am your superior!" His voice was low and thick. The doctor let his arms dangle at his side.

"So I'm supposed to choose!"

"Yes," said the officer.

"I *cannot* get mixed up in politics."

The other straightened his back. He rubbed it with his hands, his chin against his chest.

"A very respectable position," he said. "That means that you choose the other possibility."

The doctor looked up. He closed his eyes and ran his hand over his face.

The cap, thought the officer. What in the world had become of the English cap?

"Both are impossible," said the doctor. He was talking to himself, and suddenly he felt a strong longing for his father. He remembered his knees, as they were outlined through his pants when he sat in the easy chair reading—never newspapers, only books. And his hands.

"Both are impossible."

He felt distantly that someone was taking him by the arm. He opened his eyes and saw Paul's face right in front of him. It was broad and vigorous. His hair was unkempt, just like that time on the porch. Then he closed his eyes again. The other shook him by the arm.

"Heinrich!" he said. "There *is* one more possibility. A possibility no one has considered!"

The doctor looked up at him.

"And what's that?" he asked eagerly.

"That you take your family and leave the country! We have a neutral country next door, and you can go there. You need only pull up stakes, Heinrich! You can pull up stakes and actually begin a new life! I'll help you. To get across, I mean...."

He stopped and smiled.

"...not with the new life! It's easy to get you over the border."

The doctor pulled away his arm. He took a step backward.

"When one is responsible for others besides oneself," he began, "one doesn't pull up stakes just like that..."

Paul followed him. He looked him in the face.

"I *mean* it," he said earnestly. "I'll help you."

The other looked at him coolly.

"It can't be done."

The swarthy boy on the porch drew his eyebrows together:

"I think we may say that it *can* be done!"

The doctor threw up his arms.

"That's nonsense, Paul! Are you completely out of your mind? Be serious!"

The officer was excited. He grew red in the face.

"Do you really believe that one can't pull up stakes?"

He clenched his fist and ran the knuckles down his chest.

"I know it can be done! It can be done if you have a reason to do it!"

He turned abruptly and looked for the glass. Then he went ack to the desk and filled it. He lifted the glass.

"*Skaal* to those who have a reason!" he said and drank. He swallowed, and for a little while he looked straight ahead. Then he turned to the other.

"I once pulled up stakes myself," he said, and his voice rose. "And I can do it again! And again! And again! There's no limit to how often a person can pull up stakes. You can do it every minute!

"Always!"

"I cannot take responsibility for such a thing."

"It's one night's journey," said the officer. "And then you're over the border. Gerda and Claus are safe. And you'll be a free man again. It's easy!"

The doctor stared at him. For a moment he felt sweat at the bridge of his nose and on his forehead.

"Then what would we be going to?" he asked.

The officer stood before the desk. He peered at the doctor, stooping a little.

"One always pulls up stakes *from*," he said. "Never *to.*"

"For me it's important," said the doctor.

The other came over to him again. His confidence was gone now. He practically tiptoed over to the doctor and looked up into the fair, thin face. The doctor was still a bit taller than he was. With the round cap on, he would have been very tall.

"You'll get *out* of it, Heinrich, if you pull up stakes." His voice was almost beseeching.

The physician looked calmly down at him. He smiled.

"I've already made up my mind," he said.

The other raised his hands and grabbed him by the shoulders. He laughed loudly and with gasps.

"You'll pull up stakes!" he said indistinctly. "I see it, Heinrich!"

The doctor took the hands off his shoulders. For a while he didn't say anything. Then he cleared his throat.

"I know a suitable doctor," he said slowly, "who I could entrust the documents to.... and who would certainly pass them on—But I'll do it just this once! My task is of a medical—not of a political sort. And I won't go one step further in that direction! Not one step! It is completely out of the question."

The officer took hold of the bottom of his uniform jacket and pulled. He drew it taut.

"All right," he said.

"Then I assume that my family life will be kept out of it," continued the scientist.

The other was already over at the desk again. He looked askance at him. And his laughter was wholly soundless.

"You know you can count on us!" he said softly. "I certainly won't show Gerda the spots on your white coat!"

The doctor drew himself up. His fatigue was gone. His worries were gone. He felt only a glad, singing relief. At the same time he was annoyed.

"Be so kind as not to speak of this in such a tone," he said stiffly. "My work and my family life—the two have nothing to do with each other."

But the officer didn't reply. He was standing with eyes closed and head on a slant. He was listening for something—something which came from far away.

"What is it?" asked the doctor.

The other didn't reply. He was listening.

"What is it?" he repeated.

A short time more elapsed. Then the officer opened his eyes and looked distantly at him. Slowly he came to himself again.

"At first I thought it was one of the prisoners!" he said in surprise. And suddenly he bent over and laughed. He touched his elbows to his knees and stood there for a long time, bent double, laughing in the middle of the floor. And the laughter went quickly over into falsetto.

Then he slowly straightened up again and wiped his eyes.

"But it was just the rooster!" he said, half choking. "We have a poultry yard out here. And it was just the rooster. Can you imagine its being that late!"

For a while he just stood looking at the other. Then he said:

"I'll get you a car."

And he hurried across the room and out the yellow-painted door. Dr. Reynhardt saw the broad, black back violet against all the yellow. Then the door slammed shut.

And somewhere deep within him there was a bright voice which said: "I crawled in under the fence...because it was easy to see you from the street!"

6. God's Green Earth

Two days passed before Dr. Reynhardt received word that Standartenführer Paul Heidebrand was wanted by the police. The very morning after the doctor's nocturnal visit to the camp commandant the latter had left the camp in a car, accompanied by an unknown person. None of the sentries could say that they had looked closely at the passenger. However, the personnel in the camp administration could state that very early the same morning the officer had requisitioned the clothes and papers belonging the prisoner Samuel Goldmann. Goldmann himself had been fetched before morning reveille. The camp chief had said that the prisoner was to be transferred to Theresienstadt, and that he himself would see to it that this was done.

No one had found anything striking about the summons, for personnel were used to Heidebrand's high-handed and eccentric ways. The next morning a report came in that the car, a black Mercedes Benz type 170 H, had been found abandoned, fourteen kilometers from the Swiss border. The terrain had been searched, but to all appearances the fugitives were already in neutral territory.

⚬⚬

Dr. Heinrich Reynhardt was immediately called in for interrogation, and the doctor could inform them that on the evening before the previous day Paul Heidebrand had been in agitated, but fully rational state.

161

He stated further that the prisoner Goldmann had gone to the same high school as Standartenführer Heidebrand and himself, but two classes behind them. Upon further examination of the witness it transpired that on the above-named night Standartenführer Heidebrand had offered his unsolicited assistance in helping the witness and the witness's family emigrate to an unnamed, neutral neighboring country. Dr. Reynhardt assumed that the expression "neutral neighboring country" referred to Switzerland. To the question why he had not reported the incident earlier, the witness replied that he had regarded the offer as a provocation from the commandant's side, a trial balloon which Heidebrand had employed to investigate the witness's political stance.

During the examination the witness showed strong signs of nervousness, and admitted after further cross-examination that his real reason for keeping silent about Heidebrand's behavior was the personal feelings of friendship he harbored for the latter.

Dr. Reynhardt confirmed that former Standartenführer Heidebrand had charged him to seek contact with doctors within the Wehrmacht; with the aim of mediating information about the medical experiments being conducted in the local concentration camp. In response to questioning the witness declared that he remained willing to carry out the assignment.

The interrogation of Heinrich Reynhardt, M.D. was entered into the record and signed by those present.

These were:

Obergruppenführer Scholz, M.D.; Standartenführer and acting commandant Ilya Kassler, LL.D.; P. Eger, M.D.; and the recorder, Rottenführer F. Blau.

৪০ ৫৪

KARL SCHWENZEN, LL.D, opened the door and bade the strange man come in.

It was an odd time for a visit—almost eleven o'clock at night—but the guest seemed to have a reason for calling on him. And he ran his hand through his thin, fair hair while the stranger freed his big shoulders from his raincoat. He was a heavy, large man in his forties. Above the broad, round face grew wiry and close-cropped dark hair. But despite their roundness and plumpness, both face and figure seemed emaciated and exhausted. The very fact that the man had not introduced himself was striking.

"Please!" said the jurist, and opened the door to the office which abutted his private apartment. The other was ready, and went in first. The lawyer felt a strong disquiet as he followed after him.

In the office he turned on the light and went straight over to the carefully blanketed window. His hand glided probingly down the black paper.

When he was convinced that the blackout was satisfactory, he turned to the guest, who had already seated himself in the big, leather-upholstered client's chair.

"It pays to be careful," he said apologetically. "A colleague of mine recently paid a 300-Reichsmark fine because of insufficient covering."

The stranger looked up.

"Yes, cover it well!" he said. "I have nothing against it."

Dr. Schwenzen again felt uneasy. There was something about the other's intonation, an undertone, a ring which almost frightened him. He ran his hand through his wispy hair and sat down behind the desk. He leaned back slightly in the chair, and ran his thumb and forefinger down along his little double chin.

"Please!" he said wearily. "You've come to consult me, Herr…?"

The stranger did not accept the invitation to introduce himself. He merely looked at the other for a long time.

"I've come on behalf of your client and relative, Samuel Goldmann."

The jurist looked down.

There was something in the voice which told him that the other was used to speaking "on behalf of."

"He is no longer my relative," he replied. "My sister is dead now, and there exists no blood tie between us."

"I know that," said the stranger. "But I've come on his behalf all the same."

His voice sounded clearly official.

"Goldmann is interned because of his ancestry and his former political activities," replied the barrister. "I assume that you represent the leadership of the camp…?"

Some time passed before the other replied.

"Goldmann is no longer interned," he said softly. "He is at liberty in Switzerland. And I spoke with him a little over two days ago. I represent only him."

Dr. Schwenzen felt the sudden cold down his back.

He leaned forward with open eyes. Suddenly he understood why the other hadn't introduced himself, and why he had already felt such disquiet at the very sight of him.

The cold in his back grew stronger.

"He told me that you are still manage his affairs. And among them there are a number of foreign securities. Is that correct?"

The guest looked at him. But his gaze was not inquiring. He was sure that such was the case.

The barrister wanted to answer, but his throat was thick and tight.
He nodded.

And the other went on:

"Now Goldmann has asked me to get the papers from you. He is sick and unfit to work, and needs the papers to survive."

The jurist swallowed. He heard the words in the air around him, and they remained there after the other had spoken.

Then he swallowed again. Thoughts ran lightning-fast back and forth inside him—like rubber balls dancing between the walls in a room. And all the thoughts had the same confusing content.

He felt the cold in his back spreading out and settling around his chest.

He cleared his throat with all his might, and noted that his voice had come back.

"Do you have a power of attorney with you?" he asked.

And the other stuck his hand down in his breast pocket. He held out the paper and let go, so that it sank with small, spasmodic movements down onto the desk.

"Please!" he said.

The lawyer held the paper up before his eyes. The letters danced around each other. But at the bottom stood Goldmann's signature—unchanged. He hadn't seen it for seven or eight years now.

"Right," he said. "Right…."

And at that instant the front door slammed, and he jumped up.

"That's my wife," he went on. "Will you excuse me for a moment? I must say a few words to her before she goes to bed…."

Closing the door carefully after him, he went out into the hall. And for several minutes he whispered with her out there.

"Good night!" he said aloud, as he stood once again with his hand on the doorknob.

The dark, strange man looked indifferently at him as he sat down.

Then the jurist picked up the power of attorney again.

For a while he held it up before his face. His heart was beating so hard inside him that he could feel his own pulse in the fingertips which held the paper.

It's creepy how slowly the seconds go by, he thought. And the pounding of his heart suddenly made him very dizzy.

"Right," he said loudly, with a thick voice. "It looks to be in order."

And after a little while:

"The papers are American…. I had them in my bank box for a long time, but in recent years I've had them up here." He pointed quickly at the safe against the fire wall.

"They're quite valuable now," he added. "And truth to tell I'm glad to get rid of them…."

But the guest was in a hurry, and they were already standing in the vestibule when the police arrived.

⁂⁂

THE STOUT POLICEMAN leaned down over the desk. He stuck his finger in under his collar and exhaled, red and warm. Despite the summer heat which had suddenly come with full force, his face was beaming with satisfaction.

"We sure got our pigeon yesterday!" he said, smiling. "But the boys had all they could do to take him alive. The apartment looked like there'd been a good old-fashioned tavern brawl!"

He looked off into the air and smiled at the memory.

The other looked up, curious.

"Who was it?" he asked softly, almost inaudibly.

He put down his fountain pen, but picked it right up again and turned it between his fingers.

The stout one looked down at him.

The he bent again and whispered in the other's ear. And the man with the fountain pen raised his eyebrows.

"Good God!" he said when the stout man had finished. He pursed his lips and produced a long, thoughtful whistle.

"No wonder he defended himself!" he called after the broad, uniformed back.

But the stout man was already out the door.

For a while he sat playing with the fountain pen.

Then he tried to work. But he couldn't concentrate. His usual pleasure at putting together the even, same-sized letters absolutely wouldn't come. And several times he broke off the work to sit and stare straight ahead, twirling the fountain pen between his fingers.

Finally he rose resolutely and went out to the hall, took a few steps to the right, and disappeared into the office next door.

There he stopped in the middle of the floor, still grasping the fountain pen.

"Hey, Gusti!" he said familiarly.

The other looked up.

"We sure got our pigeon last night!" said the one with the fountain pen. Then he walked up to the other, bent down, and whispered for a long time in his ear.

₧₨

The five men stood in a circle on the floor.

"Pull!" called Dr. Scholz, and Max put all his weight on the rope. But the man whose handcuffs were fastened to the other end of the rope was much too heavy. He weighed more than the Balt, and the rope running over the hook in the ceiling merely pulled his hands up along his back.

Then the swarthy doctor, the one who looked like an auto mechanic, stepped forward and pulled too. And through his strained, half-closed eyes Max saw Heidebrand's boots slowly lifting off the floor.

"Now he's hanging!" said Eger.

And Max made the rope fast. He knew what was coming, and was already swallowing in advance to counteract the nausea which would soon rise up in him. For it was funny about the nausea; it didn't pass off so easily.

Dr. Scholz picked the monkey wrench up off the table. He held it in his right hand and took a step forward. Then he raised it and hit the bound man in the face with all his might. Quick as a dancer he stepped backward to avoid the blood. The blow had landed under the left cheekbone.

Then he handed the monkey wrench to Max.

It took a long time with Heidebrand. He only screamed a little, but very loudly. Once he spoke. That was when his hand was in the vise. But Max didn't hear it clearly, for the nausea always rose up violently when he heard the sound of bone. He no longer threw up, but he had trouble taking in anything else.

He heard something from far away, and then the last two words quite clearly. "…on account," said Heidebrand and fainted. They had long since taken him down off the rope, but when he fell, he remained hanging by the hand in the vise.

He was still hanging like that when Max threw water on him. And he fainted again while the water ran off him.

The same thing repeated itself several times. As soon as Hedebrand had opened his eyes from the water, he fainted again.

"Good God!" said Dr. Scholz slowly with a groan. "Don't you understand that he can't wake up so long as his hand is in the vise?"

He shook his head in despair.

Only after they unscrewed him did they succeed waking him up. But finally all the water in the world didn't help any longer. He just lay on the spot where they let him fall, as lifeless as a wet towel.

"Do you have any single cell free?" said Dr. Scholz.

"We have one under the laundry," replied one of the men. "But there's a prisoner in there already—a Norwegian name of Lyngby—We can take him out first."

"No," said the old doctor. "They can just as well live together."

So they carried Heidebrand down.

When Dr. Scholtz was about to leave, he stopped in the doorway and looked back at the others. He looked down, and shook his head for a moment.

"Dr. Reynhardt must under no circumstances know that Heidebrand is here in the camp!"

He looked around at their faces in turn.

"Under no circumstances!" he repeated, softly and threateningly. "We've had enough, now."

He turned his back on them again.

But yet again he stopped in the doorway. Half in profile he looked back.

He pointed at a big package lying on the floor, half hidden away in a corner of the room. It was in heavy brown paper, and a small lake of water had formed under it.

"Those are some roses I brought from Berlin," he said. "They've been standing in my garden."

And suddenly he was very old and very tired. He took a big handkerchief out of his pocket and carefully wiped the corners of his eyes and the bridge of his nose.

"I thought you could plant them out here, on the other side of the vegetable garden. . . It's that time of year now."

Then he left.

⁎

BY THE TIME Dr. Reynhardt began the thirty-second series of experiments, he had absolute authority over all the medical research carried on within the camp. Dr. Eger's greater political enthusiasm had long since proved less effective than the other's far more systematic mind.

This was due above all to Dr. Scholz, who had never erred in his evaluation of the doctor's unusual ability and comprehensive knowledge.

Of course it was clear to all that politically Dr. Reynhardt was a weak reed, and that he was by no means fit to bear large practical burdens. But in fact that didn't matter—first because all temptations were carefully removed from him, and secondly because his sole lasting passion was the work which the camp's operations allowed him to carry on wholly unimpeded. With Dr. Eger as practical and administrative assistant his researches proceeded without a hitch.

At this time he was also as close to being forgiven for his own great error as anyone could come. It was now nearly two years since he had failed to report former Standartenführer Paul Heidebrand's offer of help in defecting. The matter was almost forgotten, and Dr. Reynhardt never mentioned his former classmate's name.

Another thing was that by carrying out the political assignment he had been given, the doctor had done something to make amends for the incident.

In addition to his practical tasks Dr. Eger had continued with his own work as well. The surgical experiments—which at the outset had almost been regarded as his private business—now bore, with Dr. Reynhardt's help, quite significant fruits.

Eger was an able surgeon and earlier that winter had already carried out successful transplants of healthy limbs to wounded or sick SS men. And Dr. Reynhardt's own research, which had initially been confined to the area of fever research, now expanded to include infectious diseases of other types.

Healthy prisoners were inoculated with tetanus, anthrax and other diseases, which were then treated in various stages of development. A special class of experiments comprised those using pregnant women.

The only thing which was at a complete standstill was Dr. Fritze's work on the big euthanasia program with which Dr. Scholz had charged him one evening approximately two years before. Whether this was because the time was not yet ripe for it, or whether it was due to Dr. Fritze's incompetence, at any rate the program came not one step closer to realization.

Otherwise the only change within the prison was that in the course of the last year Dr. Reynhardt, out of all the camp personnel, had become the man most hated by the prisoners. The tall, genial scientist with the narrow, handsome face found himself at the focal point for the rays of several thousand prisoners' hatred. And it was now months since he had entered a ward or walked across the courtyard without an armed escort of two or three men.

And Max was gone.

Earlier that spring he had been present at one of Dr. Eger's operations, an experimental amputation done on a healthy Russian farm girl. Dr. Reynhardt was there. But the Estonian was no longer nauseated. After the operation Max went into the ammunition depot. He sat down alone on a crate and began to smoke. After a while a guard came along.

"Come out!" said the guard.

"Shut up!" replied Max.

"There's no smoking here!" said the guard.

"You go to hell!" said Max.

"Well," said the guard, turning to the door, "I'm reporting the matter."

As he was walking toward the exit, Max picked up a submachine gun and shot him down from behind.

The bullet went in between his shoulder blades.

When Max came out the door, he ground out his cigarette butt carefully with his foot. It was finished now.

The Balt went up and reported to the camp commandant. His fair, youthful face was marked with unnaturally deep wrinkles.

"There has been a fatal accident," he said and clicked his heels. "An accidental shooting."

"Accidental shooting?" said the commandant.

"Yes, an accidental shooting," repeated Max. "It was one of these damned wobbly submachine guns…."

The matter was never completely cleared up. Human judgment failed to find a reason why Max should have shot his comrade. Still, the affair didn't smell good.

Max was demoted and transferred to a Wehrmacht division on its way to the Eastern Front.

"Too bad!" said Dr. Eger. "Just when he was beginning to be useful."

But despite the scientific progress the morale among the doctors was not good that spring. And it got worse as summer approached.

At night, when the camp was quiet, and if a west wind was blowing, you could at once hear both the nightingale and the artillery from the Western Front. It had come very close now. The doctors were irritated and nervous.

Therefore it felt almost like a relief when Dr. Reynhardt was arrested. The air was so laden that every event had something of a deliverance about it.

A batch of documents belonging to the doctor had been confiscated from the baggage of a Swiss traveler. The documents contained an inventory of almost all the experiments which Dr. Reynhardt had completed since he began work in the camp.

Under interrogation the doctor explained that the dispatch was an attempt to preserve the results of his work, should enemy troops get so close as to necessitate burning the records.

Dr. Reynhardt was removed as doctor and interned in the camp. But because of his services, and the other prisoners' attitude toward him, he was interned in a separate area.

He was allowed to keep his own most necessary personal possessions, and had a room of his own, strictly separated from all others.

Within his own private barbed-wire fence he enjoyed the advantages of a certain freedom of moment, along with freedom from work.

But the internment of Dr. Reynhardt lasted only three weeks.

଼ ଓ

A LL DAY THE TWO MEN in the concrete cell under the laundry had noticed that something was afoot. The incessant uproar, the running, the shrieking—the cessation of all shouts of command, the cessation of all muster for work, the shooting which came steadily nearer; nothing needed explanation any longer.

"It's clear that they're evacuating the camp," said one of them, the one with the crushed hand. And his emaciated, deathly pale face smiled weakly.

The words were the end of a conversation they had been having.

And the other merely looked at him. He was lying on the floor, with nothing between the cement and himself. It was over two months since he had been able to stand on his legs.

Just then they heard the footsteps on the stairs.

"Are there any more down here?" said one of the voices from outside.

"There's six of 'em down 'ere inna cellar," answered another. "Two in one an' four in the other."

They heard the key being inserted and turned in the door of the next cell.

Then they heard the blows and the shrieks. More blows, groans, and at last only a little gurgling. A man's voice cursed for a long time afterward.

Then they began on the door of these two.

"Ya got the keys?" said the lightest of the voices.

"Hell!" replied the other. "Now they'll be leaving soon."

Then one of them ran up the stairs, with long, diminishing steps. And for a while it was utterly still.

The two inside the cell didn't look at each other. Then the steps came back— down the stairs.

"We gotta hurry!" said the one voice outside. The key slid easily into the lock. It opened quickly. And three men in green uniforms came in. One of them stopped in the doorway.

"You better come as soon as you're done," he said. "We're ready to leave now!"

He turned around and left.

Of the two who remained, one went over to the man lying on the cement floor. He turned the rifle in his hand and used the butt as a weapon.

Twice he thrust with all his might. Then he straightened up. Not a sound had come from the sick man. But the head was no longer a human head. Then he turned the rifle around and stuck the bayonet through the prisoner's chest.

The other prisoner was also lying on the floor now. He was blinded by the blood running down over his face. But he was groaning loudly.

And the officer, stooping over him, raised his gun again and aimed carefully.

"Hell!" he said to the other. "I missed."

He thrust twice again. And both blows landed where he wanted them.

When he had broken both the prisoner's legs, he pushed the butt into his face with all his might. Then he turned the weapon so that the bayonet was down.

But the other—the soldier with the light voice—was already out in the cellar corridor.

"Damn it, come on!" he called back. "Now they're leaving!"

And the officer looked at the prisoner. He was lying on his back, wholly still now. And the man with the rifle suddenly saw the tip of his own well-shined shoe beside the bloody face. He quickly drew back his foot.

He shouldn't have taken hold of the butt when he turned the rifle, he thought. Now it was too late. He had got dirty again. With annoyance he pulled off the ruined white glove and threw it on the floor.

Then he heard the other one running up the stairs. And without another thought he ran after him.

The six men who had remained to hand the camp over to the advancing allies were well armed, but they were a laughably small force. Practically as soon as the sound of the last column of thundering trucks had died away, the rebellion began.

When the prisoners had understood that almost the whole SS crew had been evacuated, they collected all the work tools they could find.

With amazing calm they set about removing the barbed wire barriers with picks, shovels and wooden stakes. But when connection with the other part of the camp had been achieved, there was an end to the quiet and order which had seemed to reign for awhile.

The SS contingent's abandoned food stores unleashed, as if on an agreed signal, total war between the strongest of the prisoners, while the weaker, the sick, and those who had suffered most from undernourishment, were shoved aside from the very first moment.

When the healthiest had satisfied their most gnawing bodily hunger, there appeared another hunger, of the soul—the lust for reprisals for years of torture and humiliation. And in the course of half an hour the six remaining SS man reaped the fruits of their previous work in the camp. Only a couple hours later was Dr. Reynhardt found and recognized.

Still panting from his dash across the courtyard, the doctor found his way down into the cellar under the laundry. But from the minute he realized that the key was still in the lock, and that the door could be locked from the inside, he was already clear that it would merely mean a postponement—perhaps for no more than a few minutes. Right afterwards he heard the voices from outside, the loud, excited shrieks—and the strange resonance, the echo produced by the acoustics in the cellar corridor. Still it was a while before they found suitable tools with which to open the heavy door.

And as the axe's first blows crashed into the oaken wood, the doctor discovered that he wasn't the only living person in the room. Of the two prisoners lying on the cement floor, one was not yet dead. He was a large, well-built man, but emaciated as a skeleton, and badly beaten up. He lay stretched out on his back, but both legs were unnaturally twisted sideways below his knees. A few gray threads of hair and beard protruded through the blood congealed on his head and neck. The doctor bent down and felt the pulse in the left wrist. And as he looked at the crushed metacarpal bones in the hand, he heard the shriek of splintering wood. The fingers were whole and untouched. Then the sound grew stronger.

"It's him!" shouted the first of the men. And, crowbar in hand, he squeezed through the opening in the door. He noticed distantly that his pantleg was torn by something sharp lodged in one of the boards. Stooping, he headed for the man who knelt on the cement floor. Then he grasped the warm, bent iron rod with both hands. But the doctor didn't even turn his head to avoid the blow.

After the prisoners had opened the camp, three days passed before the Allied forces arrived.

The British sanitation officer with the narrow blond face knelt down by the two men lying together on the cellar floor.

"Dead," he said. "He's stiff already."

He got a good grip on the dead man and turned him over, so that he lay with half-open eyes turned up to the ceiling.

The two men standing at the splintered door had come further into the cellar room. One of them was wearing an American private's uniform. And the other had drawn an English military jacket over his ragged prison garb.

The one in prison garb bent forward.

"That one lying there," he said in German, "is the greatest swine who ever walked on God's green earth."

The officer looked down at the chiseled, dead face. Then he slowly drew a red leather purse from under the dead man's arm. It took a little time, for the red strap was twisted around the rigid, snow-white wrist. Carefully he opened the purse and emptied the contents out onto the cement floor.

There was a toothbrush, a shaving brush and a razor. A photograph lay with the blank side up. The cardboard was greasy and dirty.

The officer turned it over and held it up to the light from the grated cellar window. It was a picture of a women in her forties and a blond, half-grown boy. Then he put the things back in the leather purse. He handed it to the American.

"We'd better send it to the widow," he said. He pulled the dead man all the way to the side, and bent over the man lying underneath.

"Hallo!" he cried suddenly. "He's alive!"

Under the battered head someone had laid a white glove. And while he examined the man, he slowly turned red in the face. Several minutes elapsed before he spoke.

"Good Lord!" he said. "Good Lord!"

He looked up at the other.

"He must have been lying like this for three days!"

Then he knelt behind the head and grasped the man carefully under the arms. The American and the German had come very near now. They bent down. The American slipped the strap of the leather purse over his wrist. In that way he freed up both hands.

And together they carried the unconscious man out of the cell.

Only on the cellar stairs did they notice how heavy he was.

JENS BJØRNEBOE

Ere the Cock Crows:

THE PLAY

An attempt to reconstruct
Bjorneboe's original play of 1949 (now lost)
from the novel of 1952

Reconstruction done in English translation
by Esther Greenleaf Mürer

CAST

SS Standartenführer Paul Heidebrand
Dr. Heinrich Reynhardt
Gerda Reynhardt, his wife
Claus Reynhardt, his son
Fräulein Emm'chen Reynhardt, his sister
Max
Aide
Dr. Schotz
Dr. Fritze
Dr. Eger
Schneider, a newspaper editor

ACT I

*A big, largely empty room. Lemon-colored wall. Windows curtainless, white-
washed, covered from outside. A large radio set under one window and
a small coke oven further along the wall. Three unshaded electric bulbs
provide light. The opposite wall covered with filing shelves from floor
to ceiling. The only furniture is a desk, on which there are three large
glasses, a bottle of French cognac, and a stack of papers.*

*HEIDEBRAND sitting behind the desk. (Powerfully built, plump, with
dark-blond, close-cropped hair showing a bullet-shaped head. Wearing
black SS uniform.) Before him in the middle of the floor the AIDE
and MAX also in SS uniforms, but subordinates, stand at attention.
The AIDE, tall and thin, is in his forties. MAX is a boy of eighteen,
with a square, pale face and ash blond, Baltic hair. Medium height,
unusually broad-shouldered Despite the deep wrinkles in his face he
does not look older than he is. He stands unsteadily, swaying.*

HEIDEBRAND: Do you know if any of the vaccination records
were *not* brought up to date?

AIDE *(as if reading from a book)*: Jawohl, Standartenführer! The transients are not included in the statistics. But all the fever experiments are registered and entered in the records.

HEIDEBRAND *(suddenly alert)*: What does "transient" mean?

AIDE: That is the designation for those who are inoculated with the
disease just so they will have it. They aren't vaccinated first. Dr.
Eger says that he keeps the bacteria cultures alive in them, so that
one can just help oneself when infectious matter is needed.

HEIDEBRAND *(ponders. Gesturing toward the window)*: Have *the ones out
there* learned the song?

MAX: It took a couple hours, but now them's singin' just fine.
(Quickly leans forward to keep his balance.)

HEIDEBRAND (*consults a paper. To AIDE*): Were there more doctors involved in the experiments besides those listed here?

AIDE: Jawohl, Standartenführer! A Danish doctor took part in the experiments, but he hasn't been here for a long time now.

HEIDEBRAND (*looks at his wristwatch. To MAX*): Obergruppenführer Dr. Scholz should arrive from Berlin before two o'clock. When he gets here, we must have a little night-time roll call and welcome him with the song. We can let them sing it a couple times first. He'll appreciate it.

(MAX *clicks his heels, fighting to stay upright.*)

HEIDEBRAND: Were you present at all the experiments for the Air Force?

MAX (*trying to sound sober*): No.

AIDE (*coming to his rescue):* Not all of them, Standartenführer!

HEIDEBRAND: I don't mean every single experiment, but at all the different *types.*

MAX: I was only at the frost and pressure experiments. But not the others.

AIDE: You can be glad of that.

HEIDEBRAND (*to AIDE, after a pause*): Did *you* attend all of them?"

AIDE (*thinks about it, then counts on his fingers*): Let's see: Air—one! The dry frost experiments—two! The wet frost experiments—three! Then we have the shipwreck experiments with salt water—four! Then there were the ones with distilled salt water! That's five. Chemical salt water—six! The others—the ones with mustard gas and the surgical experiments, they were for the Army. But I've been at all the types of experiments for the Air Force, yes.

HEIDEBRAND: Drink! Help yourselves!

(*The AIDE and MAX march forward in unison, lift half-filled glasses and drink simultaneously. The AIDE finishes first, and sets down his glass half-empty. MAX drains his, struggling to stand upright when tilting the glass toward the ceiling. He sets it down on one of HEIDEBRAND's papers.*)

HEIDEBRAND (*pushing the glass aside with irritation*): But then we have a clear overview. (*Ironically.*) That leaves just a few little things! To begin with, the wagon. It was hermetically sealed, so that the air pressure could be varied. And a window was built into it, so that one could see how the prisoner acted when the air pressure sank. How low could the pressure go inside the wagon?

AIDE (*to MAX, after a pause*): Do you remember how low it could go? Dr. Eger explained it once.

MAX: The air pressure corresponded to twenty-one kilometers above sea level.

HEIDEBRAND: Could the temperature be varied at the same time?

AIDE: No.

HEIDEBRAND: So one couldn't do frost and pressure experiments simultaneously. That's too bad, because in fact you usually have to protect yourself against both at the same time.

AIDE: Dr. Eger thought that it was easiest to work with them separately.

HEIDEBRAND: It's certainly *easiest*, yes. But for us here the point isn't whether it's easy or not…. Then there were the frost experiments. They were intended to establish exactly how much cold a human being can stand, and then to arrive at the best methods of treatment after the frostbite? Is that right?

AIDE: Yes.

HEIDEBRAND: The experiments in ice water I'm familiar with. But how did the "dry" experiments go? Only the results are written up here. Drink now, boys!

MAX (*fills his glass, drains it, points toward window*): They was just put on a stretcher and set outside.

HEIDEBRAND: And there they lay?

MAX: No, they hadda be tied to the stretchers, 'cause they din't have no clothes on—'sides it was kinda cold.

HEIDEBRAND (*gulping*): How long did they lie like that?

AIDE: They lay there from a few hours to all day and all night. And then their temperature was taken—well, the ones who got chloroform had their temperature monitored the whole time, 'cause of course we couldn't tell when they fainted.

HEIDEBRAND (*surprised*): They got chloroform?

MAX: Yeah, Dr. Eger, he couldn't get to sleep! Hah!

HEIDEBRAND: *They* got chloroform so *Dr. Eger* could get some sleep?

MAX (*with a nasty grin*): And daytimes they couldn't get no peace to work, not him or Dr. Fritze!

HEIDEBRAND: Did it disturb them so much to think of the prisoners lying out there? Imagine the doctors being so sensitive!

(*The AIDE and MAX roar with laughter.*)

AIDE: Well, the subjects screamed so horribly.

MAX (*thickly, very drunk*): Yeah, they screamed so loud it was hell to listen to for everybody 'round. Ten, twelve of 'em at once. Wasn't easy to sleep when we was doing the dry 'sperments!

HEIDEBRAND (*looking down*): Yes, I see. But the chloroform helped?

AIDE: Yes, there was just a little gurgling still.

HEIDEBRAND: The death rate?

MAX: A damn sight more'n half of 'em went up. Through the chimley….

AIDE: Nearly seventy percent.

HEIDEBRAND (*pours more brandy, then puts the bottle in a cupboard*): Please drink…. Then there were the salt water experiments. All that's recorded here are ages, daily rations, results, and so on. I don't suppose they proceeded quietly either?

AIDE: No, I should say not! They squealed like stuck pigs. Some of 'em went crazy, too.

HEIDEBRAND: Those who got salt water screamed the most, I assume?

AIDE: Yes, so long as they could. They got even thirstier from the salt. Yecch! Makes me thirsty just to think of it. (*Takes a long swig of cognac.*)

(*MAX staggers around the room, knocks over a chair, kneels in front of the radio and fiddles with it, finally tuning it very loud, midway between two stations, playing a tango and a Schubert melody at the same time. He struggles to his feet, drags the upturned chair across the floor, sets it up in front of the desk and sits down, facing HEIDEBRAND.*)

HEIDEBRAND: Are you comfortable?

(*MAX doesn't reply; his face sinks down to his chest with a jerk.*)

AIDE (*still standing at attention*): He gets drunk fast. He ain't no mamma's boy. When we were doing the pressure experiments for the Air Force, two of the other orderlies fainted—even if they'd been in the service for a long time. Those fellows were much older than him. But Max, he took it like a man! He just threw up. Hah! (*Bends down and pats sleeping boy on shoulder.*)

MAX (*mumbling*): Go 'way!

AIDE: Just listen! After all, he ain't but a lad!

HEIDEBRAND (*kicking MAX on the shin under the table*): Up with you, Max! You've rested enough. Up, I say!

MAX (*getting up and standing at attention, now steady on his feet*): Jawohl, Standartenführer.

HEIDEBRAND: So, you took it like a man?

AIDE (*from the filing shelves*): Max takes everything like a man.

HEIDEBRAND (*looking at MAX with intense distaste*): And so you only threw up?

MAX: There was one of 'em wasn't dead. Woke up while Eger was cutting into 'im. But Eger he just went on, and so I had to hold 'im. I threw up on the floor, but I di'n't let go of 'im.

HEIDEBRAND: Dr. Eger didn't say anything about your throwing up?

MAX: No. Dr. Eger just said it did me good to see what Jews looked like inside. (*Sobering*) But there wasn't no trick to holding him, 'cause after all he din't have no strength left.

HEIDEBRAND (*sholds up a sheet of paper*): And here are some more who'll be screaming soon.

AIDE: Is that the list of research subjects? As a matter of fact, I'm familiar with it from before. (*In a confidential tone.*) They'll get theirs next, the ones on that list. They're for the fever experiments. For the moment they're getting extra provisions.

HEIDEBRAND (*astonished*): What?

AIDE: They get full soldier's rations for three weeks first. Or they won't have no resistance. Hah!

(*One of the radio stations has gone off the air. The other is playing a lively polka.*)

HEIDEBRAND: No, of course not. Otherwise the experiments would be worthless, wouldn't they?

AIDE: (*Nods.*)

HEIDEBRAND (*sits motionless for a bit, then bursts into loud, shrill laughter, at times almost falsetto*): Lord! It's just like Hansel and Gretel! First they're fattened up, afterwards they go into the oven. Yes, afterwards they literally go into the oven! (*Bursts out laughing again; the embarrassed AIDE tries to laugh with him. HEIDEBRAND stops, then feels to see if his collar is straight.*) It's about time for Dr. Scholz to arrive. You're so musical, Max, see about putting a little life into them.

MAX: I'm not afraid of night work. But I had too much to drink. I've never been able to stand it. (*furiously*) Hell, I'll make 'em dance!

(*The door opens, and REYNHARDT enters. He is tall and thin. His handsome, nervous face is narrow, with finely chiseled features and a striking tan. Without looking around, he peels off his wet raincoat, revealing a grey suit underneath. MAX and the AIDE click their heels and give the Nazi salute. HEIDEBRAND stands up. REYNHARDT nods, then—after a moment's silence—listens expressionless as the conversation continues.*)

HEIDEBRAND (*to MAX, in a friendly tone*): Have you ever been whipped yourself?

MAX (*exchanges glances with the AIDE, then straightens up*): Jawohl, Standartenführer! As a boy.

HEIDEBRAND: When Dr. Scholz gets here you can both go to bed.

MAX: Thank you, Standartenführer!

HEIDEBRAND: Here we're all comrades. Take the glasses with you!

MAX: Jawohl, Standartenführer! (*He takes two measured steps forward, collects the three glasses on the desk with his left hand, and steps backwards to his place again.*) Can we sleep in tomorrow morning?

HEIDEBRAND: No.

(*Exit MAX and the AIDE, slamming the door after them. For a moment HEIDEBRAND and REYNHARDT stand looking at each other. Then REYNHARDT strides across the room, stopping with his back to the filing shelves.*)

REYNHARDT: You've found your conversational tone.

HEIDEBRAND (*lights a cigarette*): He's a child of the people, Heinrich. They don't appreciate the finer things the way you and I do.

REYNHARDT: May I find something else besides this commercial music?

HEIDEBRAND: I was just going to do so myself.

(*REYNHARDT bends over the radio, finds a Mozart concerto. HEIDEBRAND walks back to the desk, gathers up the papers, crosses and puts in them in pigeonholes. A single sheet remains on the table.*)

REYNHARDT: We keep meeting, Paul. (*Puts on his pince-nez*)

HEIDEBRAND: Yes. Again and again. (*Closes his eyes, listening to the music. Abruptly:*) But always in new circumstances. Have you noticed that, Heinrich? (*Listens some more.*) Providential meeting! How long is it since we've seen each other?

REYNHARDT: Over six years…. And you've been three days in your new position?

HEIDEBRAND (*looks at his watch*): We are two hours into the fourth day. (*More softly*) How's Gerda? I said hello to her a few days ago——

REYNHARDT: Thanks, it's going quite….

(*Loud shouted commands from outside, followed by a rhythmic tramping. They stand listening for a bit to voices going high and low in leaps and large intervals, long pauses and sudden, solo cries against the monotonous sound of boots.*)

REYNHARDT: May I assume that you're doing well?

HEIDEBRAND (*calmly, after a pause*): It's too early for me to say yet. But there's much to learn here, much to fill myself in on. I've been trying especially to acquaint myself with the records from this winter. The scientific work which has been done here, the experiments I mean, seem to have been very interesting.

(*Yells from outside.*)

REYNHARDT: The experiments are of very great significance.

HEIDEBRAND (*lights another cigarette*): And how are things with you? I assume *you're* doing well?

REYNHARDT: I'm not here all that often. Of course, it's exclusively as a scientist that I'm associated with this camp. And just for the fever experiments. My laboratory is in town—it was a surprise to hear that you'd taken over the position.

HEIDEBRAND: It's a long story. (*Closes his eyes, listening to the music*) A story of connections. But I'm here exclusively as an official.

(*More shouted commands from the courtyard. Tramping of boots faster and faster.*)

REYNHARDT (*irritated*): That's nothing to joke about. I am perfectly clear what responsibility my work entails. One day it will indeed save thousands of human lives, but for the research subjects—*now, today*—the tests are both prolonged and painful. And even if it were only for their sakes, it is my duty to ensure that the work is done in a responsible, scientific manner.

HEIDEBRAND: The mortality rate lies around seventy percent?

REYNHARDT: It will decrease—provided that the research is carried through.

HEIDEBRAND (*looks down, then looks REYNHARDT in the eyes*): Do you know anything about the surgical insertions of gangrene and tetanus bacilli?

REYNHARDT: It was Dr. Eger who started those.

HEIDEBRAND: Do you think they're valuable?

REYNHARDT: They can doubtless become so. (*Abruptly turns off the radio. Singing outside&—a large men's chorus.*) Why in the world do you have them sing such mournful songs? This one is almost unbearable.

HEIDEBRAND: It must be a very bloody series of experiments? (*Steps forward and takes him by the arm.*) Lord, Heinrich, this is an unappetizing business.

REYNHARDT: So? (*Sidesteps, pulling his arm away.*)

HEIDEBRAND: Well, I was thinking that it might not be absolutely necessary. At least not so necessary as the fever experiments.

REYNHARDT: Nothing can stop it now.

HEIDEBRAND (*with an open, shameless smile*): With your scientific and
my political influence….

REYNHARDT: I have a responsibility to my family. I can't get mixed
up in adventures. I can't allow myself to be reckless.

HEIDEBRAND: Do you think I'm trying to trap you?

REYNHARDT (*takes off his pince-nez and begins polishing them with his
handkerchief. Coolly*): How in the world should anyone trap me?
I'm a wholly unpolitical person.

HEIDEBRAND: You mean you *were*.

REYNHARDT: I am a doctor.

(*Long silence. Singing continues outside. HEIDEBRAND paces restlessly,
then sits down behind the desk and rests his chin in his hand.*)

HEIDEBRAND: You're so right, Heinrich. It *is* remarkable that we
should meet like this!

REYNHARDT: Yes, it's strange, Paul. After such a long time! (*Pause*)
I didn't know anything about you….

HEIDEBRAND: The funny thing is that we seem to meet at decisive
moments. Isn't there something in chemistry called a catalyst?

REYNHARDT: Yes. Catalyst is the name for a substance which has
the property of being able to accelerate a chemical process which
would have happened anyway—only more slowly.

(*Pause. They look at each other.*)

HEIDEBRAND: Well, well. Anyway, I have good news for you.

REYNHARDT: For *me?*

HEIDEBRAND: Yes. Your membership is in order.

REYNHARDT: What membership?

HEIDEBRAND: Yours.

REYNHARDT: In what?

HEIDEBRAND (*leans back and runs his right hand down the black uniform, patting it lovingly*): In our legion. You're accepted into the order.

REYNHARDT (*takes an involuntary step backward, then walks right up to the desk and bends forward, shouting*): But I've never asked to be accepted!

HEIDEBRAND: Oddly enough you're accepted all the same.

REYNHARDT: But I've never applied. I have never—

HEIDEBRAND: So you'll have to get a uniform. And you'll naturally want it tailor-made it, won't you? You must pay for the sewing yourself at the outset. But later we can doubtless find some line on the books to charge it to.

REYNHARDT: I haven't applied.

HEIDEBRAND: Don't forget about the tailor. You must see about getting your measurements taken as soon as possible.

REYNHARDT: Hell, no! I said I haven't applied!

HEIDEBRAND: Calm down, Heinrich! (*Smiling*) If you don't like our black uniform, you can always wear your white lab coat over it! (*Pushes back his chair and jumps up. From outside a couple of sharp cries, followed by singing.*) There he is! Now the doctor is coming!

(*A moment of silence. The door opens abruptly, and the AIDE appears in the doorway.*)

AIDE: Obergruppenführer Dr. Scholz! (*Exit*)

(*Pause. Enter DR. SCHOLZ, followed by DR. FRITZE and DR. EGER. All wear the SS uniform. DR. SCHOLZ is stout man in his sixties. He bears a high-ranking insignia and several decorations. DR. FRITZE is young and blond, also with insignia. DR. EGER is in his forties and very swarthy. He is wearing a white lab coat over his uniform.*)

HEIDEBRAND, REYNHARDT and the three newcomers all shake each other's hands and introduce themselves by name and title. The ritual finished, they group themselves respectfully around DR. SCHOLZ. He looks around, listens for a moment to the singing outside, and smiles at HEIDEBRAND.)

SCHOLZ: Wonderful song, Heidebrand! Is it new?

HEIDEBRAND (*smiling*): It's new *here*, but actually it's very old.

SCHOLZ: They sing it just splendidly!

HEIDEBRAND: We have such musical prisoners. And then we have Max, too—to put some life into them!

   (*FRITZE and EGER laugh*)

SCHOLZ: Max?

FRITZE (*laughing*): Yes, Max can make them sing, all right!

EGER: We also make them sing—in our way!

(*All laugh except REYNHARDT, who appears to be feeling extremely uncomfortable with the company in which he finds himself.*)

SCHOLZ: I don't have the pleasure of knowing Max. But I understand that his acquaintance must be worth having.

HEIDEBRAND (*drily*): He's one of our boys, Oberführer! He's a Balt, an Estonian—and Dr. Eger has him as a trainee at present.

EGER: We'll make something of him yet, but first we have to work

on him awhile. He's still a bit of a nature boy. But Lord, he's so
young!

(*HEIDEBRAND goes over to the filing shelves and finds a file which he
lays on the desk. Then he goes quietly up to SCHOLZ and taps him
on the shoulder.*)

HEIDEBRAND: If you could spare me a moment first, Herr Oberführer?

SCHOLZ: Of course, of course. (*They go over to the desk and whisper over
the papers.*)

EGER (*to REYNHARDT*): How is your son, Herr Doktor? I hope
that he continues to get better?

REYNHARDT (*with reserve*): Yes, thank you, he's making progress.

EGER: After all, he must be getting the best possible treatment!

REYNHARDT: I'm not a neurologist.

EGER (*smiling*): I would be glad to turn over any kind of case to you,
Dr. Reynhardt.

REYNHARDT (*coldly*): I don't doubt it. But I doubt if just any patient would get the same benefit from it.

SCHOLZ (*loudly, crossing to REYNHARDT with outstretched hand*): May
I congratulate you, Herr Doktor!

REYNHARDT: On what, Herr Oberführer?

SCHOLZ: On your membership, of course! Of course, we too
should be congratulated. It is an uncommonly great pleasure to
acquire a colleague of your scientific standing.
(*EGER and FRITZE congratulate REYNHARDT. SCHOLZ
crosses and leans against the wall with arms folded and eyes closed. The
others quiet down, and stare expectantly at him.*)

SCHOLZ (*clears throat, opens eyes, looks around, then draws himself up*):
And so to business, gentlemen! This time there is in fact an
order from the Führer which we are to receive. It is definitely
the so-called euthanasia program which stands on our doorstep.
This has long been a matter close to the Führer's heart. The
code name for the project will be: "Catalyst." You know that
the Greeks (I mean the ancient Greeks), like the early Germanic
tribes, used to "expose" their sickly and deformed children in
the woods. That's what they did in those times which laid the
foundation for the later, great ancient and Germanic cultures.
It was done while the peoples were still young. It was done to
prevent those of inferior stock from burdening the national body
and genetic substance. In other words, it was done for reasons of
racial hygiene.

Today, gentlemen, we are once again facing the formation of
a new culture. And we are aware of the task which confronts us.
We know that our movement, whether it is victorious or not, is a
harbinger of those cultures which belong to the future. Under *all
circumstances*, gentlemen, it is that. We pioneers, we who are present at this beginning, we bear the responsibility for that which is
to come. The future shall hibernate in us!

This is not about *ourselves*, gentlemen! We are servants. Our
task is to ensure the evolution of a race which shall give birth
to the future. And this race must be tilled like a field. It must be
weeded and tended. It must be cultivated in its purity. We are
gardeners, and our first task is a negative one. We must get rid of
the inferior genetic material. Already nature herself is working
in this direction. We shall merely assist. What is destined for destruction must be destroyed. The Germanic national body must
be cleansed and purified. But—we will no longer be exposing
children.

Today we have other means.

In 1935 the Führer received a letter from a father in Berlin.
The man begged leave to take the life of his deformed and imbecile child. The child was completely misshapen and would never
have become a human being. Well, he got permission. "Mercy
killing" we called it back then. That was the first case. Next the
euthanasia program was worked out theoretically. And then came
a difficult time. Everything was kept secret, and the program

had to work invisibly. In one of the homes, for example, we had twenty-five Jewish children. That was in '39, and we still had to take into account the foreign press and—above all, certain gentlemen in one of our neutral neighboring countries. The children had to die quietly and naturally. (*Draws a blue silk handkerchief out of his pocket and wipes the sweat from his brow and eyes, then surveys the listeners, smiling*) How do you suppose we managed it?

(*EGER puts his hand halfway up. SCHOLZ nods at him.*)

EGER: They starved them to death?

SCHOLZ (*smiling*): And if so—*how*? (*Silence*)

EGER: Hm—by cutting off their food supply?

(*SCHOLZ smiles, waves for the others to come closer. All do, except REYNHARDT, who looks down, unmoving.*)

SCHOLZ: No, *not* by cutting off the food supply. We merely cut down the daily ration—a little each day, until it finally came below the subsistence level. And then we kept it there. In practice this meant that each child had to have a precisely measured, definite number of calories per day. Each case had to be treated separately. But the payoff—and *this* is the main point, gentlemen! (*raises his index finger and looks around the circle*) The payoff was that one could have opened every single one of the children afterward, and one would have found the remains of food in their intestines! (*Pauses, takes a few deep breaths, mops his forehead*)

It takes imagination to picture what this meant in practice. Something which today we could have accomplished in half an hour, as late as '39 had to be dragged out over several weeks. Quite aside from the screaming! You can imagine what it cost in time and money. But we learned a lot from it. We gained real understanding from it.

I've mentioned this, gentlemen, to show how we began. It is probably new to most of you. But today, of course, things are luckily quite different. We are armed with all of modern science's technology and objectivity. And on this objectivity everything depends. We have no time for sentimentality. The program which goes into effect as of this evening, and which in the future will be realized on a steadily greater scale—for this program *I* bear the responsibility. (*Looking at the others*) I! I bear the full, human, medical and political responsibility. *I!*

EGER: May I ask what main categories the project will cover?

SCHOLZ: Yes, my friend—that you may! (*Pause*) It will be first and foremost: imbeciles, schizophrenics, mentally ill in general, and then the deformed and crippled and incurably ill who are unfit to work. In general, we will be removing inferior and superfluous human material. A certain number of war casualties we will regretfully be treating in the same way, along with two large population groups: the Jews and the Gypsies. That is the list. (*Looks around expectantly*)

FRITZE (*eagerly, fumbling for words*): And the technical side of it? The means of death, I mean—the cremation of the bodies? I mean, the development of the system itself? Has any decision been made about that? (*Looks around nervously, wiping his palms on his jacket*)

SCHOLZ: I'm glad, really glad you asked about that, Dr. Fritze. It is in fact our main concern at the moment. (*Looks around, fixing on REYNHARDT, who is still detached. Louder, addressing FRITZE*) It is first and foremost the technical side we must agree on here. The thing is that the [project] must be kept secret.
   (*Turns to HEIDEBRAND, who is very tense*) I've been thinking along the lines of creating big collection points all over the country. They must be built with crematoria. But to prevent the accumulation of too many people at once—which could attract too much attention—both the laboratories and the crematoria must have a relatively large capacity. It would be best if people could be liquidated the same day they arrive. So these stations must be a kind of factory. (*Pause*) The extermination method is a problem in itself. We can't let them go straight into the oven. They must be killed or stunned first, and that will prolong the process. The obvious solutions are gas or some kind of injection—*but. . .* it's

possible that someone may find better and cheaper solutions!

(*Smiles at Dr. FRITZE, who is now consciously playing the role of the youthful enthusiast. Then turns to the other doctors in turn, and finally addresses HEIDEBRAND again*): This killing procedure must under no circumstances be wholly mechanized, for we must not forget the double role these stations will come to play: first and foremost as extermination facilities, and secondly—and this is no less important!—secondly as training grounds for people we will need in the future.

Very young people can do a kind of military service at these stations, and we will be able in a relatively short time to harden them to a degree of callousness which we cannot imagine today. The main thing, gentlemen, is to begin the experimental spade-work as fast as possible. (*Leans against the wall with eyes closed, resting*)

EGER: It's a far-reaching plan.

FRITZE: Impressive! Now we have a real task ahead of us!

SCHOLZ (*pulling himself together*): Since Dr. Eger has taken over the direction of the surgical researches, I'm entrusting the administration of this work to you, Dr. Fritze. You seem to have a particular interest in it. And Dr. Reynhardt will follow it with his interest and good advice. (*To REYNHARDT*): You will be so kind as to keep an eye on the methodology, will you not, Herr Doktor?

(*REYNHARDT looks up without replying. His face has a tormented expression. He fumbles for his pince-nez and clamps them on the bridge of his nose.*)

SCHOLZ (*with exaggerated kindness*): Do you have concerns, Dr. Reyn-hardt?"

(*Silence. The others are following the incident wide-eyed. REYN-HARDT takes off his pince-nez again, draws out his handkerchief and polishes them, looking around.*)

REYNHARDT: If these things—ahem!—if these things are not handled with discretion, they will lead to the creation of rumors and an atmosphere of panic. (*Looks around the circle, polishes his glasses again and sticks them slowly back in his pocket.*) In the hands of inappropriate persons they can cause irreparable harm.

SCHOLZ: Don't worry about it, Dr. Reynhardt. I shall take care of the discretion.... Now let's think of other things! For example— *for example* of how our taking the first steps to actualize the euthanasia program means far more than mere material progress. The euthanasia project is the symbol of an intellectual victory. (*Warming to the subject*) Yes, I will go so far as to say that it is first and foremost a symbol. It confirms that we—humanity—have finally become masters in our own house. We have overcome the deep, subconscious inhibitions, the old taboos which have hitherto stood in the way of carrying out such a relatively natural thing. We have taken a step which no cultured people before us have dared to carry to its full conclusion. We are the first fully mature beings nature has produced. The day the euthanasia program becomes a reality is the new humanity's secret birthday!

A scientist, a *scientist* who is privileged to take part in this, he must feel proud! The meeting of science with the practical man has made it possible to consciously set the future to rights—to create the biological and psychological preconditions for a future the way *we* want it! Oh, he who takes part in this, he must feel proud! (*Looks around, raising his hand like a standard-bearer.*) Proud, gentlemen! Proud!

(*HEIDEBRAND bends down to the cupboard behind the desk, and takes out a bottle of cognac and five small glasses, which he places on the desk and begins filling slowly and carefully.*)

SCHOLZ: Are there more questions? (*Pause*)

REYNHARDT: I find a serious problem in the business itself. May I be permitted to mention it?

SCHOLZ (*coldly*): Please!

REYNHARDT: What about the euthanasia project's purely juridical basis?

SCHOLZ (*immediately smiling again; raises a finger and looks around in a didactic manner*): It's strange that a scientist with no political training should be the one to pose such a question. But it's even stranger that none of the others present asked it first. For that is one of the most important points of all! (*Pause, looking around*) I can assure everyone here that our lawyers at the Department of Justice have long since taken care of the juridical side of the matter. (*Pause*) What is your attitude to the plan on a purely emotional level, Dr. Reynhardt?

(*All but REYNHARDT are startled by the question. HEIDEBRAND looks up from filling the glasses.*)

REYNHARDT: I am of the opinion that one should restrict one's emotional life to the sphere where it has validity. (*Emphasizing his words*) I believe that it should be restricted to one's private life— yes, perhaps to one's family life. One must draw *very* clear lines here.

SCHOLZ: Splendid! That is a most important point of view—both scientifically and politically. (*To HEIDEBRAND*) You have not expressed yourself, Standartenführer?

HEIDEBRAND (*bowing and smiling*): I have my duties as host, Oberführer! And first among them is to keep a decent cognac. The only thing I could add to what Dr. Reynhardt has said would be a few little things I found while going through the books. (*Gesturing toward glasses*) May I? I can really recommend it! My predecessor sold some of the ashes from the crematorium as fertilizer to the farmers in the neighborhood. And he got a rather large sum for it, as a matter of fact.

(*The others take their glasses from the desk and hold them, awaiting HEIDEBRAND's further words.*)

HEIDEBRAND: I should think that something similar could be done with the waste products from the euthanasia facilities.

EGER (*holding cognac glass under his nose and inhaling deeply*): Mm—ahh! Wonderful old cognac! (*All drink*) Ahh! Lovely!

HEIDEBRAND (*smiling into his glass*): I always do what I can to keep
a good cognac. This one is older than you are, Dr. Eger…. But
the facilities will of course entail production on a much larger
scale—so one may perhaps expect them to pay for themselves,
once they have got going? (*Looks at Dr. SCHOLZ*)

SCHOLZ: Your proposals are just as distinguished as the cognac you
are holding. Do you have more?

HEIDEBRAND: Only cognac for the moment. (*Reaches backward to
the desk, finds bottle, crosses and refills SCHOLZ's glass, then the others,
still speaking*) More proposals will surely come with time! (*smiling*)
And besides—this thing with delivering the ashes to agriculture
almost has something pious about it! The deceased will get the
opportunity to rehabilitate themselves with regard to society.
They will be of use! They will pay for their own burials, so to
speak. Yes, one can say that their lives have borne—if not exactly
fruit—then at any rate cabbage and potatoes!

(*All laugh loudly, except for Dr. REYNHARDT and HEIDEB-
RAND himself. All drink. SCHOLZ and REYNHARDT
engage in conversation, the ill will between them quite gone.*)

HEIDEBRAND (*to EGER*): I would like to be present at one of the
experimental operations. When is the next one scheduled?

EGER: Well, we have a transplant operation early tomorrow. It will
be very interesting…. We're using one of these Polish girls. (*Pauses, reflecting*) They have great vitality, those Polacks. It wouldn't
surprise me if they started growing new limbs…. After we've
taken something away, I mean. We begin tomorrow morning at
nine o'clock.

HEIDEBRAND: It will be interesting to see some of this for myself.

(*A long pause.*)

SCHOLZ (*Breaking the silence*): I can't say how happy I am about this
collaboration, Dr. Reynhardt. Indeed, I can't find words for it!

But you know what? I felt in my bones all along that you would really go for this thing!

EGER (*to SCHOLZ*): It's late. And if the conference is over—is it? Dr. Fritze and I have had a long working day. And we have a day ahead of us tomorrow.

SCHOLZ: Good Lord! Go to bed at once! You need it, gentlemen! And sleep well. Good night, good night!

(*Exit FRITZE and EGER*)

HEIDEBRAND (*bent over the radio, gets a clear flute tone*): Mozart again!

(*Pause*)

SCHOLZ: But the three of us must go into town for the night! (*Wearily*) Lord, we really have to get going.

HEIDEBRAND: I'll get a car. (*Exits*)

SCHOLZ (*closes eyes, and gradually begins to sway in time to the music. Fumbling for words*): Lord, how pure and clear it is!... These pure, utterly pure single notes...one and one...(*Gestures as if trying to catch the notes between his fingertips. Aroused*): This is heaven, Dr. Reynhardt, this is heaven! So endlessly pure...this is blessedness, blessedness and purity! Oh, such unending purity! (*Silence. Opens eyes*) How are things with your family, Dr. Reynhardt? Is your son better?

REYNHARDT (*who has been watching SCHOLZ with astonishment, smiles boyishly*): He's making progress. But it takes time.... You know what a shock it was, and at his tender age! Besides he has an unusually sensitive emotional makeup. (*Pause*) Do you know that when he was a child he would throw up if he saw any of the boys fighting in the schoolyard?! He actually vomited when the others were fighting!

SCHOLZ (*smiling, calmly*): He takes after you, then?

REYNHARDT: Yes, he takes after me. And besides, you have to consider what a miracle it was that it happened just as it did! It actually exploded only a few yards away from him! But now at least he's reached the point of beginning to play the piano again.

SCHOLZ (*grasps REYNHARDT by the arm*) I sincerely wish him everything good in life! Including a complete recovery!

REYNHARDT: And how are things with your own family, Dr. Scholz?

SCHOLZ (*with a happy, embarrassed smile*): It has gotten bigger…. My wife is much younger than I am. My second son was born four days ago.

REYNHARDT: Well, congratulations! And mother and child are fine?

SCHOLZ: Yes, they're just fine! He's a big strapping fellow. (*Laughs*) He has a voice like a brass trumpet! (*Takes REYNHARDT by the shoulder and turns him around, pointing at Hitler's portrait on the wall over the desk. Lowers his voice*): Can you believe that he—*he!*—sent me a private telegram of good wishes!—And my wife a *marvelous* (*extending his arms*)…a marvelous bouquet of roses….Can you imagine him finding the time and strength to think about something like that? About me and my small private affairs! When you just think of all a man like him has to do… (*Shakes head, shrugs helplessly*) Yes, I—I… (*Turns to the radio and falls silent. Then, rapturously*): Dr. Reynhardt! Oh—Dr. Reynhardt! *Listen* to this rondo!

HEIDEBRAND (*opens door and stops on threshold*): Excuse me, but the car is ready.

ACT II

Scene 1

*A music room in a house. Sofa, chairs, grand piano. The window shows
the roofs of the houses opposite in the late afternoon sun against a
darkening sky. CLAUS is seated at the piano, practicing a piece by
Schubert. His figure is thin and delicate, contrasting with his firm and
decisive manner of playing. GERDA in the doorway, leaning against
the doorframe, listening, a dustcloth in her hand.*

GERDA: I think something completely new has come into your playing since you were sick. You play more clearly.

CLAUS (*turns to her and smiles. Stops playing, lets his hands rest a moment on
the keys, then carefully closes the lid*): They say that at the conservatory too. I've definitely made progress. (*Looks down*) But, mother,
a usable soldier is something I'll never be.

GERDA (*Dusting*): In this country we have enough soldiers. But supper is ready, my boy. You'd better come and eat.

CLAUS (*stands, gathers up the music*): Well, but they must need others
too? Musicians and…well, scientists, for example. Like Father, I
mean.

GERDA: Yes, more than they need soldiers.

CLAUS: But Mother! One *has* to admire him!—Has he always been
like this? When he was very young, I mean?

GERDA: He wasn't so *very* young when I met him, but he's always
been admirable. I've been proud of him forever…. (*dusting*)
Since you were born I don't think he has thought about much
of anything but us and his work.

CLAUS (*frowning*): I *thought* so! The way he is, you have to be born like that. You can't *become* that way!

GERDA: You know people can become however they want, Claus. If they just *will* it.

CLAUS: Do you believe that? (*Brightens somewhat*) Do you really think that for instance *I* could become like—well, now, like for instance, Father?

GERDA (*hiding a smile*): I'm quite sure of it, Claus.

CLAUS (*grabs GERDA by the arm*): But look! there's something the matter with him!

GERDA: There's something the matter with Father?

CLAUS: Of course there is! He's not happy anymore. Anybody can see that! He was completely different just after he came back— much happier, like.

GERDA (*polishing the table*): Father has too much to do. And then he brings problems from work home with him. For a doctor there's no time off, my boy.

CLAUS: I don't think it's that, Mother. It feels like there's something else— something *weighing* on him. (*Looks out window*) Mother, I think I could do *anything* for him, if it ever came down to that.

GERDA: If you'd do what you could to get well again, that would be the greatest happiness you could give him.

CLAUS: Then I'll do it. But now it's starting to get dark, Mother. Such a fine, fine veil settling over everything. First it almost shines—blue! Then it gets denser and denser, and finally the houses grow blurry. The trees get so thin against the street. Look, it's as melancholy as that waltz of Chopin's!

GERDA: Go and eat, Little Claus—don't just stand there being sad.

CLAUS: I have to laugh every time you say "Little Claus"—it reminds me of that fairy tale!

GERDA: What fairy tale?

CLAUS: The one about Great Claus and Little Claus, of course! The one who gets sewn up in the black sack and thrown into the water.

GERDA: Then I'll never call you "Little Claus" again.

CLAUS (*laughs*): You might as well. After all, there's no Great Claus here. (*Looks out window, then bends forward as if looking down into the street. Makes a face.*) Ugh! There comes one of those insects! One of those in the black uniform.

GERDA (*quickly, crossing to him*): Don't worry about them, my boy. After all, there aren't so many of them these days.

CLAUS: Oh, there are lots.

GERDA (*tries to pull him away from window*): The tea is getting cold, Claus.

CLAUS: You wouldn't believe the things I heard about them when I was outside!

GERDA: People talk so much!

CLAUS (*pointing*): There—down by the chestnut tree!

GERDA: There comes one, sure enough!

CLAUS: He's completely black.

GERDA: Yes—ah. (*Her hand is on his shoulder. Suddenly she lets it fall and straightens up. It is a gesture of the greatest helplessness.*)

CLAUS: But it's *him!* (*Turns, looks searchingly at her. Accusingly*) Does he drop in just like that?

GERDA (*coming away from window*): Oh—yes, he's been here a couple of times now.

CLAUS: But it's only a few weeks since he came to town. (*Looking out window.*)

GERDA (*by piano, putting music in the bench*): Can't you learn to put your music away, then! I always have to pick up after you've been practicing.

CLAUS (*absently*): All right, I'll do that. (*Pause*) Oh! I think it's creepy!

GERDA (*dusting piano keys*): What's creepy?

CLAUS: The uniform.

GERDA: I wouldn't call it that. I just think it's unbecoming.

CLAUS (*decidedly*): No. It's spooky.

GERDA: Can't you go eat, then, my boy!

CLAUS: It's not *my* fault! And then that death's head on the hat, too! What do they mean by *that?*

GERDA: They don't mean anything by it. It's just bad theater, Claus.

CLAUS: But what kind of *people* are they, then?

GERDA (*quietly*): I'll tell you something, Claus. There are all different kinds of people in this world. There's no such thing as "they," there's only "this one" and "that one." And *he* is a person one can very well be acquainted with—at least he used to be.

CLAUS: Has it been many years since you and Father knew him?

GERDA: Oh—yes. Quite a few.

CLAUS: He may have changed.

GERDA (*probing*): Do you think so, Claus?

CLAUS: But you said yourself that people can change.

GERDA: Yes, I did. For the better, I meant.

CLAUS: They can just as well go the other way too!

GERDA: Yes, they can.

CLAUS (*hesitant*): Maybe that's what's happened with Heidebrand?

GERDA: What do you mean, Claus?

CLAUS: That he may have changed for the worse.

GERDA: It's a serious thing to talk like that about a person.

CLAUS: But I only asked a question, Mother! Maybe he didn't have the uniform back then?

GERDA (*gently but firmly*): Perhaps you should get to know him first, Claus, and then judge him afterwards.

CLAUS (*stubbornly*): But did he have the uniform then?

GERDA: At that time there were no such uniforms. They're a more recent thing.

CLAUS (*Pauses, reflecting; then triumphantly*): There, you see! Don't you think that maybe a person's clothes can affect him *inside*?

GERDA (*softly, with irritation*): Tell me, Claus! Have Father and I conducted ourselves toward you in such a manner that you have reason to look upon our friends with suspicion?

CLAUS: But I didn't know that Heidebrand was a friend! If I'd known that, then….(*Stops and stares, then quickly springs forward and grabs her hand.*) But tell me you aren't mad at me, then! For what I said about Heidebrand, I mean!

GERDA: Not at all. But I don't like to hear people judged by the clothes they wear.

(*Doorbell rings. They both jump. GERDA looks uncertain, then smiles*)

GERDA: Now you can meet him!

CLAUS: He must have a high rank?

GERDA: Standartenführer.

CLAUS (*grabbing her hand*): Hey! Tell me a little about him!

GERDA (*laughs, rumpling his hair*): But he's here! It's too late now, Claus. If you'd shown some interest a little sooner, you'd have known a great deal about him by now!

CLAUS: You can tell me more later! But just give me a quick outline. Something that can be filled in later!

GERDA: It's hard, there's so much to tell about him. He was born in Berlin, but then. . . He was kind of a celebrity back then.

CLAUS: He was *famous?*

GERDA (*laughs loudly and heartily*): Only among us young folks. (*A knock on the door; still laughing.*) Come in!

(*Enter HEIDEBRAND. He clicks his heels, bows, looks from GERDA to CLAUS and back again, then laughs with delight.*)

HEIDEBRAND: What a joy it is to be human! (*Walks swiftly forward and takes GERDA by the hand, then greets CLAUS*)

GERDA: Is it still a joy?

HEIDEBRAND: Yes. It is simply unbelievable. (*They laugh*)

GERDA: There are lots of us who think that the party's over. (*Pause*) What's your excuse for celebrating today, then?

HEIDEBRAND (*with a dismissive wave*): A mere nothing. It's just that it's so lovely to be talked about. To know that old Paul Heidebrand is still expected and that people *talk* about him while they wait. (*GERDA looks down, digesting this. They laugh.*)

CLAUS (*agape*): But how could you know it was you we were talking about?

HEIDEBRAND (*whispers*): Because I am an old fox. The kind of really old fox who has been in the fire before. (*Pause*) That's *my* secret.

GERDA: You have just as much time to spare as in the old days?

HEIDEBRAND: That depends on what you mean by "spare." (*Doorbell rings*)

GERDA (*to CLAUS*): Now you must go and eat supper, son! You can get the door while you're about it, and if it's Aunt Emmchen, poor thing, you can help her off with her coat, please.

CLAUS: All right! (*Shakes HEIDEBRAND's hand.*) Auf Wiedersehn, Herr Heidebrand!

HEIDEBRAND: Goodbye for now, Herr Reynhardt! We would certainly enjoy having a little chat about music someday—if we could find the time.

CLAUS (*from doorway*): We *must* find time for that!

(*Exits, embarrassed, banging the door. GERDA walks over to window*)

HEIDEBRAND: (*quietly*) Uh—Gerda? (*No response. Clears throat, hoarsely*) Gerda! (*No response. Aloud:*) Gerda?

GERDA (*turns suddenly, furious and tearful*): You could at least have spared me the uniform! You see, I know what it means.

HEIDEBRAND (*Looking down*): I could have.

GERDA: It's just uncalled for to make me see you in it!

HEIDEBRAND: You must forgive me, Gerda. But I've gotten so used to it.

GERDA: Yes, I imagine you would—eventually. (*Calmer*) It doesn't bring back good memories.

HEIDEBRAND (*smiling bravely*): But it makes a statement!

GERDA (*almost spitting*): It's expressive, all right!

HEIDEBRAND (*surveying the uniform*): And yet it's missing something.

GERDA: I think it looks complete.

HEIDEBRAND: It's missing one color. It's missing red! It should really be black and red.

GERDA: It certainly should.

HEIDEBRAND (*whispers*): But the strange thing is that the red is there just the same. (*He stretches out both arms, grasps his right hand around left wrist, rubs, switches hands and rubs again*) The red is there just the same. And strangely enough it's invisible.… And do you know where it is? On my hands and wrists, all the way up to my elbows!

GERDA (*backing up*): Paul!

(*HEIDEBRAND lets his hands fall. Pause*)

EMMCHEN (*offstage*): You don't say! Is he really in there, Claus? Yes, that's a man who's done much for our country!

CLAUS (*opening door*): Yes, in here. But don't turn on the light, Aunt Emmchen, we haven't blacked out the windows yet! (*To GERDA*) It's Aunt Emmchen! (*Exit*)

(*Enter EMMCHEN. She is tall, full-figured, and broad-shouldered, with thick blond hair knotted over her nape. She looks like a Wagnerian soprano. She closes the door after her, pauses to adjust her eyes to the light, then springs forward and hugs GERDA.*)

EMMCHEN: God, how nice it is to be in your home again! (*Stares at HEIDEBRAND, abruptly lets go of GERDA and titters shyly.*) It's so dark in here, I could hardly tell you apart! Oh, God! What if I'd hugged you instead by mistake, Standartenführer! Oh, how awful! (*The last words are an ecstatic shriek.*)

GERDA: But I haven't introduced you to Herr Heidebrand! (*To HEIDEBRAND*) This is Fräulein Reynhardt, Heinrich's sister.

HEIDEBRAND (*steps forward, holds out hand and bows*): We've met before, Fräulein Reynhardt. But we haven't seen each other in a hundred years…. But tell us where you've been?

EMMCHEN (*solemnly*): I have been in Berlin, at the Chancery. We paid tribute to him with songs and flowers. Thousands of us, women from all over the country! Hailing him for the bombings of Lübeck.

GERDA: You were hailing *him* because Lübeck was bombed?

EMMCHEN (*explaining patiently, as to a child*): We wanted to show him that we women, too, are loyal—that we won't desert him because of a little adversity.

GERDA: Were people there from Lübeck too?

EMMCHEN (*to HEIDEBRAND*): No, the rail connections are broken. Imagine, they don't have a train station anymore!

GERDA: Won't you have a cup of tea after your all exertions, my friend?

EMMCHEN: Oh God! How good that would taste! But I don't have time. I'm on my way down to the newspaper to give them my impressions. You see, I just stopped in to tell you from mother that the party won't be on Friday, because it's Good Friday this week. So it'll probably be tomorrow instead. (*Looks at watch*) Oh God! I should have been there by now. Goodbye then, Gerda! (*Makes a dash for the door, then stops abruptly, turns, fixes gaze on HEIDEBRAND, raises hand in Nazi salute*)

HEIDEBRAND (*weakly, after clearing throat*): 'itler!

EMMCHEN (*to GERDA*): It's so long since Mother has seen Heinrich. So you must definitely come! She's hoping so dreadfully that he'll be there.

GERDA: I think it will work out. Give her our love!

(*Exit EMMCHEN. Silence*)

GERDA: Can I offer you something to drink, Paul?

HEIDEBRAND: Yes. We could drain a glass of cognac to Emmchen's continued health.

GERDA: If we settle for candles, we won't have to black out the big window. It's a lot of work, so we often do it this way in the music room. If that's all right with you, then please light the candles on the table!

(*HEIDEBRAND takes matches from pocket and lights two candles, then sits down heavily on sofa. GERDA draws curtains, gets glasses and bottles from cupboard, sets them on table in front of him, sits in chair opposite.*)

HEIDEBRAND (*holds out cigarette case*): An Allied cigarette? Captured in open and honest battle!

GERDA (*taking cigarette*): I didn't think you took part in open and honest battles.

HEIDEBRAND (*avoiding her gaze*): Heavens, no! I didn't capture them personally. It is our simple but loyal countrymen who captured them for us. (*Looks up at her, dead serious*).

GERDA (*fills glasses*): Please! This is Heinrich's special cognac!

HEIDEBRAND: Thanks, Gerda! (*Looks away*) Now *that* will perk us up! (*Pause*) I'm sitting here thinking…that this isn't the first glass you've poured for Paul Heidebrand.

GERDA: And it probably isn't the first cigarette his simple, loyal countrymen have captured for him, either.

HEIDEBRAND (*ignoring the barb*): It's almost like old times. Candles and glasses on the table! It's like twenty years ago. Do you sometimes think about those days? Do you still remember them?

GERDA: It would be more to the point to ask if *you* haven't forgotten them.

HEIDEBRAND: I haven't forgotten them. I often think of those days. (*Pause*) Especially of late it's been like that…I think of those trips down the Rhine and all over the country, the mountains, the woods—all the campfires in the dark, and the nights, the nights…. All that has jerked me back to life!
    You know, just as old people begin to remember more and more of their childhood, their first years, the first people they met…in the same way I've begun to remember my youth! I remember a stretch of road, an old tree, some twigs against the sky—but I've forgotten where in Germany—or in the world—I saw it. I remember the faces, the friends, the conversations, the songs…I remember a hand! A knee! Somebody's close-cropped neck! (*They both look down. An embarrassed silence.*) Do you know,

Gerda, that now and then the whole past wells up in me! And there's one song which haunts me. (*Drains glass, stands up and walks toward piano, stops and turns*) It's nothing! Nothing!—I just can't get it out of my head!

GERDA: What kind of song is it?

HEIDEBRAND: It's strange! I can't get it out of my head. There were so many of them, you see! But this particular one I can't get rid of. You see, it pops up at the most unbelievably inconvenient moments. One of the old soldier-of-fortune songs. You must know it.

GERDA: But which one?

HEIDEBRAND (*pleading*): Do you want to hear it? (*GERDA nods; HEIDEBRAND sits down at piano, plays a few chords, then sings loudly and monotonously*)

> "On a coal-black horse rides Brother Death,
> his cloak is full of the dark wind's breath!
> His cloak is full of the long, long sleep,
> full of the blessed peace.
> Brother Death, he gallops forth—
> wherever soldiers of fortune march,
> there he rides along. . .
> In Flanders we dance the meadow red—
> There it blooms double, with crimson thread!
> Flanders in distress!
> There in Flanders rides brother Death—
> To Flanders he rides along!
> His horse is as white as the snow so cold,
> and he is angel-fair to behold. . ."

GERDA (*furious, half rising*): Stop! Stop!

HEIDEBRAND (*hits a discord, stops playing and stands up, breathing heavily*): You remember that, Gerda!

GERDA: Yes, I remember it—and it has its prehistory—How in the world can you be so unbelievably cruel as to remind me of Little Jacob in that way!? After all, it was his song. (*Hesitates, then suddenly looks up*) Does it really help? Does it really help to have sung it?

HEIDEBRAND (*pacing*): Dear kind Gerda! You can well imagine that nothing helps. Nothing helps against ghosts. I can see them all here—very, very clearly! Now and then I talk with them a bit. Well, only with the dead ones, of course; I never speak with the living. But for the most part I merely hear their names—Little Jacob and, well…there were so many of them.

GERDA: First they got their hands on Little Jacob.

HEIDEBRAND: You don't need to be tactful on my account, Gerda. You can just as well say "you got your hands on"! —But you're wrong, my friend, you're wrong if you think it was us he died of.

GERDA (*yells*): When someone is "shot while trying to escape," what does that mean? What? What does that mean? Even if it were really true that he was shot while escaping…even if he *wasn't* beaten to death with rubber truncheons…who gave you permission to shoot someone because they tried to escape? (*Weeps.*)

HEIDEBRAND (*quietly*): That's part of the game. Just rules in a game, rules which we all know. Little Jacob knew them, too. We're just men playing.

(*GERDA hides her face in her hands.*)

HEIDEBRAND: What you're saying is right, Gerda. It all adds up. But just the same it's wrong. It wasn't us he died of…. He died of a sickness, a delayed childhood disease—one of those which hits much too hard if you get it as an adult. If the word weren't so ambiguous and so compromised, you could call it "morality." If he'd gotten over it, he could have been at liberty in just a few weeks. But you understand…you understand—he had his morbid little pleasure in his ideals right to the end.

GERDA: What kind of human being are you, Paul?

HEIDEBRAND: You put it precisely yourself: one of those who march in step—who collects his pay and wears a black jacket.

GERDA (*touches his uniform, draws hand back quickly as if burned*): And what made it possible for you to end up where you are today?—In *that*?

HEIDEBRAND: I pulled up stakes.

GERDA: That's no answer.

HEIDEBRAND: And that's no question. (*He leans forward, whispers*) Because you know the answer yourself. You know it yourself, if you just think of what I have attained by "getting there"—as you call it.

GERDA: You've succeeded in dirtying yourself, you've succeeded in sullying the old Paul, in befouling the image of you as you never were, but was only how Heinrich and I saw you! You've succeeded in betraying the ideals you talked about so much and so loudly!

HEIDEBRAND (*closes eyes*): You're wrong again, Gerda, if you think I betrayed anything. I didn't even betray my friends, let alone my ideals. And I didn't *lose* them either…I threw them overboard and choked and drowned them in cold blood. You mustn't believe for a moment that it was easy. They didn't let me kill them just like that! They still haunt me! Pale, shining ghosts from my adolescence. They're real ghosts, you see! They appear at night and in the dusk. They've never been able to stand the light of day. No, I haven't lost them! What I have achieved is something quite different.

GERDA: And what's that?

HEIDEBRAND (*looking her in the eye*): Money and power.

GERDA: And that's what you preferred!

HEIDEBRAND: Yes. I found that it suits me better than virtue and poverty. (*Pause*) But it's not *that* simple either. (*Frowns, thinking*) I went to school barefoot. Barefoot, Gerda! You can think about *that*, when you start seeing my black uniform all too starkly against Heinrich's white doctor's gown! (*Paces quickly across the room, then comes back, refills glass, holds it out as if in a toast, and drinks up.*) Aside from the past two years, which I spent in a province up by the North Pole, I've been *traveling* during this time. I know Italy. Rome! Naples! Pompeii! Venice! Florence! I've seen the Balkans. I know Paris, London, Budapest! I've slept in the best hotels, eaten in the fanciest restaurants. That's what money can buy! And *power*, Gerda—power is a strange thing.

GERDA: And this was while Jacob was in your camp.

HEIDEBRAND (*sits down*): Jacob was your brother. And he was six years younger than you. I know that. But he was twenty-four years old. He knew the rules of the game.

GERDA (*weeping*): While Little Jacob sat in your camp....

HEIDEBRAND (*buries his face in his hands*): That's how he wanted it. He wanted to lie under the wheel. And I wanted to sit up in the carriage.

GERDA): You were right not to visit us for so long. We were so fond of you, Paul! We were all so fond of you! And you've changed so!

HEIDEBRAND: Who hasn't?

GERDA (*wipes eyes*): Heinrich hasn't changed. He's the same.

HEIDEBRAND: Oh? Is Heinrich the same? (*Studies the candle flame*) I met him yesterday. And *I* thought he'd changed. He looked anxious and depressed.

GERDA: Inwardly he's the same. He's unchanged. He has the same character as back then, the same backbone. He's stayed out of the pigsty. And he's kept his ideals in spite of everything— I admire him more than ever.

HEIDEBRAND: If Heinrich has ideals, then he too has changed.

GERDA: Heinrich's ideals relate to his work, to science. And he's always had them—even if they weren't so noisy as yours.

HEIDEBRAND (*rises*): It's strange to hear you say that. Because in the old days he laid great stress on how there was very little room for ideals inside the frame of a scientific worldview. To tell the truth, my friendship with him was one of the things which helped me most in getting rid of my dreams.

GERDA (*stands up*): I will not stand here and listen to you trying to blame Heinrich for what you have become!

HEIDEBRAND: Don't worry, Gerda! Of course I won't set my black-and-red paw print on that white gown of his. Actually, I owe him a debt of gratitude, and I hope one day I can repay it.

GERDA: I'm not sure he'll accept the kind of help you can give him.

(*She takes a cigarette, lights it from candle.*)

HEIDEBRAND: No. That's what I'm afraid of, too.

GERDA: I don't think that this is a topic of conversation for us. (*Sits.*)

(*HEIDEBRAND paces for awhile, then sits back down on sofa.*)

HEIDEBRAND: You must forgive me. But I've been thinking about him so much lately. Ever since he came home, or rather, since I heard that he'd come home. How are things going with his research?

GERDA: He works so hard that I can't believe he'll manage in the long run.

HEIDEBRAND: May I ask what kind of thing he's working on at present?

(*Pause.*)

GERDA: You know that he took part in the African campaign because he was a specialist in tropical diseases. And that was also the reason he was called home. They were going to do research of military importance up here. And so first of all they wanted to find vaccines for some of the most widespread fever sicknesses. And also to find new ways of treating those who had already been infected. On the Eastern Front there were whole epidemics of such fevers—especially in the big swamp districts. And now Heinrich probably knows more about these diseases than anyone else in this country. Therefore, he puts all his energy into the work. Every single hour in the laboratory benefits somebody. Every moment can mean a life lost or saved. (*Ardently*) And after the war the results will belong to all humanity! Isn't it strange to think that in the midst of a world of corruption and inhumanity, there is one single person who is trying to do something worthwhile?!!

HEIDEBRAND: Absolutely.

GERDA: I'll tell you, Paul, that it's Heinrich who sustains me through these times. I don't see much of him, but I know he's there. And I know what he's doing.

HEIDEBRAND (*reaches for his glass, knocks it over*): Oh! (*Produces handkerchief and mops it up.*) And Heinrich's special cognac, yet! It'll probably take the finish off the mahogany.—Do you think it's because of the strain that he looks so bad?

GERDA: He's wearing himself out.

(*Pause.*)

HEIDEBRAND: Didn't he once think of becoming a prison doctor?

GERDA: Yes. That was years ago—just after Claus was born. Do you really still remember that? But actually, it was my idea! I was so taken up with social work back then, while it was still possible. Now of course everything goes through Party channels—Anyway, he considered it seriously for quite a long time. But of course he had the inheritance from his father, and so he chose to go on and specialize in febrile diseases. And of course he never needed to practice.

HEIDEBRAND (*smiling*): Had he become a prison doctor, many things would have looked different today.

GERDA: Yes, utterly different. Then he wouldn't have been working at the laboratory again this evening.

HEIDEBRAND (*drily*): No, he would have been at the front. (*Refills glass, savors bouquet, sips.*) By the way, do you know that Heinrich *isn't* at the laboratory this evening? He has a conference with my superior—Oberführer Scholz, M.D.

GERDA: Oh, well! Then it's a scientific conference.

HEIDEBRAND: Not necessarily.

GERDA: What else could it be?

HEIDEBRAND: It could be scientific *and* political.

GERDA: Heinrich has never been political—least of all now. Just what do mean, anyway, using a word like "political" in connection with him?

HEIDEBRAND (*suddenly serious*): I was just getting around to what I actually dropped in to tell you. I wanted to let you know that you shouldn't worry tonight.

GERDA: Worry?

HEIDEBRAND (*smiling*): Yes, you see, Heinrich may be called away a while after he gets home this evening. If anything comes of it, he'll probably get a call around midnight. But there's no reason for anxiety. We don't suspect him of anything. It's a purely routine matter. Purely routine.... But you know, in such inhuman and undemocratic times as ours, it can happen that people disappear in that way—so I just thought I could spare you some anxiety and agitation if I told you in advance that we don't wish him any ill. And then I was in this part of town anyway….

GERDA: And what kind of routine question is it that has to be dealt with after midnight?

HEIDEBRAND: It would be another conference with the same doctor, Obergruppenführer Scholz.

GERDA: And I suppose *that* will be of a scientific and political nature?

HEIDEBRAND: It may be, yes. Now perhaps you understand why I brought it up?

GERDA (*rising*): Yes, now I understand! Now I begin to understand!

HEIDEBRAND (*surprised*): Pardon?

GERDA: You said you owed Heinrich a debt of gratitude?

HEIDEBRAND: Yes?

GERDA: Because you've become who you are today?

HEIDEBRAND: For that too. He undoubtedly helped me on my way. But I don't think I quite understand….

GERDA: No, but *I* understand! You're repaying your debt by trying to drag him into your swinish affairs! Now I really begin to understand who you are!

HEIDEBRAND: Nonsense!

GERDA: Now I know what you meant by talking about "the old days"! And why you wanted to spare me worry! Have you always, always put on a comedy act like that?

HEIDEBRAND: I've never hidden who I am! And I go around dressed like this so that everybody can see it. It isn't everyone who does that. Is that a comedy act? I've admitted that I'm power-mad and greedy. That I've swung myself up using others' misfortune. That I wallow, gorge, and enrich myself. Is that a comedy act?

GERDA: No, that's true. You've been very frank. Very frank. You always have been, Paul.

HEIDEBRAND: But now when I tell you not to be afraid if they come to get Heinrich tonight—when I tell you not to be afraid that he'll be shot or put in a camp or God knows what—that's suddenly putting on a comedy act! Is it? But I'm telling you: nothing bad will happen to him.

GERDA: But what am I to believe, Paul? You've been away for so many years. And you've had such a strange career!

HEIDEBRAND: But now I've come back.

GERDA: What am I to believe?

HEIDEBRAND: You should believe what I said a little while ago: that my underwear is stained red and that I kill Jews and socialists with gas.

GERDA (*softly*): Paul.

HEIDEBRAND: And that I eat children at nght…and that I kill Gypsies with chlorine.

GERDA: Please, Paul!

HEIDEBRAND: And that just now I'm bored and have found my old friend Heinrich Reynhardt to experiment on.

GERDA: Shut up!

HEIDEBRAND: …to spot my old friend's lily-white soul and gown with blood.

GERDA (*enraged*): Now that's *enough!*

HEIDEBRAND (*looks at watch*): Yes, now that's enough. It's late, and duty calls. Coal-black duty. Just as black as my uniform. (*Wearily*) We live during a perpetual solar eclipse, Gerda…. If you just had an *inkling* of why I came.

GERDA: What is it, Paul?

HEIDEBRAND: I hardly know why anymore myself. But I think I came so that you'd see me—and so that I'd see you…. You must forgive me, Gerda! But the day began so strangely. For example, I attended an operation this morning. It was nine o'clock, and I had just eaten breakfast.

GERDA: Haven't you ever seen an operation before?

HEIDEBRAND: Yes. But it was strange all the same. It was a Polish girl they were operating on. I threw up my breakfast afterwards.

GERDA: How was the patient?

(*Knock on the door, which opens. Enter SCHNEIDER, a heavy-set man in his forties, followed by EMMCHEN, elated.*)

EMMCHEN: Good evening! We've just come from the newspaper. Editor Schneider has written such a lovely article about me— about *us*, I mean. About those of us who went in and paid homage to the Führer. Imagine, it was already finished when I got down there. It must be mental telepathy, because he knew it all in advance! It'll be on the front page. (*Looks around room.*) He has just now finished working. I hope we're not disturbing you? Gerda, this is editor Schneider. My sister-in-law, Frau Reynhardt. Standartenführer Heidebrand.

GERDA (*smiling*): You press people must always be working at night?

SCHNEIDER: Journalists have many duties. It's so dark in here. It takes a while for one's eyes to get used to it. (*To HEIDEBRAND*)

But you're sure we're not disturbing you? It was Fräulein Reynhardt who invited me up.

EMMCHEN (*sighs*): Standartenführer Heidebrand is a man who has made great sacrifices.

GERDA: Yes, he was just talking about his duties, right before you knocked.

EMMCHEN: Imagine, have you been talking about your duties the whole time!

SCHNEIDER (*produces notebook and pencil. To HEIDEBRAND*): I would very much like to hear a little about your appointment….

HEIDEBRAND: Well, I'll tell you! Just before you came, we were talking about duties. We agreed that there are different conceptions of what "duty" is. As an example, it was mentioned that there are men right in their prime, who think that it is their duty not to be at the front. There are men like that who think that they should go around demonstrating their patriotic sentiments with their mouths. You know, there are men like that who think that they can serve their fatherland best by lying in their good warm beds and thinking up lead articles.

SCHNEIDER (*nervously*): The press fulfills a great task in such times. It criticizes—where criticism is appropriate, especially of the enemy and of malcontents. And it admonishes, it arouses. It keeps the people alert. The press's eyes are always watching.

HEIDEBRAND: There are men like that who think that there are no older colleagues, unfit for battle, who can keep watch instead of them.

SCHNEIDER: I'm a sick man. A sick man, Standartenführer.

EMMCHEN: You mustn't take it personally. Herr Heidebrand always makes great demands on people.

SCHNEIDER: I'm a sick man.

HEIDEBRAND: Sometimes it's good to be sick.

SCHNEIDER: I have to eat white bread.

HEIDEBRAND: But it can happen that someone is sent to the front all the same—without white bread.

GERDA (*offering tray with glasses*): Will your stomach stand a glass of cognac?

SCHNEIDER: My God! That's medicine, Frau.

HEIDEBRAND (*holding out his own empty glass*): I'll gladly take twenty drops with him. Then the editor and I can empty a tablespoon for the soldiers. But we must be quick—our duties await us!

Scene 2

(Same scene. Darkness lit by a lamp over the pale rococo sofa and the small, unshaded bulb over the music stand on the grand piano. REYNHARDT has just come in, and faces CLAUS as he takes off his raincoat and throws it over a chair back. He runs his left hand through CLAUS's hair; with his right he pulls his pince-nez out of his breast pocket and clamps it onto the bridge of his nose.)

REYNHARDT: Well, son, he's certainly gifted in his way. He is a very gifted man.

CLAUS: But what's he like?

REYNHARDT: (*taking off pince-nez*) He's the kind who upset the chessboard when they lose at chess.

CLAUS: But what kind of a *person* is he?

REYNHARDT: There are people…. There are people whose personal morals are not entirely on a level with their talents.

CLAUS: But is he evil or good, I mean! Is he a good person—like—well, for example, you, Father?

REYNHARDT: No one is wholly good or wholly evil, you know—And it isn't for me to search people's hearts—but getting mixed up in politics has hardly improved him.

CLAUS: But maybe he's an idealist?

REYNHARDT: Idealist, Claus? Idealist! All respect for ideals, Claus—all respect for them! But you understand that when ideals come together with politics—well, those two things don't mix very well. And the ideals usually get short shrift—Everything and everyone has two sides, Claus. And one of Heidebrand's sides is shown by the fact that he quite openly, you might say *shamelessly*, goes around in this uniform.

CLAUS (*astonished*): But surely it wouldn't have been better for him to wear civilian clothes?

(*Pause.*)

REYNHARDT: I think you'd better go to bed now, son. We mustn't forget that you've been sick. (*Turns away*) Besides, I didn't say that that must necessarily be a bad side!

CLAUS: But you're in the lab all day, Father! I never get to see you. And we have so much to talk about!

REYNHARDT (*puts hands on CLAUS's shoulders. laughs*): Listen! Actually, I'm *two* people: One doctor and one father. One and one are, as you know, *two*. And the father is glad that you sit up so late waiting for him—but the *doctor* would feel safer if you got more rest. (*Turns CLAUS toward the door.*)

CLAUS: Will you come up then and say good night?

REYNHARDT (*crossing his heart*): Absolutely!

CLAUS: Is that a promise?

REYNHARDT: Yes!

(*Pushes CLAUS toward door, which opens, revealing GERDA.*)

GERDA (*smiling*): Well? Have the turtle doves found each other?

REYNHARDT: We were just waiting for you. Claus is going to bed now.

CLAUS (*kissing GERDA*): Good night, mother!—See that Father comes up to my room in a while. He promised!

GERDA: Good night, Claus! (*Exit CLAUS. GERDA leans her head against REYNHARDT's shoulder.*) Couldn't you spend a little more time at home, Heinz? He's completely beside himself when you're away for so long.

REYNHARDT (*with mock-sorrowful expression*): And his mother—how is it for her when I'm gone?

GERDA (*kissing him*): She's also a little bit beside herself, Heinz.

REYNHARDT (*draws her to him*): It will be better in a while. I'm working on a series of tests now, and I must do as many as possible every day—But say! Do you know what I'm thinking?... I'm thinking that you and I—our marriage, it's like an old, impregnable medieval fortress! The kind which rises up proudly on a cliff, with ruins all around.

GERDA: Many things around it have fallen into ruins.

REYNHARDT (*pulling out his pince-nez*): And there will be more ruination, Gerda—in every sense of the word.

GERDA: Paul was here today.

REYNHARDT (*lighting a cigarette*): Yes, Claus told me. What did he want?

GERDA: He seemed to have come mainly to talk about the old days. And he was in a dreadful state. Then he asked how you were—he thought you were looking poorly.

REYNHARDT (*indignant*): He thought *I* was looking poorly?... Actually he's the one who's looking poorly. He's pale—and even if he's stout and vigorous, in a way he looks emaciated all the same.

GERDA: That's the way Paul has always been. He can change his appearance completely in a few minutes. He can look glowing with health one moment, and wrinkled and ashen the next. He's always had that quality. Actually, he's as strong as a blacksmith.

REYNHARDT (*with suppressed anger*): I'm healthy too.

GERDA: But Paul isn't altogether wrong. (*Strokes his cheek*) I've seen it for a long time, Heinz! I don't mean that you're *thin*, that doesn't matter. But I have the impression that there's something weighing on you.

REYNHARDT: Well, you're wrong, my friend.

GERDA: But everybody can see it! Even Emmchen has noticed it!

REYNHARDT (*laughs*): But little Gerda! Emmchen, poor thing, you don't take her seriously!

GERDA: Today Claus spoke of it too. He doesn't think you look happy any more, he said.

REYNHARDT (*laughs*): This sounds like a conspiracy!... Hey! I've forgotten something! (*Bounds over to chair, finds package in pocket of raincoat, removes outer wrapping, holds tissue-paper package above his head, then takes it over and hands it to GERDA*) Here! This is from me, just from me.

GERDA (*unwrapping it*): Oh!

(*She unwraps and holds a red leather purse.*)

REYNHARDT: The strap goes around your wrist.

GERDA (*smelling the leather*): Oh! How in the world did you come
by it? You are a prince! A prince above all the other princes on
earth!

REYNHARDT: I came across it in the station this morning. There
was a man selling things from Russia. There were a few other
things too, but most of them were ordinary tourist stuff. This
purse was the only really pretty one he had.

GERDA: And the prince swooped down on it with his unerring falcon's eye! (*Smells it again*) Hey, they must use red leather in their
boots, too?

REYNHARDT: Yes.

GERDA: Think how different everything would be in Germany if
we used red boots here—instead of the black ones! Here they
always wear black.

REYNHARDT: Yes. Here they always wear black…. Did Paul tell
you that he had taken over the position of commandant at the
camp out there?

GERDA (*lays purse on sofa*): But that's disgusting! Disgusting!

REYNHARDT: He is said to have introduced a pace of work out
there, a tempo in the camp administration which is scaring the
subordinates out of their wits. He works day and night.

GERDA: So he stands in high favor with his superiors, then?

REYNHARDT: They're delighted. They believe they've come across
an idealist. But you're not particularly surprised. I was afraid it

would be a shock for you.

GERDA: Oh—no.

REYNHARDT (*relieved*): I'm glad that you can look on Paul with a certain tolerance. Such a case absolutely does have *two* sides.

GERDA: No. It does not. Such a case has only one side. If it doesn't come as a shock to me, that's because this position of his is only a logical consequence. Everybody who works with them has sold out. So it's really nothing new.

REYNHARDT (*taking her hands*): So? *I* work with them too, in a way. We must be objective, Gerda. A little bit fair! Do you think that I've sold out too?

GERDA: You work to save the sick. There's nothing wrong with giving them medicines. Nobody can misuse that.

REYNHARDT: You're right. Perhaps I have a bedrock in the nature of the work. One must have trust in science—that it will *bear fruit* in itself. (*Paces silently, then stops and raises hand.*) But—one must have trust in *people* too! In a man like Paul there is so endlessly much that's complex, all mixed up together. After all, he has….

GERDA: With Paul it's different.

REYNHARDT: Paul may come to prevent many wrongs—perhaps set some things to rights. He's not a fiend, after all…. At least one wouldn't think so.

GERDA: He can make small reforms in hell? Is that what you mean?

REYNHARDT: I mean that as the years go by you grow modest; a small, decent action counts for infinitely more than a big, beautiful dream. (*Takes her hand.*) Let's not be too one-sided, Gerda! There's no patented way through life. The side roads are there, tiny narrow paths and long, crooked detours. And everyone has his own. Paul has his own. And he must walk it alone. What will come out of it, no one can say beforehand.

GERDA: There are roads which nobody needs to walk.

REYNHARDT: Dear little Gerda! It's easier to judge others than to live yourself.

GERDA: That sounds almost like a defense of Paul.

REYNHARDT (*sighs*): It is, too. But it is just as much a defense of myself. Who can be human at all today without feeling like an accessory?

GERDA (*bends down and runs hand through his hair—as if to sick child*): My God, Heinz! Is that what's bothering you?

REYNHARDT (*laughs, pulls her down onto sofa*): Is the conspiracy beginning again?

GERDA: Don't laugh, Heinz! A true marriage is always based on honesty. Tell me what's the matter!

REYNHARDT: Gerda—my friend! A man must have one secret from his wife!

GERDA: But now if I *beg* you? You so often look downright despairing.

REYNHARDT (*Jumps up as phone rings in next room.*): There, you see! I don't *get* to answer! (*Runs out of room. Offstage:*) Yes, hello! Yes, it's me. Please!... Now, this evening?... Yes, but it's very late!... All right... Hm?... All right!... Mm-hmm... And it's already left? Any minute?... Jawohl!... Fine! (*Returns, looking older.*) I would have enjoyed getting some sleep tonight. But *no!* Good Lord, Gerda! I have to leave at once. A car is coming for me right away; it's left already. Oh, for a chance to have a good rest!—These eternal conferences, now they're beginning at night as well!

GERDA (*rising and kissing him*): You must eat first.

REYNHARDT: What energy these people have!

GERDA: Poor Heinz! I'll make a couple of sandwiches.

REYNHARDT: There won't be time. They may be here any minute…. But a cognac, now! That I think would help. (*Puts on raincoat. GERDA gets cognac and pours him a glass.*) Don't you want to join me?

GERDA: I've already had a drink today. (*Vehemently*) It's terrible, Heinz, that you never get a good night's sleep! Tomorrow evening we'll leave the party early.

REYNHARDT (*putting down empty glass*): Tomorrow evening I'm not going to any party at all!

GERDA: What do you think it's about tonight?

REYNHARDT: It's a Dr. Scholz from Berlin. I'll be talking to him about the possibility of mass producing the fever preparations. He's leaving at six in the morning. (*Car horn*) See! There they are. Goodbye for now! (*Kisses her.*)

GERDA: Try to think that all the drudgery will bring good to someone!

REYNHARDT (*stopping in doorway*): Yes…Hopefully someone will reap benefits from it.

(*Exit REYNHARDT. GERDA goes to window, opens crack in blackout curtains and stands looking down into street. Long pause. Door opens. GERDA starts. Enter CLAUS, barefoot and in pajamas.*)

CLAUS: Where's Father? He promised to come up and say goodnight.

GERDA: Father had to leave. He got a phone call. But I was supposed to say goodnight from him, Claus…. They phoned, you
see.

*(They stand there, CLAUS unmoving by the door, GERDA looking
around until her gaze fixes on the red purse on the sofa.)*

Act III

Scene: Same as Act I. HEIDEBRAND is standing in the middle of the room. REYNHARDT has just come in and is taking off his raincoat by the door.

HEIDEBRAND: Welcome!

REYNHARDT (*puts on his pince-nez*): May I ask what you're laughing about?

HEIDEBRAND: You're looking at me as if you already had me under the microscope.

REYNHARDT: Have the others arrived?

HEIDEBRAND: No one else is coming. (*Sits down on desk.*) It'll be just us two.

REYNHARDT (*staring*): Does that mean it was *you* who called me here?

HEIDEBRAND: That means that it was *I* who called you here. But first I was ordered to do it by Dr. Scholz. You know I'd never spoil a night's sleep for an old friend of my own free will!

REYNHARDT (*crossly*): Well, honestly! What's so funny?

HEIDEBRAND (*laughs*): You did have social impulses once, didn't you? You once wanted to be a prison doctor and sacrifice your-selves for the prisoners, isn't that right?

REYNHARDT: I considered it once; but it was actually Gerda's idea. Do you really think it's comical?

HEIDEBRAND: Well, after all, in a way you've become one! You *are* in fact a kind of prison doctor. (*REYNHARDT takes out cigarette case*) Did you get some sleep in the car?

REYNHARDT (*throwing match on floor*): Oh, yes! I slept a little! And what if I did? I'm tired, Paul! Tired! Tired! Tired! So what if I slept a little? Don't you need sleep yourself?

HEIDEBRAND (*jumps down from desk, crosses to filing shelves, turns*): The last few nights I've needed very little sleep. To tell the truth I've been rather excited. The very thought of sleep is physically painful. To relax—to close my eyes—lose consciousness—get away from myself! I tell you, Heinrich, I begin to be afraid every time sleep gets near. Going to sleep has something about it which reminds me horribly of being broken on the wheel. In a way it's as if my limbs are being pulled apart!

REYNHARDT: If you have something specific to tell me, then I must ask you to make it short. Tomorrow evening I'm going to a party, and what's left of tonight I must use to get a little sleep.

HEIDEBRAND (*smiles*): You're going to your mother's, to the widow?

REYNHARDT: Yes. If it's about your condition, you know that I'm not a neurologist.

HEIDEBRAND (*picks up empty glass and holds it to light*): It's not about my condition. That's as it should be. On the contrary it's about *your* condition—or if you will, your position.

REYNHARDT: With regard to that, I think that I'm already quite well oriented.

HEIDEBRAND: Not well enough. Not well enough. There are certain scattered features of the camp's history which will make you see it in a somewhat broader context. (*Puts glass down. Smiles.*) It's been decided that you are to play a significant role for our beloved fatherland.

REYNHARDT (*Takes off pince-nez, polishes them with handkerchief*): Are you sure it will interest me?

HEIDEBRAND (*brings out cognac bottle.*): It would be a great shame if it didn't interest a man with your high military and political rank. (*Hunkers down in front of cupboard, looking for something.*)

REYNHARDT: I have neither military nor political rank. Even if you appointed me kaiser, that wouldn't even make me a sergeant. I am a medical man!

HEIDEBRAND: Hell! There should have been a couple of glasses here! (*Stands up.*) Fine! But then as a *scientist* you're at least interested in *knowing!* (*Picks up glass from table.*) It looks like we'll have to drink out of the same glass, Heinrich. There's only one here. You don't mind?

REYNHARDT: It doesn't matter.

HEIDEBRAND (*fills glass and offers it*): We've done it before, years ago. Please! (*REYNHARDT takes glass and drinks*) I have a strenuous morning ahead of me, and so I must ask something of you in connection with what I'm about to tell you. That's why I'm keeping you up tonight. (*Refills glass and drinks*)

Last year there was a group of about a hundred and fifty Jews among the prisoners here. They worked in a quarry not so very far away. Now it happened that they were driven very hard—unusually hard, in fact—in this quarry. And there occurred an average of four to five accidents a day. The accidents happened when they, perhaps with help from others, fell down onto the gravel from the top. And it was rather high, you see, so it always led to fatal accidents.

The finished gravel was delivered to an ordinary private firm. But after several weeks of deliveries—and by then, of course, the supply of Jews had markedly decreased—a strange thing happened! The firm began to complain that something was wrong with the stone they received. They asked the camp to wash it before it was sent.

REYNHARDT: So—was it done?

HEIDEBRAND: Oh, no. The deliveries continued as before. And according to Dr. Eger you could study anatomy in the gravel. But eventually there were no more Jews, and then the complaints stopped as well. (*Pause*) You may remember my mentioning the ash sold to the farmers as fertilizer?

REYNHARDT: I remember.

HEIDEBRAND: Well, it too led to complaints. The farmers kept finding teeth and bones in their fertilizer, and they didn't like it. After all, they had bought it fair and square and had paid for the goods. So the cremation must have been highly incomplete, and first one farmer complained, then another, another—and so on....

REYNHARDT: Why are you telling me this? It doesn't concern me what these idiots have been up to! (*Collects himself*) Yes, you must pardon my saying it: These *idiots*!

HEIDEBRAND: And so one day a sewer main got clogged. Absolutely watertight. It was so stopped up that they had to get plumbers from the town to clear it.... Well, now! The plumbers got quite a shock when they discovered what was stopping up the pipes. Really fresh stuff, yet! The poor fellows were practically comatose when they were driven home—even if plumbers are used to just about anything.

REYNHARDT (*leans on desk*): But this doesn't concern me! It has nothing to do with me!

HEIDEBRAND: Can you think of any connection between these complaints from the firm and the farmers, and what the plumbers got a glimpse of?

REYNHARDT: Nothing—nothing but negligence, incompetence, and unforgivable stupidity in the camp administration!

HEIDEBRAND: *Nothing* but that?

REYNHARDT (*shouts*): No, I'm telling you! No! And it offends me to hear it! I've just come from my home!

HEIDEBRAND: But what effect do you think it might have had?

(*Pause.*)

REYNHARDT: Of course it would be whispered and talked about! Whispers and talk!

HEIDEBRAND: And how do you think they feel, the ones who talk about it?

REYNHARDT (*puts on pince-nez*): Well, the rumors would naturally create a certain—a certain anxiety. (*Crosses and fills glass*)

HEIDEBRAND: And don't you think that could be the whole point? The people get totally paralyzed. They go numb with fear. You see, they get a small glimpse of what happens to those who don't obey.

REYNHARDT: I repeat: It's nothing to me how one uses the remains. (*Earnestly, coming up to the desk.*) I'll tell you quite frankly, Paul, how things are with me. I am a medical man. Actually, medicine has always been an exception among the natural sciences. The conditions for research have been especially bad. In all other branches of science, one could solve problems by experiment. But not us. In medicine we were cut off from that. We had to proceed with infinite slowness. Now and then we could do research with animals. But that was a long way round. It didn't help us much. We could never experiment freely. We could never get past the scruples we had to observe. Imagine a chemist having to experiment with phosphorus when he wanted to know something about sulfur! That's how it was for us.

I don't give a damn about politics! I don't give a damn about the war! I don't give a damn about corpses and sewers and uniforms! *This* is what interests me. And it interests me *truly*! It has opened up whole new avenues for medicine. (*Grabs HEIDEB-*

RAND by the sleeve.) *It's so interesting, Paul!* It's so interesting. And therefore, it's completely immaterial to me what they use the remains for. Utterly immaterial! That's the way it is. (*Lowers his voice.*) You have no right to keep me awake at night with this. (*Yawns.*)

(*Pause.*)

HEIDEBRAND: Right. I understand. I understand. And as a private person you are probably justified in that. But not in the position you are in today. Not there! (*Crosses to filing shelves.*) As a scientist, as a representative for today's intellectual elite, you stand only and solely in the service of the *state*—and you ought to be interested in what political aspects your work has. You ought to be flattered that we have a use for you. As a professional man you possess an enormous asset in your reputation.

REYNHARDT: And as a private man I have another asset. I have my morality, my emotional life. I quite simply have my decency to protect! I will under no circumstances get involved in politics. That you'll have to manage by yourselves. Without me. I'm not taking one step in that direction.

HEIDEBRAND: You won't be involved in it. You'll just be giving us some purely technical help. (*Refills glass, holds it out to him. Lights cigarette.*) You know these surgical experiments Eger is working on? They would acquire an enormous psychological clout if they were to leak out as secrets. As secrets, mind! Dr. Eger can't do it himself. He's been so compromised for so long that no one will believe a word he says. But if secret, purely factual reports about the operations were to leak out, that would be more effective than anything else. And a man with your scientific prestige would be very well suited for just that sort of thing.

    You understand that there are certain officers' circles within the Wehrmacht who could doubtless use a little enlightenment about what happens to rebels. And of course, you could make a show of indignation over these experiments.

REYNHARDT (*tries to clamp pince-nez on nose, they won't stay put*): But th—th—that would be a misuse of science!

HEIDEBRAND: It's not a misuse at all. It's in perfect accord with the scientific spirit. After all, it's just a matter of conveying the pure truth: This is what happens to rebels. And that can be a good thing to know—if one is a rebel. An excellent thing to have before one's eyes. (*Pours glass for himself. Confidentially.*) How could these things get into their hands, Heinrich? How could we arrange it?

REYNHARDT: I'm not employed by the Ministry of Propaganda.

HEIDEBRAND: But that's exactly what you are! You're employed by the backside of the Ministry of Propaganda. One could say you're employed as a public bogeyman: Watch out! Or science will come and get you! We have negative propaganda, and it must be managed in tandem with the positive. For example, you could just inform one of the army doctors, show him a few documents and a couple of photographs. Everything is at your disposal. The rest will take care of itself. It will reach the appropriate people, and it will help them maintain the right attitude. (*Warmly.*) You will help us, Heinrich?

REYNHARDT (*pacing*): I can't. I cannot drag my private person into this. If I do just one single thing which goes beyond the purely medical, then I've involved myself politically. I have my family, Paul. And as its head I have very definite obligations.

(*A long silence.*)

HEIDEBRAND: Has the husband and father told his family about his scientific work?

REYNHARDT (*stops pacing*): Those things have nothing to do with each other! Be so good as to keep them separate!

HEIDEBRAND: Why haven't you told Gerda about your experiments?

(*Pause.*)

REYNHARDT: If I were experimenting with rats, I wouldn't entertain my family with that either. There's no reason for her to know.

HEIDEBRAND: Still, she's bound to hear about it someday!

REYNHARDT: Did you mention anything today?

HEIDEBRAND (*smiling*): Gerda has no feel for our disciplines. I'd never dream of talking shop with her…. But this is interesting! The paterfamilias does not acknowledge the scientist! Not even the vivisection of rats does the paterfamilias find wholly fitting!

REYNHARDT: (*Irritated*) Of course I acknowledge it! My work has the very greatest significance for the future…in a purely human sense. (*Pause*) What do you mean, she's bound to hear of it?

HEIDEBRAND (*goes to desk, sits down, pours glass, drains it, refills it, holds it out to REYNHARDT, who takes it and drinks*): You're enchanting, Heinrich! I'll always have a soft spot for you. You have a peculiar fossil charm. (*Stands up, shouts angrily.*) Why in hell should anyone have a decent private life? I thought your race was extinct!

REYNHARDT: Well, it isn't.

HEIDEBRAND: No, that's clear enough. It certainly makes itself noticed. It has its second youth now!—Thanks to us! We gave you another chance. But just wait! (*Stops.*) Just wait! (*Quietly.*) Which actually came first, Heinrich? The white coat or the black uniform?

(*A silence.*)

REYNHARDT: So you won't be so good as to tell me what you meant by saying that Gerda is bound to hear it? It's an extremely painful thought, for I don't believe she'd be able to understand it quite…quite objectively.

HEIDEBRAND: I meant that you should have a chance to tell her about it yourself—before others do.

REYNHARDT: What others?

HEIDEBRAND: Sooner or later Dr. Scholz will make sure that Gerda is carefully informed. Carefully! And he will have his reasons for doing it. Therefore, you should put her in the picture yourself.

REYNHARDT: But it's Dr. Scholz who bears responsibility for the work!

HEIDEBRAND: Well. Then of course it's a question whether Gerda will understand *that*.

REYNHARDT (*taking HEIDEBRAND by the arm*): But this is inhuman! Gerda won't understand anything at all. She'll judge it by a standard which is alien to our work.—*She* can't understand that it involves another world with different values than hers! She won't understand that, Paul! She *can't!* After all, she's a romantic! She's a child!

HEIDEBRAND: It will be worse for her to hear it from outsiders. You must do it yourself.

REYNHARDT: (*Bewildered*) You can't demand such a thing of me! It would destroy my home.

HEIDEBRAND (*wearily*): We aren't *demanding* it. No one is demanding anything of you. I just think it would be best if she heard it from you.

REYNHARDT: There must be a way to avoid it.

HEIDEBRAND: Dr. Scholz will certainly understand your situation, but means what he said—he was completely frank about there being no room for sentimental considerations. There really isn't any place for them. Not in his book. He's a hard man, Heinrich—and just as hard on himself as on others.

REYNHARDT: But what can I do?

HEIDEBRAND: Tell her yourself.

REYNHARDT: I can't do that.

HEIDEBRAND: It would be the wisest course.

REYNHARDT: I *can't*. It's wholly out of the question.

HEIDEBRAND: And then there's one more thing. You have a grown son!

(*Pause.*)

REYNHARDT: *Grown* is putting it strongly.

HEIDEBRAND: He's at most a couple of years younger than Max. You should tell him about your work.

REYNHARDT: Are you crazy? Don't you know the boy's sick?

HEIDEBRAND: You'd better tell him all the same. That would be best. If you do it yourself, if you steal a march on them, then you can tell him in a way that softens the shock.

REYNHARDT: Claus is much too nervous to tolerate anything so upsetting. You know that very well! And besides, he is nowhere near mature enough to understand it.

HEIDEBRAND: He's old enough to begin to understand.

REYNHARDT (*stumbles over to the desk, puts hands on it, leaning forward*): Lord God in heaven, Paul! He's sick. And besides, he's hardly come up against reality yet!

HEIDEBRAND (*holds out a glass*): Sooner or later the boy must learn about the world.

REYNHARDT (*refusing glass*): It would destroy him!

HEIDEBRAND (*drinking*): You're the one who's destroying him—by shutting him up in an ivory tower.

REYNHARDT: He'd kill himself! He'll misunderstand everything— my position—the work—everything, everything!.... Just think how he clings to me! Think what I *mean* to him!

HEIDEBRAND: As you will. But I have to tell you that none of this cuts any ice with Dr. Scholz.

REYNHARDT: But Dr. Scholz? Why should he…. What pleasure would he get from informing Claus and Gerda?

HEIDEBRAND: Dr. Scholz isn't after pleasure. Dr. Scholz is after results.

REYNHARDT: But what benefit can anyone get from destroying and sullying my family life?

HEIDEBRAND: To make a long story short, Heinrich! I'm speaking here on behalf of Dr. Scholz himself: He values your work, and can certainly appreciate your point of view. He is glad that you're helping us. He is grateful for your exertions…. But he is your superior. And now he wants you to do him a service.

REYNHARDT: And that is?

HEIDEBRAND: That you tactfully turn certain secrets over to your colleagues, the doctors inside the Wehrmacht.

REYNHARDT: But I've already said that I can't engage myself po- litically! That is out of the question.

HEIDEBRAND: And therefore he is going to inform Gerda and Claus. That is, provided that you don't change your mind.

REYNHARDT (*tearing hair*): But that's blackmail! So he's trying to force me to do it!

HEIDEBRAND: You can't call it blackmail. You have a perfectly
free choice.

REYNHARDT: Yes, between two impossible things!

HEIDEBRAND: No. Between two possible things.

REYNHARDT: And you go along with things like this!

HEIDEBRAND (*softly*): Now don't forget that I too am your superior!

REYNHARDT: So I'm supposed to choose!

HEIDEBRAND: Yes.

REYNHARDT: I *cannot* get mixed up in politics.

HEIDEBRAND: A very respectable position. That means that you
choose the other possibility.

REYNHARDT (*closes eyes*): Both are impossible…both are impossible.

HEIDEBRAND (*shaking him*): Heinrich! There *is* one more possibility. It's a possibility no one has considered!

REYNHARDT: And what's that?

HEIDEBRAND: That you take your family and leave the country!
We have a neutral country next door, and you can go there. You
need only pull up stakes, Heinrich! You can pull up stakes and
actually begin a new life! I'll help you. To get across, I mean…
(*smiles*)…not with the new life! It's easy to get you over the border.

REYNHARDT (*pulling away*): When one is responsible for others
besides oneself, one doesn't pull up stakes just like that….

HEIDEBRAND (*earnestly, following him*): I *mean* it. I'll help you.

REYNHARDT: That's nonsense, Paul! Are you completely out of your mind? Be serious!

HEIDEBRAND: Do you really believe you can't pull up stakes?.... I *know* it can be done! It can be done by anyone who has a reason to do it!

REYNHARDT: I cannot take responsibility for such a thing.

HEIDEBRAND: It's one night's journey. And then you're over the border. Gerda and Claus are safe. And you'll be a free man again. It's easy!

REYNHARDT: Then what would we be going to?

HEIDEBRAND: One always pulls up stakes *from*. Never *to*.

REYNHARDT: For me it's important.

HEIDEBRAND (*almost beseeching*): You'll get *out* of it, Heinrich, if you just pull up stakes.

(*A long silence*)

REYNHARDT (*Clears throat*): I know a suitable doctor, who I could entrust the documents to. . . . and who would certainly pass them on.— But I'll do it just this once! My task is of a medical—not of a political sort. And I won't go one step further in that direction! Not one step! It's completely out of the question.

HEIDEBRAND (*pulling his jacket tight from the hem*): All right.

REYNHARDT: Then I assume that my family life will be kept out of it.

HEIDEBRAND (*back at desk, laughs soundlessly*): You know you can count on us! I certainly won't show Gerda the spots on your white coat!

REYNHARDT (*stiffly, drawing himself up*): Be so kind as not to speak of this in such a tone. My work and my family life—the two have nothing to do with each other.

(*HEIDEBRAND doesn't reply. He stands with eyes closed and head cocked, listening.*)

REYNHARDT: What is it? (*No reply.*) What is it?

(*Pause.*)

HEIDEBRAND (*opening his eyes*): At first I thought it was one of the prisoners! (*Bends double, elbows on knees, and laughs and laughs, going over into falsetto. Then slowly straightens up and wipes his eyes. Half choking.*) But it was just the rooster! We have a poultry yard out here. And it was just the rooster. Can you imagine its being that late! (*Stands looking at REYNHARDT.*) I'll get you a car.

(*Hurriedly crosses and exits through the yellow door, slamming it behind him. REYNHARDT looks after him.*)

FINIS

Jens Bjørneboe's *Ere the Cock Crows*:
The Novel and the Play

Esther Greenleaf Mürer

Jens Bjørneboe's early novel, *Før Hanen Galer* (*Ere the Cock Crows*), contains seeds of much of his later writing. Although *Duke Hans* was written earlier, *Ere the Cock Crows* was his first novel to be published. It is a chilling look at medical experiments in Nazi concentration camps.

Bjørneboe first wrote *Ere the Cock Crows* as a play. However, he was unable to get it produced; the Studio Theatre turned it down in 1950 with the comment, "The public runs away from this kind of thing." He then used the play as the core for a novel, which was published in 1952.

The process of turning play into novel resulted in a two-tiered structure which often creates problems for readers. It seemed to me that an examination of the structure and content of the play might shed light on the difficulties. The first task was to sort out which elements belong to the play and which were added in the novel. Since the original play is lost, I attempted a reconstruction.

In outline, my findings are as follows:

First, Steinar Løding's identification of the novel's "part II" (chapters 3-6) as the original play and chapters 1-2 as a novelistic addition, while correct in broad outline, requires some modification and fine-tuning.

Second, Bjørneboe's intense involvement with Anthroposophy at the time of writing affects the structure of both play and novel in ways that are not immediately apparent.

Third, the addition of new material in the novel profoundly alters the central focus of the work.

Reflections on these findings, with particular reference to the play, form the substance of this essay.

Background and Plot Summary

Bjørneboe's obsession with Nazi atrocities dates from the shock he received as a young, unprepared teenager from reading *Die Moorsoldaten*, an account of one of the early Nazi concentration camps by an escaped prisoner, Wolfgang Langhof. Bjørneboe tells of this event—which he regarded as his "confirmation," the beginning of his conscious life—in *Ere the Cock Crows*, in *Jonas*, and in *The Silence*.

> The sun stood almost still in the sky. But while I was reading, it became gray. For it was a strange thing I was reading; it…dealt with people who had their eardrums punctured because they could not stand in a straight line, and who were beaten to death with leather belts because they were sick. And, even while I was reading, it became clear to me that those things that were written there I would never be able to forget. And what happened while I was sitting there reading during the quiet, sunny afternoon hours I would never be able to undo.[1]

Elsewhere Bjørneboe says of the genesis of the work:

> That my first literary effort concerned Nazism's atrocities in general, but in particular the doctors' experiments, is due to circumstances which were not accidental. Shortly after the war I traveled to Germany, and there a German scientist, chemist and lawyer gave me the documents from the doctors' trials, and I studied them closely....
>
> Later I became personally acquainted with the very closest relatives of the doctor who had directed the experiments with the prisoners, a certain Dr. Rascher. I met his brothers, his father and his stepmother, and thereby gained an intimate acquaintance with Dr Rascher's character; this butcher of humans was a fine son and a fine citizen beside activities in vivisection of human beings.
>
> He is the key to the essence of Nazism and of bestiality.
>
> I began by writing articles on the subject in newspapers and magazines, but wasn't finished with it. I then tried writing it as a drama, let it lie, and then rewrote it as a novel. This process took several years. It was begun in 1947, and the novel was finished in 1952—at any rate for five years I was almost continually occupied with the material....And today I

---

1. Jens Bjørneboe, *Ere the Cock Crows*, 47. Page references for both the novel and the reconstructed play are to the *Samlede Verker* edition of *Før Hanen Galer* (Oslo: Pax, 1995).

am sure that the insight into this ocean of human evil and cruelty was the reason for the many years' depression which followed....I think that this book almost destroyed me.[2]

A brief summary of the novel is as follows:

The first two chapters are narrated by a Norwegian journalist who is sojourning in postwar Germany. We follow his observations, thoughts, and emotions as he meets with a community of relief workers, including the saintly Lyngby, who purports to be a Norwegian survivor of one of the camps who has chosen to stay in Germany. He also meets Max, a bedridden but unrepentantly sadistic SS man lodged in a makeshift hospice, who delights in torturing a blind fellow inmate; and Gerda and Claus Reynhardt, widow and son of the doctor in charge of the experiments. From these meetings an incredible story gradually emerges—a story with Reynhardt and the mysterious Lyngby at its center.

In the ensuing chapters the narrator disappears, and his reconstruction of the story is presented as a flashback to the early 1940s. Paul Heidebrand has just come to be commandant of the camp; while being oriented regarding Dr. Reynhardt's experiments he learns that a childhood friend, Samuel Goldmann, is a prisoner and is due to be experimented on shortly. He and Dr. Reynhardt are also childhood friends; Reynhardt accuses Heidebrand of having sold out, while insisting that he himself is there purely as a scientist. During a site visit by the high-ranking Nazi official Dr. Scholz, Reynhardt goes along with the plan to build the crematoria, saying that he believes in restricting his emotions to the private sphere. Heidebrand visits Gerda and learns that she knows nothing of her husband's activities. He uses this knowledge to pressure Reynhardt into making political use of his scientific prestige; Reynhardt capitulates, still insisting on his ethical neutrality.

Heidebrand then leaves the camp, taking Samuel Goldmann with him. He apparently succeeds in getting Goldmann across the Swiss border, but is himself caught, tortured, and put in a cell in the camp

---

2. Jens Bjørneboe, "Fra en litterær injurieproces" (1968) *Samlede Essays: Kultur I* (Oslo: Pax, 1996), 211f.

with a Norwegian prisoner named Lyngby. During the next two years Reynhardt continues his experiments and becomes thoroughly hated by the prisoners. As the Allies approach, the fleeing guards kill Heidebrand and Lyngby; Reynhardt tries to hide in their cell but is found and killed by the prisoners. When the Allies arrive, they find that one of the three is still breathing.

Structural Problems

Virtually everyone who has written about the novel has trouble with the two-part structure and the abrupt shift in form and point of view.

Janet Garton notes that efforts to piece together the novel's two parts—"to work out for example how the original narrator could possibly have been informed by the survivors about what Dr. Reynhardt thought when he was on his own in a taxi, or to wonder when the man Lyngby, who is obviously so important in the first part, is going to appear in the second"—may distract the reader from the central theme.[3]

Leif Longum argues that Bjørneboe's intention is not to *explain* Reynhardt, but to use him to show the reality of evil, the mysterious and demonic aspects of existence. Yet while the documentary style of the opening chapters has a prophetic intensity, the conventional realism of the novel's second part has no place for evil and mystery; it can only speak of pathological cases with rational explanations. Longum therefore concludes that "Bjørneboe is trying to share with us a reality which is too overwhelming to be contained in the literary form he has chosen."[4]

Steinar Løding, recognizing that Part II was the original play, comments that in the first part "the narrator lives desperately into the questions, and the other characters appear as experienced by another, as interpreted," while Part II purports to be an objective account by an omniscient narrator. Assuming that Part I was written at the time the play

---

3. Janet Garton. *Jens Bjørneboe: Prophet Without Honor.* (Westport, CT: Greenwood Press, 1985), p. 39f.

4. Leif Longum, *Et speil for oss selv. Menneskesyn og virkelighetsoppfatning i norsk etterkrigsprosa* (A mirror for ourselves: View of man and conception of reality in postwar Norwegian prose), 50-54. Oslo: Aschehoug, 1968), 54.

was recast as a novel, Løding asks why Bjørneboe "did not then rewrite Part II in a language which opens to the interpreting 'I,' in some form or other write himself away from this task of the omniscient author?"

> I read Part II as a withdrawal, as a surrender to a more unambiguously postulated objective form of presentation and understanding; also in the moment of writing five years later he was overwhelmed....This was not just the undoubted difficulties of translating from one genre to another....A linguistic structure against the chaos of gruesomeness had to be created; to write oneself over into a more exterior form may have had the character of existential necessity. But...I read Part II without meeting the executioner in myself.[5]

In sum, the principal charges made against the novel are: the structural difficulties are distracting; psychological realism as a form has no place for the mystery of evil that Bjørneboe is trying to convey; and the pretense of objectivity is a defense which prevents him from fully living into the questions.

I agree with Janet Garton's assessment that "Bjørneboe always knew the importance of choosing the right medium in order to convey his message with maximum intensity."[6] Moreover, it is my experience that the seeming flaws in Bjørneboe's writing always repay study; they provide vital clues to the author's intention, and perhaps to unconscious aspirations as well.

It does not seem to me that anyone has grasped the full significance of the play, and how its structure affects the shape of the novel. In addition to the first two chapters, I believe that the first part of chapter 5 and chapter 6 are also novelistic additions. The original play, as I reconstruct it, consists (with modifications) of the novel's chapters 3, 4, and the second part of 5. These passages strike me not as "objective" or "conventionally realistic" or indeed as novelistic at all, but as *stagy*. They consist almost entirely of dialogue and gestures, each section is

---

5. Steinar Løding, "Smerte og struktur: Om 'For hanen galer' av Jens Bjørneboe." *Vinduet* 40 (1986), no. 2:20-22.

6. Garton, 40.

limited to a single setting, and the entire action takes place within a twenty-four hour period.

In reconstructing the play, I chose to work in English for the sake of my own clarity. After making a rough translation of chapters 3-5, I then subtracted the characters' thoughts and feelings, and everything that cannot be seen by the audience within the confines of a single stage setting for each act. On the assumption that in turning the play into a novel Bjørneboe tried to flesh out the dialogue by minutely imagining details of body language, I cut much of the latter. What remains is dialogue and a highly abbreviated form of Bjørneboe's exhaustive indications of gestures, facial expressions, and tones of voice.[7]

Some preliminary observations: I suggest that the abruptness with which the narrator disappears is itself part of the problem, and would have been softened considerably by the simple insertion of a couple of pages saying "Part I: 1947" and "Part II: 1940"

Contra Løding, the fact remains that during the events of first two chapters the narrator was present; during those of the second part, seven or eight years earlier, he was not. A blow-by-blow account of how he pieced the facts together, and his emotional reactions to each revelation, would be uneconomical, intrusive, and distracting. It conjures up the irritating, but currently fashionable, habit of overloading a text with interjections of "for me" and "in my opinion." He has said at the end of chapter 2 that he is going to attempt a reconstruction, so why need he keep reminding us of the fact?

Moreover, if we regard the last chapter as belonging to the frame, it provides a transition back to the beginning, both by taking a longer view (telling instead of showing) and by breaking out of the play's restrictions—first of place and then, in an accelerating fashion, of time,

---

7. I leave it to those who know more about theater than I do to gauge how exhaustive the original stage directions were. Joe Martin, translator of *Semmelweis* (Los Angeles: Sun and Moon, 1998) and author of *Keeper of the Protocols: The Works of Jens Bjørneboe in the Crosscurrents of Western Literature* (New York: Peter Lang, 1996) was immensely helpful in advising me about what would be customary now.

bringing the story forward to 1945 and implicitly pointing ahead to the present of Part I.

It might help to think cinematographically. Voiceovers might be used here and there in the first part, while the final paragraphs of chapter 2—

> The same evening I talked at length with Frau Reynhardt, naturally about her husband....On top of the information from Max and Lyngby it was her narrative—and she continued it in the days that followed—which made it possible to reconstruct the events as they actually happened in a city in Germany at the beginning of the 1940s. (58)

might be thought of as turning into a camera dissolve, zooming into the closed set of chapter 3 after the motion of shifting scenes in the first part. The voiceover would return in the last chapter; when we reach the section beginning "By the time Dr. Reynhardt began the thirty-second series of experiments, he had absolute authority over all the medical research carried on within the camp...." (160) we are fast-forwarding, and the trajectory from the end of the book back to the beginning is not long.

The Anthroposophical Background

Both play and novel were written during the period of Bjørneboe's most intense involvement with Anthroposophy, the "spiritual science" of Rudolf Steiner. The problem of Steiner's influence on Bjørneboe's writings is difficult to approach. Anthroposophy is not a system of thought to be grasped intellectually, but a path of spiritual formation which one should come to understand by following it; its adherents therefore view attempts by outsiders to get a purchase on it as illegitimate.[8] One might justifiably argue that the primary message of *Ere*

---

8. Anthroposophist commentators on Bjørneboe's work take the view that once Bjørneboe had abandoned the Anthroposophical path, any Anthroposophical content in his writings was notional. This view impelled Kaj Skagen to take strong issue with Inge S. Kristiansen's exhaustive analysis of Anthroposophical motifs in Bjørneboe's later novels, particularly *Moment of Freedom*. See Inge S. Kristiansen, *Jens Bjørneboe og Antroposofien* (Oslo: Solum Forlag, 1989); Kaj Skagen, *Metafysikk eller selvmord : et essay om Jens Bjørneboe og*

the Cock Crows comes through loud and clear without reference to any Anthroposophical subtext. Still, that subtext must be there. Though I am in no position to undertake an analysis of it, I have gleaned a few passages from Steiner's writings which seem to me to shed light on the book's underlying structure, and offer them for what they are worth.

The title, *Ere the Cock Crows*, is of course an allusion to Jesus's words to Peter: "Thrice wilt thou deny me Ere the cock crows" (Matt 26:34 and parallels; John 13:38). Since I intend to show that the play is structured around the three denials, a word is in order about the Anthroposophical understanding of Christ. It is particularly important to point out that we are not dealing here with a simple conflict of Christ vs Antichrist, good vs evil, white hats vs. black hats.

---

antroposofien (Oslo: Cappelen, 1996). See also Karl Brodersen, "Jens Bjørneboe og antroposofien," *Arken* 4 (1981), no. 4:28-30.

For a close look at Anthroposophical subtexts in a work from Bjørneboe's anthroposophical period, see William Mishler: "Jens Bjørneboe, Anthroposophy and *Hertug Hans*." *Edda*, 1987 no:2:167-178. I have not seen Eldrid Skaar's unpublished dissertation, *Antroposofisk tankegods i Jens Bjørneboes lyrikk*, Univ. of Oslo, 1995. I have found Kristiansen's book invaluable; whatever the merits of his analysis of *Moment of Freedom*, he provides an immensely helpful introduction to Anthroposophical motifs which may be looked for in Bjørneboe.

I have found only one direct quote from Steiner in Bjørneboe's writings, in "Istedenfor en forsvarstale," in *Uten en tråd* (Samlede verker, Oslo: Pax, 1995), 152. It appears that in his early works, at least, Bjørneboe does quote Steiner without attribution, probably more often than has been recognized. Mishler quotes a passage from Bjørneboe's essay "The Fear of America Within Us" (published the same year as *Ere the Cock Crows*) which he says "derives almost verbatim from Rudolf Steiner," though he does not say where in Steiner's work it occurs. In his later work Bjørneboe tends to cite Goethe—whose thought is of central importance to Steiner—when alluding to esoteric matters.

I appreciate the dangers of trying to approach Steiner from the outside; moreover, given that Steiner's works comprise 350+ volumes, it is difficult to know where to start. I have tried to take my clues from what I know of Bjørneboe's preoccupations, and from the novel itself. Sources for Steiner's writings which I have used are: *The Essential Steiner: Basic Writings of Rudolf Steiner*, edited by Robert A. McDermott (San Francisco: Harper & Row, 1984); *Evil: Selected Lectures*. Translated or revised by Matthew Barton, compiled and edited by Michael Kalisch (London: Rudolf Steiner Press, 1997); and *The Gospel of John*, rev ed. (Hudson, NY: Anthroposophic Press, 1962). The online Rudolf Steiner Archive at http://wn.elib.com/Steiner/sumries.txt.index.html has helpful summaries of Steiner's works—some of which I found to have a familiar ring.

Kristiansen notes that for Steiner "Christ is not a personified compassionate savior, but an 'Impulse,' a kind of 'catalyst' which sets in motion a process of transubstantiation."[9] Mishler adds that Steiner follows the author of John's gospel in his focus on the Logos, the Cosmic Christ, which he sees as "the yeast of history, as a seed buried in the soil of time which impels consciousness through the phases of its unfolding.... Steiner sees the process as one which is at work on the individual level, as well as on the level of the cosmos...."[10]

According to Steiner, human beings are constantly exposed to the influence of two polar spiritual powers, Lucifer and Ahriman:

> Luciferic energy...causes people to view the world from an aerial perspective, like birds high above the earth. All the wonderful programmes for turning the world into a better place, all those beautiful ideas for bringing about some kind of golden age, arise through the luciferic streams flowing in us.... Another luciferic aspect of human nature is to lose interest in our fellow-men....
>
> Dreams of world power, on the other hand, which arise in fragmented, separate realms of human activity, are of an ahrimanic kind.... It is ahrimanic to wish to bring the whole world under the sway of one particular, circumscribed sphere of human life or activity....A person possessed by Ahriman...wishes to have as many people as possible under his thumb, and to rule over them—if he is clever enough—by using and manipulating their weaknesses....[11]

Steiner's point, as I understand it, is not that the faculty for abstract thinking and the use of power are evil in themselves, but that they become so if not brought into right subordination to the Christ-Impulse. Without the mediating Christ-Impulse, they are eternally at war with one another. (This tendency is expressed in another image from Steiner,

---

9. Kristiansen, 58.

10. Mishler, 168f.

11. Rudolf Steiner, "The relation of Ahrimanic and Luciferic beings to normally evolved hierarchies." (1918) In *Evil: Selected Lectures*. Translated or revised by Matthew Barton, compiled and edited by Michael Kalisch. London: Rudolf Steiner Press, 1997, 80-84.

which Bjørneboe uses elsewhere: "When the knights lose sight of the Grail, they kill each other").[12]

Steiner continues, "Only in the center of the heart is there a space that cannot be reached by either Lucifer or Ahriman, and it is from this tiny spot that the human being must maintain his balance and thus his true humanity in the face of these cosmic opponents."[13] This center is the seat of the Christ-Impulse— which, if well-tended, enables one to subordinate Luciferic dreams and Ahrimanic desires for power to love for the concrete individual:

> Seeing human nature for what it truly is and being clear that everyone, just in their "unimproved," ordinary state—yes, even the criminal—actually has more to tell us about the real nature of the world than our most elevated fancies and beliefs about the human being, establishes the right equilibrium in us, counteracts the sway of the luciferic.... The point is not to cherish a general idea but to penetrate to the actual reality of every individual, and to develop a loving (or perhaps more accurately, an interested) understanding for each specific instance of humanity.[14]

In the novel, as we shall see, the Christ-Impulse is central; it transforms Heidebrand, and permeates the frame as well.

The play as I have reconstructed it focuses on the battle between Lucifer (Reynhardt) and Ahriman (Scholz, assisted by Heidebrand). The Ahrimanic forces eventually succeed in bending the Luciferan to their purposes. The thrice-denied Christ-impulse is represented chiefly by Gerda, who sees her husband as a healer. We learn in Act II that she knows nothing of his activities; it is her understanding that he is working to develop vaccines for febrile diseases:

> Every single hour in the laboratory benefits somebody. Every moment can mean a life lost or saved. And after the war the results will belong

---

12. Jens Bjørneboe, "Hans Jæger." *Norge, mitt Norge* (Oslo: Pax, 1968), 125; *Samlede Essays: Kultur I* (Oslo: Pax, 1996), 114.

13. Rudolf Steiner, "The Balance in the World and Man—Lucifer and Ahriman." (1914) Summary from the Rudolf Steiner Archive.

14. Rudolf Steiner, "The relation of Ahrimanic and Luciferic beings to normally evolved hierarchies," 81f.

to all humanity! Isn't it strange to think that in the midst of a world of corruption and inhumanity there is one single person who is trying to do something worthwhile? (114f)

A word about the names of the characters: "Heidebrand" can be taken to mean "Burner (brand) of heathen (heide)." In the novel he subsequently becomes Lyngby--"city (by) on the heath" (lyng = heather, a plant which grows on the heath, where the heathens live). He is transformed from a persecutor of those who are deemed outside the pale into a universalist, living in community with them.

"Reynhardt" could perhaps be construed as either "purely hard" (rein + hard) or, stretching a little, "pure of heart" (hertz). In an ironic sense both of these meanings are certainly apt. But the spelling with y is significant: it suggests that the primary reference is to Reynard the Fox. In his 1953 essay "Two Years in a Rudolf Steiner School," Bjørneboe retells one of Reynard's many unsavory exploits and notes that all the other animals "know that Reynard is intellect incarnate, pure and absolute reason."[15] That we are meant to see Reynhardt as a picture of reason gone amok is further indicated by the novel's dedication "to the memory of the victims of the blindness of heart and coldness of mind which have long characterized modern science," and the epigraph to chapter 3—the putative beginning of the play—from Jeremiah 4:9: "And in that day—declares the Lord—the mind of the king and the mind of the nobles shall fail, the priests shall be appalled, and the prophets stand aghast."[16]

The Play: Reynhardt

The shape of the play, as I reconstruct it, is simple: In each of the play's three acts Reynhardt is presented with—and refuses—the opportunity

---

15. In *Under en Mykere Himmel* (Oslo: Gyldendal, 1976), p. 54.

16. Jewish Publication Society (JPS) version. This was the only English version I could locate that agreed with the Danish version that the *mind (Forstand)* of the rulers shall fail; all other translations used "heart" or "courage." The Hebrew word can mean any of these, but in Hebrew the heart is the seat of the intellect.

to reject the false light of Lucifer and instead choose love: compassion for the concrete individual as illuminated by the light of Christ. Each refusal to allow the Christ-Impulse to flourish increases his vulnerability to the forces of Ahriman. When he chooses Lucifer for the third time, the cock crows, signaling that he has passed the point of no return. The Ahrimanic forces have won.

Let us now look at the denials in greater detail:

Act I (chapter 3) begins with Heidebrand, the new head of the camp, interviewing two underlings to orient himself (and the audience) about the nature of the experiments. The most directly gruesome material in the play thus comes at the outset, providing a context for the drama which follows. (The Oslo theater official who rejected the play on grounds that "the public runs away from such material" had a point; the play's opening scene is not for the squeamish.)

After this Reynhardt is introduced. Heidebrand gently but consistently challenges Reynhardt's assertion that he is "wholly unpolitical." He then informs Reynhard that his membership in the S.S. has been approved. Here the dialogue parodies the language of grace:

Heidebrand: Anyway, I have good news for you…Your membership is in order.
Reynhardt: What membership?
Heidebrand: Yours…In our legion. You're accepted into the order.
Reynhardt (*takes an involuntary step backward, then walks right up to the desk and bends forward, shouting*): But I've never asked to be accepted!
Heidebrand: Oddly enough you're accepted all the same. (74f)

During the ensuing meeting with Dr. Scholz and other doctors involved in the research, Reynhardt keeps aloof. But when given a chance to voice his objections, Reynhardt expresses concern first about discretion and then about legality. Scholz assures him that both are taken care of, and launches into a panegyric designed to exploit Reynhardt's Luciferan bent:

The euthanasia project is the symbol of an intellectual victory. Yes, I will go so far as to say that it is first and foremost a symbol. It confirms that we—humanity—have finally become masters in our own house. We have overcome the deep, subconscious inhibitions, the old taboos which have hitherto stood in the way of carrying out such a relatively natural thing. We have taken a step which no cultured people before us have dared to carry to its full conclusion. We are the first fully mature beings nature has produced. The day the euthanasia program becomes a reality is the new humanity's secret birthday!

(*Carried away with excitement*) A scientist, a *scientist* who is privileged to take part in this, he must feel proud! (85)

The first denial is crystalized when Scholz challenges Reynhardt:

Scholz: What is your attitude to the plan on a purely emotional level, Dr. Reynhardt?

Reynhardt: I am of the opinion that one should restrict one's emotional life to the sphere where it has validity. (*Emphasizing his words*) I believe that it should be restricted to one's private life—yes, perhaps to one's family life. One must draw *very* clear lines here. (86)

In the second act we see how bogus this ideal is. During the first scene we see that Reynhardt's wife and son are worried about his mental health. The ensuing scene between Gerda and Reynhardt begins with Reynhardt telling her:

I'm thinking that you and I—our marriage, it's like an old, impregnable medieval fortress! The kind which rises up proudly on a cliff, with ruins all around. (124)

The falsity and irony of this becomes evident in what follows. What he really means is that he needs Gerda's ignorance of his activities to enable him to maintain the illusion of being above politics.

He tests the waters but cannot face Gerda's moral judgment:

Reynhardt: I'm glad that you can look on Paul with a certain tolerance. Such a case absolutely does have *two* sides.

Gerda: No. It does not. Such a case has only one side. If it doesn't come as a shock to me, that's because this position of his is only a logical consequence. Everybody who works with them has sold out. So it's really nothing new.

Reynhardt (taking her hands): So? I work with them too, in a way. We must be objective, Gerda. A little bit fair! Do you think that I've sold out too?

Gerda: You work to save the sick. There's nothing wrong with giving them medicines. Nobody can misuse that.

Reynhardt: You're right. Perhaps I have a bedrock in the nature of the work. One must have trust in science—that it will bear fruit in itself. But—one must have trust in people too! In a man like Paul there is so endlessly much that's complex, all mixed up together. After all, he has…
Gerda: With Paul it's different.

Reynhardt: Paul may come to prevent many wrongs—perhaps set some things to rights. He's not a fiend, after all….. At least one wouldn't think so.

Gerda: He can make small reforms in hell? Is that what you mean?

Reynhardt: I mean that as the years go by you grow modest; a small, decent action counts for infinitely more than a big, beautiful dream. (*Takes her hand*) Let's not be too one-sided, Gerda! There's no patented way through life. The side roads are there, tiny narrow paths and long, crooked detours. And everyone has his own. Paul has his own. And he must walk it alone. What will come out of it, no one can say beforehand.
Gerda: There are roads which nobody needs to walk.

Reynhardt: Dear little Gerda! It's easier to judge others than to live yourself.

Gerda: That sounds almost like a defense of Paul.

Reynhardt (*sighs*): It is, too. But it is just as much a defense of myself. Who can be human at all today without feeling like an accessory?

Gerda (*as if to sick child*): My God, Heini! Is that what's bothering you?

Reynhardt (*laughs, pulls her down onto sofa*): Is the conspiracy beginning again?

Gerda: Don't laugh, Heini! A true marriage is always based on honesty. Tell me what's the matter!
Reynhardt: Gerda—my friend! A man must have one secret from his wife! (127f)

Gerda offers him an opportunity to open himself to the Christ-Impulse. But that would entail an inner crucifixion and rebirth, a possibility beyond his ken. Instead he belittles her moral judgment. As he later tells Heidebrand:

Gerda won't understand anything at all. She'll judge it by a standard which is alien to our work—*She* can't understand that it involves another world with different values than hers! She won't understand that, Paul! She *can't!* After all, she's a romantic! She's a child! (146)

Reynhardt's evasions and jokes in response to both Gerda and Claus show that he takes neither of them seriously; his "family values" are an enabling mechanism in support of his own luciferic self-delusion. He is called to a meeting and leaves without keeping his promise to say good night to Claus.

Act III is a sustained confrontation between Heidebrand and Reynhardt. The latter speaks in a Luciferan voice when he tells Heidebrand:

I'll tell you quite frankly, Paul, how things are with me. I am a medical man. Actually medicine has always been an exception among the natural sciences. The conditions for research have been especially bad. In all other branches of science one could solve problems by experiment. But not us. In medicine we were cut off from that. We had to proceed with infinite slowness. Now and then we could do research with animals. But that was a long way round. It didn't help us much. We could never experiment freely. We could never get past the scruples we had to observe. Imagine a chemist having to experiment with phosphorus when he wanted to know something about sulfur! That's how it was for us.
I don't give a damn about politics! I don't give a damn about the war! I don't give a damn about corpses and sewers and uniforms! *This* is what interests me. And it interests me *truly!* It has opened up whole

new avenues for medicine. *It's so interesting, Paul!* It's so interesting. And therefore it's completely immaterial to me what they use the remains for. Utterly immaterial! That's the way it is! (141)

Under pressure of blackmail, Reynhardt agrees to leak SS disinformation to the scientific community. Heidebrand presents him with honorable alternatives——telling Gerda about his activities and submitting to her moral judgment, or fleeing to Switzerland and giving up his research. But Reynhardt rejects both courses and opts to continue deluding himself that he can pursue "pure" science and remain ethically neutral:

Heidebrand: Heinrich! There *is* one more possibility. It's a possibility no one has considered!

Reynhardt: And what's that?

Heidebrand: That you take your family and leave the country! We have a neutral country next door, and you can go there. You need only pull up stakes, Heinrich! You can pull up stakes and actually begin a new life! I'll help you. To get across, I mean…(*smiles*)…not with the new life! It's easy to get you over the border.

Reynhardt: When one is responsible for others besides oneself, one doesn't pull up stakes just like that….

Heidebrand: I *mean* it. I'll help you.

Reynhardt: That's nonsense, Paul! Are you completely out of your mind? Be serious!

Heidebrand: Do you really believe you can't pull up stakes?… I *know* it can be done! It can be done by anyone who has a reason to do it!

Reynhardt: I cannot take responsibility for such a thing.

Heidebrand: It's one night's journey. And then you're over the border. Gerda and Claus are safe. And you'll be a free man again. It's easy!

Reynhardt: Then what would we be going to?

Heidebrand: One always pulls up stakes *from*. Never *to*.

Reynhardt: For me it's important.

Heidebrand: You'll get *out* of it, Heinrich, if you just pull up stakes.

(*A long silence*)

Reynhardt (*Clears throat*): I know a suitable doctor, who I could entrust the documents to…and who would certainly pass them on—But I'll do it just this once! My task is of a medical—not of a political sort. And I won't go one step further in that direction! Not one step! It's completely out of the question.

Heidebrand (*pulling his jacket tight from the hem*): All right.

Reynhardt: Then I assume that my family life will be kept out of it.

Heidebrand (*back at desk, laughs soundlessly*): You know you can count on us! I certainly won't show Gerda the spots on your white coat!

Reynhardt: Be so kind as not to speak of this in such a tone. My work and my family life—the two have nothing to do with each other. Heidebrand doesn't reply. He stands with eyes closed and head cocked, listening.

Reynhardt: What is it? (*no reply*) What is it?

Pause.

Heidebrand (*opening his eyes*): At first I thought it was one of the prisoners! (*laughs and laughs, going over into falsetto. Then wipes his eyes. Half choking*) But it was just the rooster! We have a poultry yard out here. And it was just the rooster. Can you imagine its being that late! I'll get you a car. *Hurriedly crosses and exits, slamming door behind him.* **Reynhardt** *looks after him.* (150-2)

Play into Novel: Heidebrand

It appears that the play does not include Heidebrand's transformation into Lyngby. If this is so, then how does Samuel Goldmann fit into the structure of the play? Heidebrand's strong reaction to learning that Goldmann is in the camp is a dramatic high point for our putative Act I, but leads nowhere. There are a few references to Samuel in chapter 4, usually coupled with references to Gerda's dead brother, Little Jacob—who is not mentioned elsewhere. In chapter 5—our hypothetical Act III—Samuel isn't mentioned at all. It would seem, then, that Samuel Goldmann is tied to Heidebrand's transformation, and must therefore be a novelistic addition. And, in fact, it takes only minor surgery to remove him from the play.[17]

In the play Heidebrand is a morally ambiguous figure. Perhaps the audience would have perceived him as purely evil; familiarity with the novel makes it difficult to tell. Did Bjørneboe, at the time he wrote the play, have an inkling of how Heidebrand would develop? As a writer he seems always to have had so much to say that his problem is one of carving out manageable pieces and finding or inventing a form to fit them. His works are never finished; they always have loose ends that lead to the outside, to other works, written and unwritten. So perhaps this play is no exception.

One problem I had with the reconstruction was an uncertainty about the intensity of Heidebrand's urging Reynhardt to pull up stakes at the end. It seems important to the play, but: if Heidebrand is merely acting the provocateur, the intensity seems overdone; was it more muted in the play. His laughter at the very end might well have been interpreted as diabolical, the stuff of melodrama, but that was surely not Bjørneboe's intention.

Heidebrand is haunted by a mournful song about a mercenary soldier; in Act I he has ordered it taught to the prisoners to sing for Dr. Scholtz; in Act II he sings it to Gerda:

> On a coal-black horse rides Brother Death,
> his cloak is full of the dark wind's breath!
> His cloak is full of the long long sleep,
> full of the blessed peace.
> Brother Death, he gallops forth—

---

17. Another serious flaw in the novel, it seems to me, is that the friendship with Samuel Goldmann is never made credible. He never appears directly, nor are we shown any of Heidebrand's or Reynhardt's memories of him, as one would expect if they were a triumvirate. The name "Goldmann" implies the intrinsic value of the concrete individual, a negation of the Nazi rubric of "inferior and superfluous human material." Still, Samuel remains an abstraction, a plot device, a catalyst for Heidebrand's embarkation on the way to Golgotha.

wherever soldiers of fortune march,
there he rides along....

Gerda (*furious, half rising*): Stop! Stop! How in the world can you be so unbelievably cruel as to remind me of Little Jacob [novel: Samuel] in that way!? After all, it was his song. (*Hesitates, then suddenly looks up*) Does it really help? Does it really help to have sung it? (107f)

Is he then an opportunist (soldier of fortune) who tries to keep his options open? It may be that in the play Little Jacob, who died in a concentration camp, is Heidebrand's Christ-Impulse, denied in the service of Ahriman:

Gerda (*yells*): When someone is "shot while trying to escape," what does that mean? What? What does that mean? Even if it were really true that he was shot while escaping...even if he *wasn't* beaten to death with rubber truncheons...who gave you permission to shoot someone because they tried to escape? (*weeps*)

Heidebrand (*quietly*): That's part of the game. Just rules in a game, rules which we all know. Little Jacob knew them too. We're just men playing.... What you're saying is right, Gerda. It all adds up. But just the same it's wrong. It wasn't us he died of.... He died of a sickness, a delayed childhood disease—one of those which hits much too hard if you get it as an adult. If the word weren't so ambiguous and so compromised, you could call it "morality." If he'd gotten over it, he could have been at liberty in just a few weeks. But you understand...you understand—he had his morbid little pleasure in his ideals right to the end.... He knew the rules of the game. That's how he wanted it. He wanted to lie under the wheel. And I wanted to sit up in the carriage. (108-12)

But if Heidebrand is "an opportunist who tries to keep his options open," he is also an existentialist, attuned to the possibility of choosing anew at every moment, as shown in his impassioned words to Reynhardt about pulling up stakes. The version in the reconstructed play given above is toned down from that in the novel, which reads in full:

> The officer was excited. He grew red in the face.
> "Do you really believe that one can't pull up stakes?"
> He clenched his fist and ran the knuckles down his chest.
> "I know it can be done! It can be done if you have a reason to do it!"
> He turned abruptly and looked for the glass. Then he went back to the desk and filled it. He lifted the glass.
> "Skaal to those who have a reason!" he said and drank. He swallowed, and for a little while he looked straight ahead. Then he turned to the other.
> "I once pulled up stakes myself," he said, and his voice rose. "And I can do it again! And again! And again! There's no limit to how often a person can pull up stakes. You can do it every minute! Always!" (150f)

This, Heidebrand realizes, is true freedom, as opposed to freedom in material things—power and wealth. Joe Martin comments:

> there are different definitions of freedom. One is Heidebrand's other definition: to have power and wealth—to be sitting up on the carriage rather than being under the wheel. To do this you have to accept the morality around you, whatever it is, and seek "success" in those terms. The other freedom carries terrifying responsibility. That is to not accept the ethos and morality with which you are surrounded, unless you test their metal and find it based on truth and on compassion. This leads to the higher freedom, the spiritual one, which is Freedom-in-Truth.[18]

In more conventional Christian terms, repentance (*metanoia*) is always a possibility, at least for those who are open to it (as Reynhardt clearly is not). At this point it may be well to look at some passages elucidating Steiner's view of conversion:

> It is one of the golden rules of life that we all carry in us a wiser man than we ourselves are...one who reigns in the depth of our unconscious and who remains inaccessible to ordinary consciousness. He directs our

---

18. Joe Martin, personal communication, May 2000.

gaze away from easy enjoyment and kindles in us a magic power that seeks the road of pain without our really knowing it.... He always acts in such a way that our shortcomings are guided to our pains and he makes us suffer because with every inner and outer suffering we eliminate one of our faults and become transformed into something better.[19]

Steiner's view of conversion hinges on the experience of the Cross (which he calls "the Mystery of Golgotha"). It seems to have much in common with 12 Step principles:

Everyone who is honest in this striving [for self-knowledge] will have to concede that he cannot actually attain what he seeks, that his powers are insufficient, that he feels weak and powerless to achieve his aims.... If we experience this feeling of powerlessness strongly enough then we can suddenly turn the corner, receive the opposite experience: the feeling that if we refrain from immersing ourselves in what our physical powers alone can provide, if we immerse ourselves instead in the gifts of the spirit, then we can overcome this inner soul-death. We can find our soul again and unite with the spirit. We can sense the emptiness of existence on one hand and its glorification through ourselves on the other, once we step beyond our feelings of powerlessness. We can sense our illness and incapacity through our powerlessness; but we can also sense the Saviour, the healing power, by plumbing the depths of this powerlessness and acquainting our souls with death. When we sense the Healer we feel that we bear something in our soul that can at any moment resurrect from death within our own inner experience. These two experiences belong together. When we seek both of them we can find Christ within our own soul.[20]

Heidebrand appears to have plenty of self-knowledge; in his way he too is an experimenter, without Reynhardt's self-deceptions. He conducts his own experiments on his primary research subject—Reynhardt—with an attitude of surface detachment, while the wiser man within does his work.

Pain is heaped upon pain: the orientation concerning the experiments, the reunion with Reynhardt and the spectacle of his stubbornly held

---

19. Rudolf Steiner, "Facing Karma," *The Essential Steiner*, 155.

20. Rudolf Steiner, "How do I find the Christ?" In *Evil: Selected Lectures*,181.

delusions about his own ethical neutrality, the encounter with Gerda and Claus and the knowledge that what they have already suffered is nothing compared to the pain that lies in store for them—in order not to be affected by all this, even without Reynhardt's indifference to the news that their old friend Samuel is about to become an experimental subject, Heidebrand would have to be a monster—as great a monster as Reynhardt.

In the play Heidebrand's final response is not action, but what the narrator of *Moment of Freedom* (1966) calls "Florentine laughter." In the novel it is the presence of Samuel which sets Heidebrand on the road to Golgotha, leads finally to action, and thence to a multi-leveled death and resurrection.

His rescue of Samuel results in his being caught and tortured. His subsequent imprisonment in a cell with the real Lyngby consolidates his inner transformation. As he describes it in the novel:

> Once I was with a man day and night for two years. We had eight square meters to move around in, and got very little to eat. But he knew the Gospel of John by heart—word for word. And after a few months that came to take the place of both the motion and the food. (23)

Steiner, in his *Lectures on the Gospel of John*, describes the ancient process of initiation into the mysteries. After a lengthy period of instruction, the neophyte "was put into a deathlike sleep by the initiator or hierophant who understood the matter and there he remained for three-and-a-half days...."[21]

I cannot begin to fathom the esoteric details of Steiner's interpretation of John's gospel; but a central point, as I understand it, is that Lazarus, after a three-and-a-half-day sleep, was transformed into John the Beloved Disciple. Similarly Heidebrand, when he is found by the liberators, has lain under his dead cellmate in a deathlike sleep for three days. Those of us not versed in esoteric lore will probably read his "transformation" into Lyngby simply as an appropriation of the dead man's identity, though

---

21. Rudolf Steiner, "The raising of Lazarus," *The Essential Steiner*, 237.

there may be other interpretations. (I wonder about the significance of the novel's final sentence, "It was only as they carried him up the cellar stairs that they noticed how heavy he was"). (167)

Conclusion

However bitter the theater's rejection of the original play was for Bjørneboe, it appears to have worked out for the best. The response that "the public flees from such stuff" was on target; the opening of the play anticipates *Amputation* (1970) in its uncompromising brutality. After the intense opening scene, however, the play gradually settles down into a conventional drama in the Ibsen mold. It may have been Bjørneboe's karma that he could not emerge as a dramatist until he had found a way to break free of the dead hand of Ibsen.[22]

But perhaps the reconstructed play is of more than academic interest. I am indebted to Joe Martin for his incisive comments on my reconstruction, and in particular for his suggestions of how it might point to turning the novel—whose formal problems are indubitable—back into a play. He says:

Though in theatre these days—especially European theatre—this kind of realistic approach is beginning to vanish, as it can't compete with film—perhaps the very thing that might make this work is the apparently realistic set-up, conflicting with the absolutely shocking and mentally dislocating material which is coming out of the characters' mouths. If the medium is the message, then we've got Hannah Arendt's "banality of evil" on stage. (Which is not to say the play is banal.)
I think the play is sharp, well written, well translated, deals with the evil in one man brilliantly (Reynhardt). But the novel's frame device was a step forward, not a step back. Heidebrand's purpose is unfulfilled, and so he is simply ambiguously evil.... For the stage in the US and Europe, at this time, I think an abbreviated *adaptation*—a flexible, free and theatrical one—of the frame device—perhaps one in which the actor playing Reynhardt might play the investigating journalist "B"—would make it a better play. Instead of simply introducing the play, the material from

---

22. See my essay "Mad Scientists and Moral Outrage: The Genesis of Jens Bjørneboe's Amputation," in Jens Bjørneboe, *Amputation: Texts for an Extraordinary Spectacle* (Los Angeles: Xenos Books, 2002).

the first chapters could create a complete "frame." It could be divided in two parts, so that at the end, the rather "epic" events of Heidebrand's capture, and the final days before the liberation of the camp, could be partly narrated by "B" and partly enacted. This would flesh out the Samuel Goldmann subplot (which Lord knows, I don't think should be cut). The insight provided by Heidebrand's death and resurrection could be provided by a live performance.[23]

Naturally the above merely skims the surface; much more could be said about the function and interplay of other characters and images in both play and novel.

A final thought about how the Anthroposophical subtext may bear on the novel's problematical shift in form. I suggested above that the trajectory may be viewed as circular, the end pointing back to the beginning, toward the present of Part I. The play itself has a great intensity and an immediacy, but the novel creates distance by interposing descriptions of body language and tones of voice, thoughts and memories, departures from the single scene, etc. Perhaps Bjørneboe's choice of form is meant to mirror the way the Christlike compassion for the concrete individual remains the background; the "omniscient authorial" voice mirrors both the Luciferic tendency to "view the world from an aerial perspective" and the Ahrimanic "to rule over them...by using and manipulating their weaknesses."

Heidebrand's resurrection at the end points us back into a present dominated by the Christ-Impulse—most of the characters exhibiting compassion for the concrete individuals they encounter, however heinous their past acts; the whole reflected as part of the narrator's own concrete "meeting between a human mind and the world." The singular lack of demonization in Part I contrasts sharply with the Nazi rhetoric about "inferior and superfluous human material" in Part II.

Part I is set on the eve of the currency reform, a time which the narrator of *Moment of Freedom* describes thus:

---

23. Joe Martin, personal communication, May 2000.

I've never met such human people as the Germans at this time among the ruins; calm, resigned people, on the way to becoming nature, they too—philosophic, thoughtful people, content and almost happy, if naked want were kept away. There was a kind of lethargy over the land, something which resembled a coma, a languor and a quietude as after one has lived through a severe illness. In all the misery there lay a peace over land, cities and people....

There was something brewing in Germany before the currency reform; I'm not the only one who saw it. There was a new humanity present, a brotherliness, a depth—a first seed, an infinitely weak and tender germ of something new, of something non-Teutonic in Teutonia. This one night, between the worthless currency and the strong hard currency, decided Germania's new development, and thereby the fate of Europe in the years which are to come.[24] (194)

---

24. Jens Bjørneboe, *Moment of Freedom*. Translated by Esther Greenleaf Mürer (Norwich: Norvik Press, 1999), 194.

About the Author

Jens Bjørneboe (1920-1976) was a Norwegian poet, playwright, essayist, and novelist who was arguably one of the most important experimental writers of the mid-twentieth century. He was also a visual artist, a Waldorf School teacher, and a renowned social critic. Although little known in the English-speaking world, his work has been translated into a number of European and world languages and is still highly regarded in Scandinavia. His last major work was *The Sharks* (*Haiene*, 1974) and his most critically acclaimed were the three volumes making up the *The History of Bestiality* trilogy; all have been translated into English by Esther Greenleaf Mürer.

About the Translator

Esther Greenleaf Mürer is a poet and translator who resides in Philadelphia. She has previously translated Bjørneboe's novels *The Sharks* (Norvik/Dufour, 1992), *Moment of Freedom* (Norvik/Dufour, 1999), *Powerhouse* (Norvik/Dufour, 2000), and *The Silence* (Norvik/Dufour, 2000) as well as a number of his essays and poems. She was responsible for the "Jens Bjørneboe in English" website, which was the premiere source of information about Jens Bjørneboe written in English and included translations of his poetry, essays, and excerpts of other works

Jens Bjørneboe: Works in English

Plays

Amputation
Edited by Karl August Kvitko
Two versions of the play, translated by Solrun Hoaas +
supplementary essays
Xenos Books, 2003

The Bird Lovers
Translated by Frederick Wasser
Sun & Moon Press, 1994

Semmelweis
Translated by Joe Martin
Sun and Moon Press, 1999

Novels

Ere the Cock Crows
Translated by Esther Greenleaf Mürer
Includes a re-creation of the original play by the translator
Frayed Edge Press, 2021

Winter in Bellapalma
Translated by Esther Greenleaf Mürer
Frayed Edge Press, 2021

Moment of Freedom: The Heiligenberg Manuscript
Translated by Esther Greenleaf Mürer
Norvik Press/Dufour Editions, 1999 (Re-issued 2017)

Powderhouse: Scientific Afterword and Last Protocol
Translated by Esther Greenleaf Mürer
Norvik Press/Dufour Editions, 2000 (Re-issued 2017)

The Silence: An Anti-Novel and Absolutely the Very Last Protocol
Translated by Esther Greenleaf Mürer
Norvik Press/Dufour Editions, 2000 (Re-issued 2017)

The Sharks: The History of a Crew and a Shipwreck
Translated by Esther Greenleaf Mürer
Norvik Press/Dufour Editions, 1992

Without a Stitch
Translated by Walter Barthold
Grove Press, 1969

The Least of These: A Novel [*Jonas*]
Translated by Bernt Jebsen and Douglas K. Stafford
Bobbs-Merrill, 1959

Essays

The Fear of America Within Us & Other Essays on Politics and Society
Translated by Esther Greenleaf Mürer
Xenos Books, 2016

Degrees of Freedom: Anarchist Essays By and About Jens Bjørneboe
Protocol Press, [1996]

About Bjørneboe and His Work

Jens Bjorneboe: Prophet Without Honor
By Janet Garton
Greenwood, 1985

Keeper of the Protocols: The Works of Jens Bjørneboe in the Crosscurrents of Western Literature
By Joe Martin
Peter Lang, 1996

Website

Jens Bjørneboe in English
Includes translations of essays, poems, and excerpts from larger works, and information and essays about Bjørneboe and his work. This site is no longer being maintained; archived copies can be found at: https://web.archive.org/web/20100105183016/http://emurer.home.att.net/